TREASURE TROVE
OF THE ISLAND KING

Golden plate was stacked in profusion like so much crockery. Giant vases of hammered bronze held the riotous plumes of exotic birds. Casks overflowed with gems and pearls. The nostrils stung with the scents drifting from hundreds of spice chests. Ivory sculptures were heaped with fine instruments of bronze and glass, and everywhere were piled bolt upon bolt of precious fabrics.

Some of the strangers made strangled sounds, but the leader retained his composure. Subdued, they followed her from the building to one only slightly smaller. Once again the sides were raised and they went within. This time the strangers gasped unashamedly.

The building was not a treasury, but an arsenal. Here there was no gleam of gold or warm glow of colorful jewels. Instead everywhere they looked was the deadly glitter of steel.

Tor books by John Maddox Roberts

Cestus Dei
King of the Wood

THE CINGULUM

The Cingulum
Cloak of Illusion
The Sword, The Jewel, and The Mirror

THE ADVENTURES OF CONAN

Conan the Bold
Conan the Champion
Conan the Marauder
Conan the Valorous
Conan the Rogue
Conan and the Treasure of Python

THE STORMLANDS

The Islander
The Black Shields
The Poisoned Lands
Queens of Land and Sea
The Steel Kings

QUEENS OF
LAND AND SEA

JOHN MADDOX ROBERTS

A TOM DOHERTY ASSOCIATES BOOK
NEW YORK

This is a work of fiction. All the characters and events portrayed in this book are fictitious, and any resemblance to real people or events is purely coincidental.

QUEENS OF LAND AND SEA

Cover art by Ken Kelly

A Tor Book
Published by Tom Doherty Associates, Inc.
175 Fifth Avenue
New York, N.Y. 10010

Tor® is a registered trademark of Tom Doherty Associates, Inc.

ISBN: 0-812-52307-5

First edition: September 1994

Printed in the United States of America

0 9 8 7 6 5 4 3 2 1

ONE

The palace stood atop a knoll a few hundred strides from the shore, commanding a splendid view of the small bay and the twin capes that embraced it like grasping arms. Brightly painted war canoes rested on the glittering sands of the bay. Idle as the canoes, warriors lounged on the beach, some wrestling, some gambling, a few practicing with weapons. They wore the clothing, ornaments and paints of a dozen tribes, but all had the black shields, symbol of their allegiance, close to hand.

In lines from the bottom of the knoll to the top, rank on rank of the elite Shasinn warriors stood guard. They were magnificent men, bronze-hued of skin and hair, blue-eyed, so splendidly proportioned that mainland artists considered them to be the only adequate models to employ when sculpting the likenesses of gods. On the lower slope stood the junior warriors of fifteen to twenty years, their long hair dressed in hundreds of tiny plaits. Nearer the palace stood the senior warriors: formidable men, their many scars painted proudly. All the Shasinn bore long spears made entirely of bronze save for their inset steel edges.

On the wide verandah of the log-built palace Queen Larissa sat brooding. In years past the sight of her warriors in their thousands had filled her with pride and excitement. Now she felt foreboding. For the first time since childhood she was afraid.

"Too many warriors doing too little," she said, addressing the tall, powerful warrior who stood beside her. "They are as useless as livestock in this state."

"Something must be found for them to do," the warrior said.

"When the king is recovered, he will lead them back to the mainland. Then we will regain our lost territories."

"The king may not recover," the man said grimly.

Hissing, she turned to glare at him. "The king will recover! You dare to think that he will not?"

"Forgive me, my queen, but the king and I were boys together. To the others he is a god, but I know that he is a man. He is the greatest warrior of the age, but he was wounded as a man and he may die. I never saw a man take such a wound and live for a full turning of the sun."

"And yet he has lived for fully half a year! Does that not mean something? Does that not prove that he is not as other men?" Haughty as she was, Queen Larissa's voice was full of pleading. She needed reassurance that her world had not been utterly destroyed.

"No one doubts that he is not as other men, nor that you are not as other women. But those who revered him as a god are now filled with doubt. Had it been any other man save King Hael who struck him down, even the Shasinn might have deserted him."

"Hael!" she said venomously. "Must that man plague us to the end of our days?"

"Hate him as you will, men recognize that he, too, is more than an ordinary man. The spirits are strong with him. The duel between Hael and King Gasam was no common fight. Both kings received wounds that should have been mortal. Now the people do not know what to do or think. The folk of the islands obey you without question because you struck Hael down with your own hand."

"Surely he is dead by now! I saw my spear strike him. I saw him fall, pierced through! Everyone saw it!"

"And your glory will live forever, my queen. But the word we have from the mainland says that the Canyoners keep him alive with magical arts."

"King Gasam needs no magic. He lives because of his own godlike strength. He will recover, Pendu. The wound will heal, and the king will again be as he always was!"

Pendu smiled faintly. "If the power of your will were enough to drag him back from death, it would be so even now. But all this is beside the point, my queen. The king cannot command, but the Shasinn are loyal to you. Let me take these idlers south. Some of the Islanders there are slipping back into their old ways, wanting their own tribal chieftains. They have forgotten that there is only one king over them. They need a lesson."

"We cannot have backsliding here in the islands," she said. "The islands are our power base, home of the only warriors worthy of the name. Yes, assemble a war band and get some use out of those vessels.

Where you find sedition, kill the ringleaders, but there must be no wholesale slaughter. The king values . . . what is that?" She pointed to the high headland of the southernmost cape, where a thread of black smoke ascended toward the high-piled clouds.

"A ship coming," Pendu said. "It is early in the season. Only the bravest captains defy the late storms."

The queen clapped her hands and a serving woman came from inside the palace. "Fetch my spyglass," Larissa ordered. A few moments later the woman reemerged holding a long box of polished wood. The queen unfastened the bronze clasp and opened the lid. Inside was an exquisitely wrought telescope of polished flamewood with bronze tips. It was a Nevan device, loot of war like almost all of her possessions. She took it and set it to her eye, adjusting its length until she had focus.

"A blue flag," she reported. "Strange ship coming. No, three ships."

"It must be a merchant," Pendu said. "No war party would come here in only three ships. But what nation?"

"The blue flag means unknown. Perhaps they are still too far to identify. There is a runner coming this way from the lookout point. We should know more soon." She clapped twice and a half dozen of her women appeared. "I may be receiving visitors. Prepare me." Then, to Pendu: "Get that rabble out there in shape. We cannot have spies detecting weakness or disorder."

The warrior bowed. "As my queen commands." He left the verandah, shouting orders. As if by magic, the lounging warriors formed disciplined units awaiting their instructions.

Quickly and efficiently her Nevan cosmetician be-

gan applying the slightest of colors and accents.
Larissa had long scorned such artificialities, but she
had become self-conscious about the tiny signs of
aging that had appeared when she passed her forti-
eth year. As a race, the Shasinn resisted the ravages
of age longer than any other, but even their legendary queen was not immortal.

"The red silk gown, my queen?" asked a woman.

"The new blue one, with the gold trim and the
pearls." Among her own people, Larissa often wore
no more than her jewelry, defying the power of time
to reduce her beauty. She was careful what she ate
and was extremely active. From ten feet away she
could be mistaken for a woman of twenty years. Receiving strangers, though, she usually dressed more
demurely, at least by her own standards.

The women finished their ministrations just as the
runner from the lookout point bounded up the steps
and flung himself at the queen's feet. He was a
Shasinn junior warrior, sweating only slightly despite his long run and not breathing hard at all.

"Well, what is it, Mana?" The boy was a member
of her personal bodyguard, with whom she was always familiar and affectionate. In return, they worshipped her with more fevor than the mainlanders
accorded their gods.

"Three ships, my queen, such ships as I have
never seen before!"

"You have traveled only among these islands,
Mana. Perhaps they are Chiwan. No such ships have
visited here since you were a child."

"The officer of the watch is Captain Utho, my
queen. He is a veteran of many voyages. He studied
them long through the great spyglass, and he says to
tell you he has never seen such craft."

She leaned forward, feeling stirrings of excitement

for the first time in long, despairing months. "Describe them."

"He says that they are smaller than the great Chiwan warships, but larger than any Nevan merchant craft. Each has three masts . . ."

"Three!" She had never before seen a three-masted ship.

"Yes, my queen. Some of the sails are square and some are three-sided. That is all that was clear when I left the point."

"Do they look like they intend to stop here?"

"They sail straight for the harbor. We could see them come about when they spotted the capes."

Out on the waters of the harbor, canoes set out, bristling with warriors. Pendu came back up the hill, moving at an easy lope.

"We are ready to receive visitors," he said, grinning.

The queen told him what the boy had reported. "I thought we had seen every sort of ship in the world. Where could these be from?"

Pendu shrugged. "There is always more of the world. I remember when we thought the whole world was these islands and a bit of mainland, just over the horizon. Every nation we took, there was another just beyond. There is no end to it."

"No," she insisted. "King Gasam is destined to conquer the whole world. It is just going to take longer than we had thought."

"As you say, my queen. How shall we handle these strangers?"

"Let them know we are powerful, but otherwise we shall be hospitable. I cannot imagine that they will be hostile, with only three ships, but they could be a threat if they have the Mezpan fire weapons. Determine that before you allow them ashore."

"As my queen commands." He saluted and went back down the hill to take charge of the reception.

Larissa disliked waiting, so she rose and went into the palace. Its interior was immaculate but severely plain. In the conquered territories the royal couple lived amid barbaric magnificence, but in the home islands they preferred their ancestral simplicity. The palace was wood, its roof thatched. Except for the great throne room there were only an armory and a few chambers. The guards slept in huts behind the palace.

Larissa passed through a doorway flanked by two of the savage women of the king's bodyguard. The grotesquely ornamented women bowed as she went between them. Their devotion to Gasam was fanatical and his defeat had done nothing to lessen it. Inside the bedchamber four more women guards stood watch over the king. Also in attendance was a physician, a famous surgeon taken prisoner during the conquest of Neva. He knew that the king's last day would be his own and was consequently solicitous.

"How is he?" Larissa asked in a quiet voice.

"No change since your last visit," said the physician.

The king lay upon a mattress stuffed with herbs believed to promote healing. His great frame was wasted, the flesh of his face fallen in to reveal the contours of the skull. His chest rose and fell with each slow breath.

"Show me the wound," she ordered. The physician lifted the bloody pad of bandage to reveal the rent Hael's spear had torn through Gasam's chest. It did not gape wide as it had in months past, but the healing was terribly slow. She feared greatly that a vengeful spirit might enter the king's body through the wound and kill him. Spirits not powerful enough to kill might already be keeping him from healing. Gasam had never been ill and had always recovered quickly from his wounds.

"I think it has closed somewhat these last few days," she said.

"Perhaps a bit, my queen," the physician said. "His pulse is strong and his breath is much improved over what it was a month ago. The damage to the lung seems to be healed."

Larissa leaned over and kissed Gasam's brow. His eyelids fluttered open and he smiled weakly when he recognized her.

"A gown, little queen?" His voice was barely above a whisper. "I trust you are not preparing for my funeral."

"Do not speak so!" she chided gently. "In a few days you will be up and planning your next campaign. There are some ships coming in and I must greet them. They seem to be strangers. The ships are of a sort we have never seen. There could be advantage in this."

"If there is advantage, you will find it, my queen, you always do. The strangers must be told that I am nearly recovered."

"I will tell them you are touring your lands in the interior. They will not know you are ailing at all."

"Even better . . ." His eyes rolled upward, his lids lowered. Even these few words had exhausted him. At least he had known her this time. There were days when he did not.

When she returned to the verandah, the first ship was just entering the channel between the headlands of the capes. She sat and picked up her telescope again. Through it she studied the ship and she knew that what Utho had said was true. In no port had she ever seen such a vessel. The two foremost masts bore square sails. The very short rear mast had a slanting yard from which depended a small, triangular sail. The hull of the ship was deeper and more tublike than those she was accustomed to, but it seemed to sail handily enough. A spiderweb of ropes made up its complex rigging.

The once-bright paint of the ship's woodwork showed the effects of a lengthy voyage. She could make out little more. As she watched, the vessel dropped all but a few small sails and a boat was lowered over the side. It was rowed before the ship and she saw that the men aboard it were engaged in some painstaking activity, probably taking soundings. She hoped this was not going to take too long.

Canoes full of her warriors paddled out to meet the arriving ships. The men stood behind their shields, spears upright at their sides. They made no outcry or other demonstration, but the Shasinn radiated a palpable menace even when at rest. Those of the other island races were only slightly less intimidating.

The second ship, slightly larger than the first, eased into the channel. A few minutes later the third, largest of all, came in between the capes. The ships shared the same rigging plan and seemed to differ only in size. A red banner hung from the foremast of the largest ship, its device the head of a creature with two spreading horns worked in gold. The artistic style was completely new to her.

There must be advantage here, she thought. Everything had been taken from them save the home islands. Now something new had come upon the scene, something that might tip the balance that had turned so irrevocably against them.

At last the three ships rested safely in the center of

the bay. A large boat was lowered from the biggest
ship and men climbed into it. It pulled away amid a
flash of oars, and across the water came a creaking
of oars working in metal oarlocks. Already she had
learned something: These people were rich enough
in metal to use it for so mundane a purpose. Possession of gold, silver, copper and bronze meant wealth.
Possession of steel meant power.

"Don't laugh at them, whatever they look like,"
she warned her men. "These are my guests until I
decide otherwise."

A double line of canoes formed a corridor leading
to the landing just below the palace. The longboat's
progress was unhurried, stately. Larissa sensed that
this was a conscious effort on the part of the mariners. They knew that they were about to call upon
royalty and they wished to emphasize their own importance. It was the sort of diplomatic game-playing
to which she had grown accustomed in her years as
queen.

The landing party climbed onto the wooden jetty
and came ashore, Pendu leading them up the slope,
between the ranks of warriors. Six men led the party
of foreigners, another half score men in light armor
bearing weapons. The latter were a laughable precaution amid the armed might of her warriors, but
she saw among them none of the fire weapons she
had come to dread.

The foremost of them was a tall, burly man with a
great, fan-shaped beard spreading over his breast.
Larissa detested facial hair—her own people had
none. But the man was striking. Both hair and beard
were striped in tawny and crimson. She could not
tell whether this was natural or dyed. She had never
seen stripe-haired humans before. His clothes were
loose-fitting and voluminous, a combination of

leather and fabrics, all in bright colors. The men behind him were dressed similarly.

She noted both bronze and steel among the weapons carried by the guards. The notables wore long swords sheathed at their waists. Their hilts sparkled with gems set in silver. Even the common guards wore silver bracelets and silver chains around their necks. These people were rich in silver, if nothing else. The leader halted before her and bowed deeply, but with a grace and ease that suggested this was a courtly compliment rather than a sincere obeisance.

"Their language is strange," Pendu told her, "but it sounds like some sort of Southern."

The leader spoke a few words and they did, indeed, have the sound and cadence of the tongue spoken in Chiwa and Gran. She spoke, in the dialect of the Chiwan court, very slowly and precisely.

"More slowly, please."

His eyes widened slightly. "Long life to you, chieftainess. I did not expect to be understood." The accent made it difficult to understand his words, and the syntax was different, but she could follow him.

"The correct form of address is 'Your Majesty,' and you must be far from home."

"We are, indeed. You are the queen of this island?"

"Of all the islands, and of the mainland as well, although there are some usurpers there who will dispute that."

His flickering glance at the modest buildings of the village spoke volumes of his skepticism. She had expected no less. She knew the great store that mainlanders set by architectural show. She would educate him, by and by. He turned and said something to the others, too swiftly for her to understand. All speakers of Southern tended to speak rapidly and run their words together. Only in the most formal speech did they make clear breaks between words. It seemed these strangers were no different.

Slowly the other five important men went down each upon one knee. The leader and the guards remained standing. The guards seemed reasonable enough. Nobody expected bodyguards to relax their vigilance. But the leader declining to render her royal honors—that was going to take some explaining. A deep growl began among her warriors but she signaled for silence. The man had to know the sort of danger he courted, but he showed no sign of it. This she admired.

"I am Grand Sea Lord Sachu, and I bring you greetings from Her Majesty Isel of Altiplan."

"Have you credentials from your queen?" she asked coolly.

This time he registered surprise. He had not expected such a request from one who appeared to him to be a mere savage chieftainess. He turned and one of his followers opened a decorated satchel. Sachu reached inside and withdrew a flat tablet of ornately carved wood, inlaid with ivory. This he opened ceremoniously and presented to Larissa.

She took the hinged tablet and studied it. The interior was lined with fine parchment illuminated with colored inks together with silver and gold leaf. It was closely covered with lines of complex script that made little sense to her, but she could make out a word here and there. It seemed to be a royal commission giving Sachu command of a fleet for purposes of trade and exploration. At the bottom was appended a small, golden seal bearing the beast-head device. Above the seal was a bold, scrawling signature.

"This script is ornate beyond my experience,"

Larissa said, "but your queen's signature is plain enough." Sachu was perfectly serene, but she could see that the men behind him were fearful. This was not transpiring as they had expected. She decided that it was time to ease the pressure somewhat. She favored them with her dazzling smile. Patting the cushion beside her, she said, "Come, sit beside me, Lord Sachu. You other gentlemen, please join me on the verandah. My servants will provide seats for you. Pendu, clear a space for the guards to take their ease. Bring them food and drink."

The warrior gestured for the guards to accompany him, but they ignored him and kept their eyes on their captain. Sachu spoke a few words and they shouldered their weapons and followed Pendu.

"You are most gracious, Your Majesty," Sachu said, sinking gratefully onto the cushion beside her.

"I am Queen Larissa," she said. "My husband, King Gasam, is not here at the moment. He is away surveying his domain. I am fully empowered to act in his behalf. It has always been our greatest goal to establish and maintain the friendliest relations with our fellow monarchs."

"Such is my queen's wish."

"I must confess, though, that I have never heard of your nation. Your ships show all the marks of a lengthy voyage, so your land must be far away."

"Far to the south. Our historians maintain that another great continent lies to the northwest of ours, and my queen commissioned this fleet to sail in search of it. We left the last northern islands of our own land more than two months ago."

"And this is your first landfall?"

"Some days ago we found some small islands south of here. We put in at one to take on water but we saw no inhabitants. This was the first good harbor we spied. Our water casks are full, but we are very short of other provisions."

"You shall have all you need."

"You are most gracious."

"Tell me, Lord Sachu: How did it come about that you found these islands but missed an entire continent?" She smiled sweetly and pretended not to notice the reddening of his face.

"These are unknown waters to us, Your Majesty. We kept a generally northwesterly course, but there are strong currents and powerful easterly winds between our two lands. And it seems that this is the stormy season this far north. At home this is the time of calm winds."

"How fortunate that you found these islands. Another day's sailing to the west and you would have been upon endless waters."

"There is believed to be yet another continent in that direction, but so far that our ships could never make the voyage. Finding your kingdom was indeed fortunate." He paused to take a beaker of wine proffered by a slave woman. After taking a sip he went on. "But you say this northerly continent exists indeed?"

"Oh, it does. You may wish to sojourn here for a while before proceeding there, though. The nations there are in a considerable state of turmoil." She gazed at the three ships in the little harbor. "Three ships, large as they are, seem a small fleet to send on so great a voyage."

"We had eight smaller vessels in the beginning. Two were lost in a great storm a month ago. The rest were scattered in another storm ten days past. We hope they will overtake us before long."

"Another good reason for you to abide with us awhile. I shall order the beacon fires to burn day and night. Also, I will dispatch craft to all the other islands to search for your lost vessels."

"You are more than generous, Your Majesty." The captain touched his spread fingertips to his beard-sheathed breast and bowed his head slightly.

"Your sailors must be greatly in need of rest. Why not have them come ashore? I will have quarters prepared for them."

"You are too kind. However, there is much repair work to be done on the ships. The men had better remain where they are for the time being. Perhaps later, a few at a time."

"As you will." Clearly the man was too cautious to trust her fully. He wanted to keep his ships ready for a quick escape. Of course, none of them would get ten paces if she decided to have them killed or taken prisoner, but they had no way of knowing that.

When food was set before them, the men on the verandah showed self-restraint, although it was clear they were famished. She saw that the guards were wolfing down their food like starving men. Sachu was not lying about being low on provisions. She spoke only polite nothings while they ate, and Sachu introduced the others, all of whom proved to be high nobles or influential burghers.

Only one showed anything like the personal force of Lord Sachu. His name was Goss and he was not prepossessing, having a lean, deeply pocked face and lank black hair. His small beard came to an abrupt point. He had a lazy, sardonic air, and little gestures and attitudes indicated that he had little love for his captain. Larissa decided to cultivate him.

"Now that you are refreshed," she said as the platters were cleared away, "you must tell me all about your country, and about your sovereign, my sister queen." She found that her fluency in Southern was returning, and she was having less trouble in following Sachu's word.

"To tell all would be the work of years," he said, "but I can tell you a little. My homeland, the continent to the southeast, is a vast realm of high mountains and mighty rivers, of broad plains teeming with wildlife, of wild jungles where only savage men dwell." His voice had a rolling sonorousness and his words a metered cadence. She guessed that he was reciting a form of poetry.

"Great as are the wildlands, even greater are the cultivated lands: productive grain and orchard and grazing fields. In all this great land there are many small kingdoms but only one great nation, and that is Altiplan. Sovereign of Altiplan is Isel the Ninth, First Lady of the House of the Bull."

"The Bull!" she said.

"Yes. It is the sacred beast of the royal family." He frowned slightly. "The name surprises you?"

"Only because we have never seen such a creature. There is a constellation of stars we call the Bull, and legend says that it was once a herd animal, like the kagga. But none has been seen since the days of legend. The horned creature on your banner and on the royal seal—is this the bull?"

"Indeed. We maintain great herds of the animals, of which the bull is the male. They are as common as grass in our country. It is only the sacred breed that figures in our holiest rites."

"Imagine!" Knowing that the strangers had actually seen the fabulous beast rendered them truly exotic to her for the first time. Men were just men, but these had seen bulls!

"Queen Isel during her reign has vastly expanded the merchant fleet of Altiplan and sought out new trade routes. It was for this purpose that my fleet was formed."

"How splendid that my sister queen, like all sensible monarchs, desires mutually beneficial trade with her neighbors. At a later time, we must discuss at length the articles of exchange that each of us finds desirable." She did not point out that her people had very little use for trade. They were conquerors and plunderers, preferring to take by force what others had produced.

"I am sure that we have many things your people need," Sachu said. "Altiplan produces wonderful textiles and ceramics, weapons, wines, tools, dyes and paints . . ."

"I am sure. And what sort of goods do you look for in exchange?"

"Well, this is an unknown land to us, and we must see what sort of products it has to offer. I can tell you, though, that you will find a ready market for spices, pearls and gemstones, the skins of interesting beasts, fine feathers and so forth."

The man called Goss leaned forward. "I noticed, Your Majesty, the splendid spears your warriors bear. Whence come these?" Sachu looked annoyed at the interruption, but he said nothing.

"They are ancestral heirlooms, handed down from generation to generation of warriors. The great spears embody the very soul of our race."

"And a comely people you are," said Goss. "I have never seen handsomer men, nor women so beautiful." The others with him nodded in agreement with his compliment. "And if I may say so, Your Majesty's beauty can be compared only with that of our own sovereign."

"How kind of you to say so." She was perfectly conscious of her own beauty. As for this queen of

Altiplan, she knew that her subjects would praise her looks even if she were a shriveled hag. "But now, gentlemen, I know how tired you must be. Let us discuss no more serious matters until you have rested. I will have quarters prepared for you."

"Thank you, Your Majesty," Sachu demurred, "but we are required by ancient law to sleep on our ships while upon official duty. If it pleases you, we will come ashore again in the morning."

"Just as you wish. My steward will arrange for boats to be loaded with provisions and rowed to your ships. I think fresh fruit will do your sailors a world of good after so long a voyage."

Sachu bowed. "Your Majesty is knowledgeable about maritime matters."

She smiled at him. "My people get about quite a bit on the great waters."

That night she knelt by her husband's bedside and reported to him. King Gasam breathed easy, but he showed few other signs of life. His eyelids were half-closed, but she knew he heard and understood her words. They had been so close for so long that she would know instantly when he slipped into unconsciousness.

"As I thought when I saw them walking up from the beach, they take us for primitive savages."

"We are," the king said, his voice barely above a whisper.

"Of course we are, my love, but we are savages who have seen a good deal more of the world than they imagine. Like most such people, they expect to come here and dazzle us with great quantities of the low-cost manufactures of their land. In return they want low-bulk items of high value, items that we, as mere savages, will not appreciate. My speech and bearing obviously impressed them. Otherwise they would have tried to capture my simple, greedy mind with mirrors and bright cloth."

He managed to chuckle gently. "It would be amusing to take their ships and cook them all over a slow fire, but first we must know much more about their land and how these people may be turned to our advantage."

"I agree." She frowned slightly, wrinkling her smooth brow. "I am not entirely certain how to play this game, my love. There is advantage to be had in keeping them contemptuous of us. People will speak freely before those they consider to be ignorant and unimportant. On the other hand, I have always hated to negotiate from any but a position of strength."

The king thought for a while. "No, we must impress them with our power and wealth. When they leave here, they will sail straight for the mainland. They will know that there is far more trade to be had there, and diplomatic agreements to negotiate with many nations. They must be assured that these islands are a reservoir of the greatest warriors in the world. They will hear a great many stories about us from the mainlanders and they must not be allowed to think that we are a beaten people."

"I agree. I shall take them on a little tour, show them a bit of our treasury and armory. And the man named Goss seems like one with his own games to play. I shall cultivate him."

"It is the sort of activity at which you excel, little queen."

"You understand, my husband, that the balance of the whole world has shifted again?"

"It has occurred to me. A new continent, and a rich one. We must learn about these ships of theirs. Perhaps, with knowledge of the winds and currents and when to avoid the great storms, it is not so long a voyage. There may be something there that will give us the opportunity to rebuild our strength, so that we may return to the mainland and retake my empire, and destroy Hael."

"So much talk is exhausting you, my king. Leave these strangers in my hands and I will wring every drop of advantage to be had from them. Our fortunes have gone down for a long time now. I believe that they have just taken a turn for the better."

"I think so," Gasam said, almost slipping away from her. "My destiny will not be thwarted . . ." Then he was asleep.

Larissa rose and walked from the royal bedchamber, past the ferocious women who guarded her husband. Outwardly she was serene, but inwardly she exulted. If Gasam was dreaming of new conquests, he had to be on the mend!

The next morning she greeted the strangers as they came ashore. Behind her stood her bodyguard of Shasinn junior warriors and she held the miniature spear that was her emblem of power. It had been made to replace the one she had lost when she cast it into King Hael's chest. She saw how the eyes of the strangers were drawn to the little spear. It was made entirely of steel.

"Gentlemen, do you feel up to a little exercise? I would like to show you some little part of my husband's realm. I have riding cabos if you wish, but here in the islands we generally prefer to get about on our own feet."

He smiled broadly. "We have never heard of the beast, and I know it is inadvisable to mount an unfamiliar animal. After so long a voyage some leg-stretching exercise would not come amiss. Lead on, Your Majesty."

They set off inland. She had ordered the young warriors to keep to an easy pace. Ordinarily they ran or trotted wherever they went, but effete foreigners would have to be coddled. Sachu did not walk with the rolling gait of the habitual mariner, but kept up with her with easy, long-legged strides. This was a marvel to her because he wore heavy boots with thick soles and heels, their wide tops extending half-way up his thighs. She could not imagine how any-one could move about with such weights attached to his legs, nor how he could keep his balance with so much leather between his soles and the earth. She had felt clumsy and uncomfortable on the few occa-sions that she had worn light sandals.

By the end of the first mile most of the strangers were sweating, but none made a move to shed any of their heavy, voluminous clothing. Goss took off his broad, beplumed hat and fanned his face.

"Would you like to stop and rest awhile?" she said sweetly.

"Your Majesty has the wonderful resilience of youth," Sachu said gallantly, clearly nettled that a woman showed no effects from exertion that was straining his companions. "And your young warriors are wonderfully fit. Still, I think we middle-aged sailors can keep the pace a while longer."

"Excellent. A little way higher up is a sight I think will please you." Their road led up from the low coastal land toward the high interior. The escarp-ment was not steep, but the climb was strenuous for the overburdened strangers. Goss looked about them in some puzzlement. The foliage of the slopes was heavy and riotous with bright birds and small man-of-the-trees, but a great deal of the growth was clearly new.

"Your pardon, Your Majesty," Goss said, "but am

I correct in thinking that this land was but recently cultivated?"

"It was," she affirmed. "Much of the lowlands of these islands used to be tilled by farming tribes. Some years ago my husband decreed that these islands should raise nothing but warriors. Those among the farming people who could not make the change were killed or transferred to our mainland territories."

Sachu looked shocked. "*Nothing* but warriors, Your Majesty? Surely that is impossible!"

"Search these islands as you will," she said, "you will find no male above the age of fourteen who does not bear arms, or who does anything else for his livelihood."

"But—but," one of the strangers sputtered, "how do you eat? Those fruits you sent out to the ships yesterday . . ."

"Those the women and slaves gather wild. We are a race of herdsmen, and we live on the meat and milk and blood of our herds. The tending of animals is a part of the warrior's way."

"Their blood?" somebody said queasily.

"Oh, yes. Traditionally the junior warriors are permitted no food save milk and blood, except on special occasions."

"There is a ceremony in which we drink bull's blood," Sachu said, "but it is not something we do ordinarily." He looked admiringly at the shining bodies and limbs of their escort. "A strange diet, to our way of thinking, but it seems to have done your young men no harm."

Another hour's walk brought them to the rim of the escarpment, where the terrain sloped inland from a jagged outcropping of black stone. From the rim they could see for miles inland and the sight made the strangers forget their sore feet and tired bodies. The interior plain of the island was rich grassland, and the grass abounded with game and domestic herds. From their vantage point they could see hundreds of thousands of head, from tiny, hoofed creatures to huge, shaggy lumberers. They ran in enormous mixed herds all over the great plain. Smaller, more homogeneous herds of domestic beasts were tended by herdsmen. They could see the morning sun glittering upon the spears of the young warriors on herd duty.

"But, this is magnificent!" Sachu said, awed. "It is like something from the creation of the world! I thought I had seen spectacular wildlife in my homeland, but we have nothing to compare to this!"

"Actually we prefer more cultivated, productive land," Goss said coolly.

"We Shasinn feel very close to the beasts of our homeland," she told them. "It is against the forces of nature that the youths must first test themselves. The great cats are forever hungry for the flesh of our kagga, and many junior warriors die protecting our herds. Now, come. We have only a little farther to go."

They descended the short but steep slope and as they rounded a curving hillside they saw below them a warrior encampment along a small stream. There was no attempt at fortification, but the warriors' huts surrounded a number of large, thatch-roofed buildings.

The moment the queen came in sight around the side of the hill, the warriors below began to swarm like ants, swiftly forming into orderly regiments. Their deep-voiced chanting thundered up toward them and echoed from the hills nearby.

"Your warriors are enthusiastic," Sachu noted.

"They worship me," she said simply.

As they entered the encampment the tall braves shook their spears and their black shields rhythmically, chanting and stamping in a near ecstasy of devotion. Their uniformly blue eyes held the disturbing light of fanaticism.

"So alike they might all be brothers," Goss mused. "Scarce more than a finger's difference in height among them, all bronze of hair and skin." He shook his head in wonderment. "I have never seen such men."

"These are my people, the Shasinn," she told them. "You saw some of the other warrior peoples back by the shore. But the Shasinn are the finest and they have never mixed their blood with that of lesser people." In truth, the queen herself, with her near-white hair, her dark brows, her paler skin and violet eyes, differed startlingly from the Shasinn norm. No one ever dared to mention the fact.

They walked between the ranks of the warriors until they came to the first of the large buildings. "These are storehouses for some of our treasures," she explained. "My husband has hundreds of such treasuries scattered about the islands." She exaggerated, but not greatly. At her orders, warriors raised the hinged wall panels of the building, leaving it little more than a huge, roofed shed.

"There. That will give us enough light to see by. Come with me." She led them into the cavernous area beneath the thatched roof and took a quiet satisfaction in the widening of their eyes. The floor was of finely cut wood resting on a stone foundation, but little of it was visible. Covering the floor was a treasure trove to stun the senses of the most jaded.

Golden plate was stacked in profusion like so much crockery. Giant vases of hammered bronze

held the riotous plumes of exotic birds. Casks overflowed with gems and pearls. The nostrils stung with
the scents drifting from hundreds of spice chests.
Ivory sculptures were heaped with fine instruments
of bronze and glass, and everywhere were piled bolt
upon bolt of precious fabrics.

Some among the strangers made strangled
sounds, but the leader retained his composure.
"Your lord is truly a monarch of substance. And this
is only one storehouse among many?"

"Yes. These are a few things we picked up on our
visits to the mainland." She turned to Goss and regarded him with cold eyes. "Fertile land may be productive, Lord Goss, but warriors are acquisitive."
His face flushed darkly but he gave her a curt nod,
his eyes full of new respect.

"Now come and see something not quite so pretty
but equally impressive in its way." Subdued, they
followed her from the building to one only slightly
smaller. Once again, the sides were raised and they
went within. This time the strangers gasped unashamedly.

The building was not a treasury, but an arsenal.
Here there was no gleam of gold or warm glow of
colorful jewels. Instead, everywhere they looked was
the deadly glitter of steel. Sunlight glanced from polished edges and points. Long swords and short
swords and daggers dangled by their wrist thongs
from long poles. Rack after rack of steel-pointed
spears stood like disciplined troops. Sheaves of steel-
tipped arrows were heaped like grain and the curved
edges of steel axes made shining crescents where
they hung on the roof pillars. The air was redolent
of the sweet fistnut oil that protected the metal from
rust.

As she watched their jaws drop, Larissa once

again thanked the gods whom she did not believe in that she and the king had had the foresight to ship home a huge store of the world's most precious metal before they lost control of the great steel mine. She let the strangers gaze until she felt they were fully satisfied, then she turned to face them. She had their fullest attention.

"My honored guests, I hope this dispels any illusions you may have harbored about the simple, childlike savages you have discovered."

Sachu cleared his throat. "Your Majesty, I never intended any disrespect . . ."

"Let us speak plainly. You sailed into our harbor and you found a town of huts. You saw naked warriors and met their queen, who lives in a palace of wood smaller than one of your ships. A convenient place to stop and reprovision, you thought, but nothing to compare with the riches that await you upon the mainland, is that not so?"

"Well, Your Majesty, I mean to say . . ." Sachu was flustered and the others looked nervously through the open walls at the legion of fierce-eyed warriors.

Abruptly she smiled. "Do not be upset, it is natural enough. As you will find, my husband is a great monarch, the terror and wonder of the age. When we reside on the mainland, we live amid great magnificence and accept tribute from our many subject kings. But in our native islands we prefer to observe the simplicity of our ancestors. You may be excused for thinking us a primitive people. My husband believes that too long a sojourn amid the luxuries of the mainland weakens the men, and that may not be tolerated. Here, at home, even the king lives much as a simple warrior."

"That is most sagacious, Your Majesty," said Goss, sweating now with relief rather than from the heat.

"We, too, hold the plain ways of our forebears in highest esteem."

"That is so," Sachu said, shooting Goss an impatient glance. "And again, I apologize to Your Majesty for any erroneous impression I may have—"

"Think nothing of it," she said airily, knowing that men like Sachu hated to be interrupted in midsentence. She knew that she had seized the initiative and would not lose it. The sight of her vast wealth, the armory of steel and her sudden menace had struck them like three successive blows of a foeman's weapon.

"Now," she went on, "let me show you a few more of our storehouses. I am sure you will find their contents to be of interest. Then we will make our way back to my humble palace, where I have ordered a banquet prepared for you. Don't worry, you will not be expected to drink kagga blood." At this the strangers laughed uneasily. She wound an arm through one of Sachu's and smiled up at him as they walked. "I am so happy that we now understand one another."

He bowed slightly without breaking stride. "Indeed we do, Your Majesty."

TWO

Queen Shazad of Neva paced the broad terrace of her palace like a restless cat. Her court ladies watched her with apprehension. The queen had never been exactly indolent, but in the last few months she had positively crackled with nervous energy. She slept little and ate less, so that her seamstresses were constantly busy altering her elaborate gowns. Back and forth she walked, her body pivoting at each silk-rustling turn, but her head remaining fixed, her eyes trained to the west, past the great lighthouse, toward the open sea.

She was nearing her fiftieth year, still a beautiful woman despite her gray-shot hair and rather haggard appearance. The fine bone structure of her face had gained in strength and dignity as she aged, and her spine was as erect as a guardsman's spear shaft.

"It is time to eat, Your Majesty," said Luoma, her first lady and chief of the royal household.

"I am not hungry," Shazad said, running her fingers absently through her long, still predominantly black hair. Her rings snagged on the pearls strung through her hair on fine silver wire, but she seemed not to notice.

"My lady," Luoma said firmly, "you must eat. You have had nothing today and last night you did not touch your food."

"Yes, I did," the queen protested.

"No. I was watching. What you did was drain a good-sized flagon of wine. You will destroy your health this way. Come eat."

The other ladies watched to see how the queen would accept this defiance. After glaring for a few seconds, she released an impatient sigh.

"Oh, very well."

Shazad walked to the table and slaves snatched up the jeweled covers that concealed the lavish platters. Luoma signaled the musicians and they switched from spring morning music to an ancient dining tune, one believed to promote the appetite. Everything worn by everyone on the terrace was appropriate to the season and the time of day, as was the music. This adherence to ritual was stubbornly maintained by the courtiers and servants.

Other matters of court procedure had been totally wrecked by the queen, who had long since lost patience with what she considered her people's decadent obsession with the niggling little details of custom and ritual.

She sat and began to pick idly at the plates before her. Slaves behind her chair stirred the air with broad feather fans. The day was cool but the insects were no respecters of royalty. Nibbling at a sliver of smoked fowl, she signaled the winebearer to fill her goblet. Luoma waved the boy away and herself filled the goblet with water.

"You try my patience, Luoma."

"You have a council meeting to get through, my queen. You will need a clear head if you expect to keep it on your shoulders."

"All too true." Shazad knew well how precarious was the foundation of any throne. Her own father had usurped the crown from a king who had died mysteriously. She had contended with a number of pretenders and had to make liberal use of the headsman's sword in her earlier years. She had executed the woman who last held Luoma's post. Those closest to the queen had greatest opportunities for treason. Shazad would never oppress her people, but she had long lost any illusion that she could trust her nobles or courtiers.

"One would have thought that driving away those dreadful Islanders would have calmed things down," Luoma said, putting a plate of fragrant baked fruit before her mistress. "Instead, all is in turmoil."

"Say what you will about Gasam, he thoroughly crushed our neighbors and he had my nobles too terrified to plot against me much of the time. With him gone, it is as if the lid were lifted from a great cauldron, letting it boil over."

Luoma sighed. "If only King Hael were able to stand by you as before."

"But he is not and the plainsmen will do nothing until he recovers. If he dies"—her voice was calm but her eyes held dread—"then I am alone."

It had been Hael and his hard-riding mounted archers, not her own soldiers, that had crushed Gasam's armies, although she had supplied many for the campaign. Her nobles had resented having a barbarian king set in command over them. At the time, they had been glad enough to see the enemy fall to Hael's brilliant strategy and headlong tactics, but now they belittled the plains king's contribution and bragged over their own mediocre performance.

Hael was the strangest friend she could imagine, but as long as she could call on him as an ally against Gasam she had a sort of security. One balanced the other in a way, and her nobles feared both. And now there was a new power, Mezpa, far to the east. It was expanding and had masses of the new fire weapons and its armies were said to be surging into lands depleted by Gasam's ravening.

She shook her head. Mezpa was too far away to worry about. It would be many years before that nation could threaten her borders, if ever. She had more immediate dangers to engage her attention.

"Summon the council. I will meet with them in half an hour."

As the messenger scurried away she looked once again toward the sea. But two days before, the fire had been kindled atop the great lighthouse, signaling the opening of the spring sailing season. Ships that had lain in sheds for months were being prepared for sea, and the smoke of pitch fires drifted over the city. A great column of smoke ascended from the massive bronze fire-basket atop the tower. In another season the sights and smells might have gladdened her heart, for it meant that her merchant argosies were preparing to sail to distant ports and return with more treasure and prosperity for her land.

Now she had only one thought: *When will the Islanders come back?*

In the council room the great men stood and bowed deeply as she entered. They were landowners and generals, high priests and masters of the highest guilds. Her father's council had been smaller, but she had expanded it to include those formerly thought too lowly for such exalted company. She knew that narrowness of vision had brought many a king to grief. The merchant mariners had warned of the danger from the island long before the nobles of the council had deigned to take notice. The result had been near conquest by Gasam.

She had formed a smaller, personal council made up of men less prominent than these. She would be meeting with them later, and listening to their words just as attentively.

The queen took her high seat at the head of the table and gestured for the councilors to take their chairs. First to rise was her minister of foreign affairs. He was a white-haired noble of long experience in the diplomatic corps.

"Majesty, noble colleagues, my business today concerns the state of anarchy in Chiwa. The palaces are shattered, and all direct male line, which I remind you is the only sort of succession recognized in the south, is obliterated. A dozen pretenders fight over the carcass, and their warfare is all the more bloody for the store of steel weapons that have fallen into their hands."

"Yes," she said boredly, "there is nothing new about this. What of the exile we took in when Gasam seized the land? Does he yet live?"

"He holds the north and a part of the western coast, but for how much longer we know not."

A general stood. "My queen, the armed forces of Neva are now thoroughly reorganized and stronger than they have ever been. The situation to the south is one of opportunity for us. Before long, if there is no action, our troops will lose their fine edge. The difficulties of the south can be settled by superior force. It will bring peace to that land and quiet to our southern border."

"You mean conquest?" she said. "Never have I sought to take the territory of another nation."

"My queen," said the foreign minister, "our ancient agreements with the lands to the south were with the kings of those lands. Those kings and their lines no longer exist. We can assert our territoriality without loss of national honor." Clearly these two were in collusion.

"We have other problems, gentlemen. The last thing we need right now is to take on someone else's. It would take a generation to reorganize and settle a vast land full of troublemaking people who resort to human sacrifice at the least opportunity. The trouble would be far greater than the possible gain. Gasam stripped the place bare."

"Nevertheless, Your Majesty," said another general, resplendent in dress armor, "we must find employment for our expanded forces. There is an old soldier's saying: 'The trouble with a dagger is that you can do almost anything with one except sit on it.'"

"There is another option, Your Majesty." The speaker was the admiral of the Nevan fleet, Harakh. He was also her husband and prince consort, but in council he had to show her the same deference as the others.

"Tell me, Admiral. I will be most grateful for some sensible suggestions."

"Take the war to the enemy."

She gazed at him levelly. She trusted his judgment and loyalty above all others, but she knew better than to let affection color her decisions. "You mean invade the Storm Islands?"

"I mean just that. The fleet is in perfect order and

the winds will soon be favorable. Let's put an end to this threat forever."

There were some grumbles of assent around the table. Others looked doubtful. War to most of them meant seizing land and parceling it among themselves. There would be little land to take in the islands, and although there were rumors of great treasure stored there, there was no certainty.

She hesitated. "Gasam may be waiting for us." She hated to show weakness, but she knew Gasam personally and she feared him as she feared nothing else in the world.

"Gasam is probably dead by now," Harakh said. "Dead or alive, the myth of his invincibility is destroyed. His warriors followed him fanatically because they thought him to be a god. His enemies fell before him because they were half-convinced it was true. He can never be as effective as he once was, and if he is dead we will fight nothing but disorganized tribal bands. We can snap up the islands one by one until we have cleaned them out."

"He turned the place into a breeding ground for warriors," she said, her objections weakening.

"But they know they can be beaten, and so they shall be." He leaned forward and spoke urgently. "Let me take the fleet north, my queen. I will bring back Larissa and cast her at your feet in chains."

The image was enough to make her feel faint. "I think we can never know peace or security until those islands are scoured. Make a full plan of naval operations and bring it to the next council session. Before we can make any final plans we must have a full intelligence report. I will see to that. I will make my decision before the reliable southerly winds blow."

Not everyone on the council seemed happy, but

many appeared pleased that some sort of action was being taken. A few more matters of little importance were discussed before the queen called an end and her advisors took their leave.

When the sun had set, another group of men arrived at the palace. These did not enter through the ceremonial arch between the files of splendidly uniformed guardsmen. Rather, they came in surreptitiously, through the service entrances on the stable side of the palace. Most made no great effort to conceal their identities but a few were cloaked and hooded. Two or three were armed, and they handed their swords or daggers over to the postern guard without demur. It was a familiar routine to the palace guards.

Most of the men gathered in a small courtyard near the queen's living quarters, but one man was escorted in upon arrival. He was a salty, gray-bearded man who swayed slightly as he walked. Drink had not unsteadied him. His rolling gait came from a lifetime spent with a pitching deck beneath his feet.

Shazad looked up as the man entered her privy chamber. "Good evening, Master Malk."

He bowed deeply. "Long live Your Majesty." He straightened and got straight to the point, as was his custom. "You have never summoned me separately before. I trust no calamity looms for the merchant fleet." Malk was master of the Mariners' Guild, the most powerful of all the many guilds of Neva.

"Not at all. I called you here to tell you that I have summoned Ilas of Nar to this meeting and I want no unseemliness from you or the others."

"Ilas?" The master mariner frowned. "I thought I saw his sour face beneath a cowl out there. The man's nothing but a common pirate. He needs a hangman's rope, not an invitation to council."

"If he is what you say, he has yet to be caught plundering my territory or my ships. I am in the planning stages of an unprecedented naval project, and I have work for him that may not be carried out by my more . . . conventional sailors. Be civil to him, Malk. I hold you responsible."

"It shall be as you wish, Your Majesty." The seaman bowed again.

A few minutes later Shazad entered her privy council chamber. It was much smaller and less splendid than the formal chamber, but that made it a better setting for serious business. The men who rose at her entrance all had hard, serious faces. None held state office but they rendered the sort of services a state could not do without. Some were spies. Others served her as bribers and fixers in foreign lands. Mostly they belonged to such trades as allowed them to travel: sailors, caravaneers, even the impresario of a troupe of entertainers.

Shazad took her chair. "Be seated," she said without preamble.

One among them looked apprehensive but made a valiant effort to appear nonchalant. He had a finefeatured but somewhat ravaged face. Empty sheaths at his belt displayed that he had arrived bearing short sword and long knife.

"I thank you all for coming on short notice," the queen said. "I have an extraordinary project afoot for which I shall require your services." She was gratified that they did not afflict her with courtesies and assurances, but rather listened attentively. "Most of you know each other. One of you is here for the first time: Ilas of Nar."

The man inclined his head toward her with a pre-

cision that seemed well schooled. It went far to con-
firm a rumor she had heard: that Ilas of Nar was the
ruined son of a once-prominent noble family.

"I find myself pleasantly surprised, Majesty," Ilas
said. "But an hour ago I was taking my ease, as is
my custom of an evening, in the Drowned Sailor,
when two of the constable's man braced me and
marched me up the hill. I expected to be cast into a
dungeon, but instead I find myself basking in your
radiant presence."

"Do you feel that imprisonment is imminent?" she
asked.

"An innocent character is no defense against scurrilous gossip, Your Majesty," he replied.

For the first time that day, the queen smiled.
"Serve me well and you need fear neither prison nor
slander."

"Such is my fondest desire," he said, bowing
again.

She found herself liking this engaging rogue, and
was instantly on her guard. Likableness was more
often an accomplishment than a true quality, and
more to be suspect in men of evil repute.

"Neva is soon to commence naval operations," she
said. "As part of the preliminary work for these operations, I require current intelligence of all the maritime nations and islands." She said this in hope of
keeping her true military intentions unclear as long
as possible. It was a forlorn hope, she knew. These
men would know that Neva had only one credible
enemy approachable by sea. She just hoped they
would stay closemouthed about it.

Of course, the story would be all over the nation
as soon as serious preparations began. There was no
way of keeping any plan so ambitious a secret, and

unlike King Hael's, her forces could not fly ahead of the news of their coming.

One by one she gave each man an assignment. The inland probes were not entirely for purposes of misdirection. With her nation concentrating upon an expedition over the sea to the west, her nearer, landward neighbors might discern an opportunity to snatch pieces of Nevan territory. Her agents would know how to recognize the signs of such ambitions.

In truth, though, she had no real fears on this score. None of her neighbors were powerful or well organized enough to contemplate an invasion, but border disputes were endemic and petty campaigns to adjust the borders were a constant headache of the ruler.

As each man received his task he rose and left, until only Malk and Ilas remained. "Master Malk, to you I assign the most important of the mainland seaboard duties. You must find out everything pertinent along the shore from Kasin north past our borders. I have to know whether the Islanders have been raiding, whether they have any secret harbors, whether any of my subjects or my neighbors have been treating with them. I have to know if any of my port facilities have fallen into disrepair. I cannot trust the reports of my local royal officials in these matters."

"I understand, Your Majesty," Malk said.

"Very well. You will draw your funds from the privy purse as usual. You have my leave."

Malk looked doubtfully back and forth from the queen to Ilas of Nar. "Is this wise, Your Majesty? This rogue . . ."

"That is all, Master Malk," she said firmly. "I am quite safe, I assure you."

Frowning, he bowed and left. The queen turned to Ilas.

"You have the reputation of a pirate and reprobate."

"As I have said, Your Majesty—"

"Silence. I know the difference between malicious talk and genuine villainy. As you have seen, my intelligence sources are efficient and reliable. I know for a fact that you are a slaver."

He shrugged. "A perfectly lawful trade."

"But disreputable. It is sufficient that I do not care. The task I have for you does not require virtue, rather the opposite. You are a man of little scruple, some wit and with a sure sense of how to preserve his own hide."

"Your Majesty is acute," he said.

"I want you to go to the Storm Islands and spy out the situation there."

He said nothing for several seconds, then sighed. "I had a small wager with myself that such was Your Majesty's intention. Is there some reason why I should choose this form of suicide?"

"I will reward you richly. And I will not throw you into that dungeon you dread so reasonably and, no doubt, deserve. Besides, a man of your qualities should not find it all that dangerous."

"The homeland of Gasam and Larissa is not some coastal village. Their short way with enemies is legendary."

"Yet they must have trade with the mainland. What would be one more merchant among the others? You can pay visits to a number of the islands, making sure to drop in at whatever port those two are using for their court these days. I need to know whether Gasam is alive and, if alive, whether he is up to another fight. I need to know if the other island peoples are still loyal."

He considered it. "Ordinarily merchants among those islands get their business done and get out as quickly as possible. One who lingers and asks questions will stand out."

"Use your ingenuity."

"My ship is not at present up to such a voyage."

"Use my shipyards for whatever work you need. Or I will give you another ship."

"There is the matter of my crew. Men are reluctant to sail in those waters . . ."

"Doubtless your piratical friends will prefer the water to my rope. Promise them rich rewards. They and the Islanders are brothers under the skin."

"Your Majesty has little patience with objections."

"None at all, in fact."

He leaned forward upon his elbows and laced his fingers before him. "Then let us speak of my reward."

"Name it."

"A peerage for life, together with gold and land sufficient to support high rank."

She smiled. "You place a high value on your life."

"On my life, very little. It is the service you wish me to render that is valuable."

"Do you think titles and lands lie about unclaimed?"

He snorted derisively. "Half your nobles are of no use to you. Dispossess one and give me his holdings."

She studied him for a while. "Very well. When you return with reliable intelligence, you shall have what you ask."

He bowed with an ironic smile. "Then consider me to be at Your Majesty's service."

She smiled warmly. "Now, it might occur to you to go to Larissa with what little you know. Larissa would be the one to approach, by the way—she handles all of Gasam's intelligence and planning. Be assured that your punishment would be severe beyond your most heated imaginings. You would find the island life little to your taste, and they would never trust one who is not of the island blood. Sooner or later, if they did not kill you, you would fall back into my hands again. Remember this."

He assumed a look of hurt innocence. "You wound me."

"I can do far worse than that."

Now he smiled, showing a humorless crescent of long, sharp teeth. "I think we understand one another now, my queen."

"Excellent. Make your preparations and I will stand your expenses. You must sail at the earliest possible moment. Go now." She would have liked to speak further with this engaging villain, but she had much serious work to do and the last thing she needed was a presumption of familiarity from Ilas of Nar.

The messenger from the master of the port came to her the next morning, while she was at the royal stables, choosing a cabo for her morning ride. The master of the port begged her to come to the port to witness a most unprecedented marvel. She summoned her mounted guard and bestrode her own cabo as soon as it was saddled. She was proud that she could still mount unaided, and dreaded the day when she would need a boost from a handler. The beast tossed its four-horned head and danced about with early-morning fractiousness, then settled down. She spurred for the port.

The townspeople were accustomed to seeing their queen clattering through their streets in her riding habit. It was a thing that would have scandalized earlier generations, but this woman had so shattered the previous customs of monarchy that her informality on all save official occasions no longer raised an eyebrow. They cheered lustily at her passage, and it was not the enforced toadying of a downtrodden people. Shazad was genuinely popular with her subjects, who regarded her as their savior upon several occasions. She had turned a decadent land back into the paths of vigor and earned the respect of all neighboring kingdoms. She was stern but just and was far harder on her nobles than on her humbler subjects.

She rode down the slope over the streets paved with patterns of colored stone, past temples draped with garlands of the earliest flowers of spring. The fountains gushed water high toward the cloudless sky. In afternoon the dark clouds would come across the sea like invading mountains, loosing curtains of rain and gusting winds.

But the mornings were perfect at this time of year, and she gloried in the beauty of it, flaring her nostrils to take in yet more of the pure air.

The party rode out onto the great esplanade that fronted the harbor of Kasin, lined with multistoried warehouses. To the north stretched the naval harbor, where the warships were being prepared for the cruising season. The air was sharp with pitch smoke and the pleasant scent of wood being sawed and planed. A cheer went up from the dockside workers and idlers when she appeared in their midst.

A knot of officials welcomed her as she dismounted and they led the queen to a long wharf that jutted from the esplanade.

"What wonder have you for me this morning, Master Elvon?" she asked.

"Something most unusual, Your Majesty," said the fat official, mopping his sweaty face despite the coolness of the morning. "Look, even now it comes!" He pointed to the harbor entrance, where a long, oared ship was towing a rounder vessel into the still waters. A small boat was rowing out to meet them.

Puzzled, she studied the stumpy masts and rags of sail. "A derelict vessel? It's an unfortunate sight, but far from uncommon. Why did you send word to me?"

"But, Your Majesty, the ship is of a sort completely unknown to us! A coast guard ship found it yesterday, almost washed onto the rocks to the south of here. It had been damaged in a storm and its crew in no shape to help themselves. The guard ship took them in tow and sent a cutter ahead to inform me. Here is the report they sent." He handed the queen a sheet of parchment. She scanned the laconic, hastily scrawled words.

"Completely unknown!" she breathed. "What can this mean?"

"I do not know," said the fat man. "No such thing has happened in my lifetime. Vessels from Mezpa and points even farther away are rare, but we know their hulls and the cut of their rigging. This is such a ship as no one has seen."

Now she could see a few wan-faced men leaning on the rails of the strange ship. "They look sick. If there is contagion aboard, they must not contact anyone onshore."

"The physician of the port is on that launch, Your Majesty," Elvon assured her. "If they carry disease, he will run up the yellow flag and they will be towed to the quarantine island."

"Very good. I hope they are not ill. I must talk to these men!" She turned to another official. "They are in some distress. Have food and casks of water brought down here, and fit out one of the warehouses as a hospital."

"At once, Your Majesty," the official said. He bowed and scurried off, shouting orders.

Shazad's face remained impassive, as befitted a queen, but inwardly she was in turmoil. In keeping with his standing orders, the captain of the coast guard vessel had not boarded the stranger, since there was a possibility of contagion, but had merely cast a line onto her and taken her in tow. He had no idea what tongue the strangers spoke.

Word of the prodigy had spread through the city with mysterious speed and the esplanade grew crowded with the citizenry. The unexpected break in routine brought out a holiday mood, as if this were a spectacle being put on for their benefit.

The physician of the port signaled that there was no contagion aboard and the towline was taken ashore and wound around a capstan. With port slaves turning the capstan and the coast guard vessel pushing, the strange ship was gently nudged against the wharf.

"A good thing the tide is low," the queen mused. "This ship has higher sides than any of ours. At high tide I would need a ladder to get aboard."

The official eyed the decrepit vessel doubtfully. "Surely Your Majesty does not intend to board her? This tub is filthy."

"Nonsense. This is too important for delicacy. I am in my riding habit and I'll be no worse off than after a day in the saddle."

A gangplank was laid from the wharf to the deck and Shazad's guards preceded her onto the ship.

Most of the crew sat or lay on deck, sunken-faced and apathetic. Only four were strong enough to stand and look relieved. The physician of the port came up to her and bowed. He wore the long black robe, flat hat and insignia of his profession.

"Your Majesty, these men suffer from starvation and severe dehydration. They must have water at once, and food soon thereafter."

"It is being fetched now," she said. She studied the standing men, wondering if one was the captain of the vessel. Their tattered clothing had once been fine and two of them had had enough strength to get to their sea chests and change into new garments before entering port. One wore what looked like a silver whistle on a long chain around his neck. This man she guessed to be some sort of bosun or sailing master. The other wore a jeweled sword at his waist. He seemed to be the only armed man, so she addressed him.

"Are you the master of this vessel?"

The man tried to speak, but his swollen tongue and cracked lips would not form words. She gestured for him to be silent as a dockworker arrived with a pail of fresh water and a dipper. The eyes of the standing men widened with desperate yearning. The armed man took the proffered dipper in shaking hands and gulped greedily at the water.

The physician took the dipper from the man's weak hands. "Do not overdo it." His assistants took water to the others, and the armed man leaned back against the ship's rail, his eyes closed and an expression of near ecstasy on his face. The physician turned to the queen. "He will not be able to talk for a while. Perhaps not for an hour or more."

"Then," she said to her officials, "let's have a look at this ship." First she looked all over the deck and what was left of the masts and rigging. "Three masts. I'll wager these people have knowledge of sailing that we lack. Is this all storm damage?"

"The deterioration of a long voyage followed by storm damage, Your Majesty," said her master shipwright. "It looks as if the rudder is shattered, and I want a look at their steering gear."

"As soon as I leave," she told him, "get all your wrights aboard. Study and make drawings of everything and send a full report of your findings to me. Bring it personally and be prepared to explain everything to me."

"It shall be done." For several minutes she fired off orders to everyone present for instant action. They had seen her like this before and they scurried to do her bidding. The queen saw everything and forgot nothing. She would forgive no oversight and regarded inefficiency the way others did loathsome disease.

She noted that the fore and aft sections of the ship bore elevated sections topped with separate decks. Warships of many nations had such structures, but she had never seen a merchant ship so built. And it was clear that this vessel was not a warship. It had no ram, its masts carried no fighting tops, there were no provisions for oars to maneuver in battle, the rails were not fortified. Merchant? Explorer? She suspected a little of both. Nowhere did she see a tiller. How was the thing steered?

Her men swarmed below and soon some of them returned, carrying near-comatose sailors. "Their goods are not to be disturbed," the queen ordered. She turned to her ministers and said in a lower voice: "Though I would love to have a look at them. Still, we may be establishing relations with a new nation here, and it behooves us to show restraint."

She itched to know where this ship had come from. Was it alone? What new things might the people of this distant land have to teach her? The master shipwright came up on deck.

"The tiller is below," he said, looking bemused. "There is a contraption of ropes and pulleys attached to it. I think it is steered from up here on deck, with that thing." He pointed to a shedlike structure just before the afterdeck. It sheltered a sort of stanchion that bore a large, spoked wheel.

"Find out how it works," she ordered. "If it is better than our own tillers, I want it installed on all of our vessels before the fleet sets sail."

The man scratched his bearded chin. "Your Majesty, what we need is to get some of these men into talking condition."

"That is being attended to. But if they are friendly, we cannot force them to speak. It may be that these people prefer to keep their navigational skills secret. If nothing else, you can build me a copy of this ship, every plank of it, and we can find out for ourselves how it differs from ours."

The wright sighed. "As Your Majesty wishes."

"Now I want to go below."

"Your Majesty," Master Elvon said, "the deck is bad enough. Surely belowdecks is far worse."

"Nonetheless, I wish to see. If my riding habit is ruined, I will get another. I can afford it."

They descended a wooden stair and found themselves in a low-beamed chamber that apparently ran the length of the vessel. The open space was broken up by the masts and support beams. Along the sides were hung hammocks and there were racks of weapons: short pikes, axes, small shields. There were some cases made of waterproof leather that, by their shape, held bows and arrows. Here, away from the storm damage of the deck, all was neat and orderly.

"Not too bad," Shazad said, "except for the smell. It seems to go farther down. Let's look."

A smaller, narrower stair led them deeper into the bowels of the ship. Below was an even more cavernous chamber, this one containing stacked crates and bales. Beneath the overwhelming bilge stench she could detect spicy smells. She longed to know what was in the boxes, but she would not disobey her own order. She turned at the clatter of boots on the stair behind her.

"The sea has delivered you a fine present this morning, my dear." It was Harakh, her consort. He wore his marine dress armor and he smelled of pitch from the naval yards. He wrinkled his nose. "I thought our ships smelled bad during a long voyage."

"It could be promising, though," she said.

"On my own authority I've sent out every able coast guard vessel to search for more of these. Surely she wasn't voyaging alone."

"I was about to issue the order myself. You've saved me the trouble. There may be more of them in distress."

"I am more concerned that some may be in fine shape. We could be facing an invasion." She could see that he was not joking.

"You can see that this is not a warship."

"That means nothing. This could be a tender or transport, separated from the main fleet. Our own fleet uses two or three support ships for every war galley."

"I had not thought of that," she admitted. Harakh was not terribly clever, but he had a good mind for naval matters.

He leaned close and went on in a lower voice. "Besides, this gives us an opportunity to get the fleet prepared on an emergency schedule without raising suspicion."

She looked up at him and smiled. "Excellent. See to it, and have any other of these ships brought here, disabled or not. If there is a new nation sailing these waters, I want them treating with me first."

He took her hand and kissed it. "As my queen commands."

She went back up to the deck and gratefully inhaled the fresh sea air. From a boring morning, this had turned into a most eventful day. And she had yet to interview the mariners. She looked around and saw the armed and well-dressed man trying to address her, producing only croaking sounds. She gestured for silence and turned to the physician.

"I am returning to the palace now. I shall send litters for these four. You are to accompany them to the palace. My servants will see that they are bathed and, if need be, freed of vermin. Order whatever food you think good for them. I would like to be able to speak with them by this evening. I entrust their health to you."

The physician bowed. "They shall be as my own children."

The queen left the vessel and remounted her cabo. From the merchant harbor she rode the short distance to the naval yards and gave formal orders that the fleet was to be put in order as if a state of war existed. She spread the word that this was a precaution against the strange ship portending an invading fleet. The ruse pleased her. The ship could not have appeared at a more opportune time.

Even as she watched, some of the great hulls were hauled on rollers from their storm season sheds as slaves hurried up with paint pots and brushes. Officials broke the seals on storehouses and sail lofts were opened. Rope walks were laid out and a clattering of metal came from the arsenal. The grand fleet of Neva, greatest military sea power afloat, prepared for war.

That is, it had been the greatest naval force until today, she thought as she rode back to the palace. Now that status was in doubt. Until she knew whence came this strange ship and how many more its home nation had, she could not be certain that she owned the world's greatest naval power. Her knowledge of nautical matters was not comprehensive, but even to her eye this damaged vessel was of a design more advanced than anything she commanded. Three masts!

At the palace she changed her riding habit for a formal afternoon gown. Luoma suggested one suitable for receiving ambassadors, but the queen declined. Until the status of the newcomers was cleared up, she did not want to do anything that would have inconvenient political significance. Foreign rulers had agents at her court who would pick up instantly on the faintest signal. She had to know more about the land these people came from. A sovereign, acting through ignorance, could unwittingly establish relations with the losing side in a rebellion or civil war and earn the enmity of the winner. It was a tedious process, but she knew that she would have to employ the evasions and generalizations of diplomacy until lengthy, official correspondence with the actual sovereign of this new land would enable her to settle upon an official policy.

In midafternoon the physician sent her a report that the strangers were recovering quickly and had no infirmities save those of deprivation. He had, however, ordered medicinal baths for them, as they were infested with vermin. Their clothes were being fumigated. Luoma wrinkled her nose as she read the report to Shazad.

"These are filthy barbarians, my lady," the chief lady said.

"They did not strike me as uncleanly," Shazad said. "I've taken many voyages and I know how difficult it is to keep clean on a ship. And I have plenty of servants to help me. On such a voyage as these men have seen, even the most fastidious of people are liable to pick up some unwanted livestock. My father used to shave his head before setting out on a long naval campaign. He said he would get clean when he got home or captured an enemy bathhouse."

"I hope you are right. It would be nice to treat with some gentlemen of foreign origin instead of savages like the Chiwans and Sonoans and Omians and King Hael's nomads. Even the most courteous of them are uncultivated. The Sonoan ladies wear far too much cosmetic and their perfume is overpowering. The Chiwans practice human sacrifice when they grow alarmed. I do hope these new people are civilized."

"We shall know soon."

Luoma rose from her chair and examined the chains of amber beads woven through the queen's hair. "I think we should change to amethysts, my lady. It is almost time, and . . ."

Shazad slapped her hands away. "You're just looking to see if any of those bugs got on me! I bathed and had my clothes burned as soon as I got back. Now, sit down and act sensibly or I shall dismiss you."

"Yes, Your Majesty," Luoma said primly, smoothing her skirts and radiating disapproval.

Two hours later the foreigners were brought into her presence. She had chosen a small terrace shaded by a vine-laced arbor for the interview. It had none of the formality of the throne room or a privy chamber, but it was sufficiently luxuriant. The courtiers and foreign ambassadors could see everything from a distance, without intruding. She had summoned a few scholars to aid with what was sure to be a language problem. She even had a mime who was skilled at transmitting ideas through bodily gesture alone.

She studied the four men as they walked toward her between two files of bodyguards. They bore themselves well, but could not resist glancing at the gleaming weapons of the guardsmen. She knew that this was not fear. It was because the weapons of the guards were made of steel. So the unknown land was as poor in steel as her own had been just a few years ago. That was valuable information.

The men were quite presentable, and amazingly recovered from their condition of but a few hours before. They strode confidently and they had that indefinable look of well-being peculiar to those who have just enjoyed their first decent meal and bath after a long period of deprivation and squalor. They halted before her and bowed vigorously but without grace. It appeared they were not accustomed to courts. The man who wore a sword addressed her at some length and she did not interrupt.

"He speaks Southern!" she said when he was finished.

"Southern of a most corrupt variety," said a scholar who was a specialist in that language. "Even the most remote mountain provinces of Sono do not use so heavy a dialect."

"Even so, this will be far easier than I had anticipated." She rose and bestowed a formal welcome, using her most cultivated court Southern. The strangers looked surprised and pleased. She turned to her scholars. "All who are not experts in the Southern tongue have my leave."

All but three of the men made their obeisances and withdrew.

Within an hour a great deal of information was transmitted back and forth. Much of it was exciting, much was frustrating. Shazad sensed a great, unprecedented event in the making, yet felt that she was only on the fringe of it, not solidly in control. Still, she persevered, did not alter her demeanor and treated the newcomers as graciously as if they were visiting royalty.

The leader was Shipmaster Orga. His vessel was only one of a great fleet of trading vessels sent north by a queen. He was not the leader of the expedition, but the mere captain of a freight-bearing ship. His ship had been separated from the others during a violent tempest that had wrecked their rudder and much of their rigging. They had been adrift, completely without provisions, for days.

His sovereign was one Isel the Ninth, queen of a nation called Altiplan. He was not empowered to treat in his queen's name, and he bore no documentation from her. His leader was one Lord Sachu, who was a great noble of the court and a famous soldier. They had not seen him or the flagship since the storm, but it and the principal vessels were much larger craft than his own and probably had not sustained as much damage.

She assured the strangers that she had vessels

looking in all directions for signs of their companions, and in the meantime they were to be her most honored guests and she would be delighted to fulfill their slightest wish.

That night she spoke with her foreign minister.

"We must proceed very carefully, Your Majesty," he cautioned.

"I know that all too well. I need no more enemies, and this Queen Isel might be a powerful ally."

"Perhaps. But then, it seems that the distances are vast. This is more likely to be important to our commerce. The arrival of a single trading fleet in a season can mean much, but a military alliance would be impracticable."

"There is so much we do not know!" she said, exasperated. "There are seas and currents and winds to consider. Doubtless they arrived here by sheerest accident. They might have landed in Mezpa and all the advantage would have gone to those loathsome people! We must put together an embassy at once. I want my people at her court before the sailing season is out."

"That would be most advisable."

"We shall need people fluent in Southern, and people skilled in diplomacy. There should be scholars and experienced explorers to make a survey of this new land and send me a report."

"With the royal fleet preparing for war . . ." The minister gestured eloquently.

"Let the minister of the treasury complain about that," she said. "This will be a trifling expense compared to the war. From you I need a list of likely prospects to man the embassy and the mission of exploration. You know the sort of men they must be: The journey will be long and full of hardship. Only the young and fit can be considered. I shall personally choose rich gifts for them to take. We need to know what we have that these people lack. That is the only way to dazzle a wealthy monarch."

"And to lead this expedition?" the minister asked.

She frowned. "Let me think about that for a while. You have my leave."

The minister knelt, kissed her hand and left. Shazad thought long into the night. Who to send to command so delicate and difficult a mission? Surely there had to be someone.

THREE

The plainsmen sat their cabos upon a hilltop overlooking the river's broad floodplain. The beasts tossed their horned heads impatiently, scenting the north wind. The men who rode them wore clothing of finely dressed animal skins and brightly embroidered cloth. The garments were much worn and stained from long, hard campaigning, but the weapons the men bore were immaculate.

A smaller group of the riders had ridden their mounts a little in front of the others. Their brown hair, blue eyes and lighter skin set them apart from the others. They were clearly brothers, and the others deferred to them somewhat, although nothing else about them bespoke rank. Like the other men, they were grim-faced.

The reason for their expression stood in orderly ranks on the plain below them: an army of men who fought more like machines than warriors. They had hand weapons at their belts—short swords and axes—but each man carried a whitish tube slanted across his shoulder. Even as they watched, an officer took one of these tubes from a soldier and raised it to his shoulder, pointing it toward the men on the hill. A puff of white smoke and a tongue of orange flame spat from the end of the tube. A second later something kicked up a spray of dirt a score of paces before the riders. Another second after that they heard a flat, malicious pop.

A rider raised his great bow and sent an arrow arching high. The onlookers observed its progress as it reached the apogee of its arc, then plunged downward into the mass of men below. They could not tell if a hit was scored. Behind the ranked men was a vast earthwork enclosure filled with soldiers. The enclosure had three sides. On the fourth was a great river, and yet more soldiers were being ferried across on barges.

"We've still range on them," said the younger of the two brothers.

"Splendid," the other said drily. "That was an arrow we'll not replace until we get home where the arrow-makers live. They have tons of fire-powder and shot. They turn it out in factories and ship it downriver by boat."

"Aye," said the younger. "With enough arrows we can beat them, but only if we can catch them in the open field, and they're too cautious for that. We attack—they retreat behind their earthworks and mantlets and laugh at us. And we can't sit here forever."

"Forever!" said an older warrior with a barking laugh. "We cannot stay here for another day! Look at this place." He waved his arm in a broad gesture, taking in the inland plateau as far as the eye could see. The grass was cropped so short that the sandy soil was visible. "If we don't head home quickly, our cabos will starve and those ant-men will swarm over us."

"True," said a ranking subchief. "We are losing men to the sickness of the lowlands as well. This is not the host that King Hael led from the plains more than a year ago."

The older warrior, whose name was Jochim, was of a different race from the subchief, but they were devoted followers of King Hael. The two young warriors they addressed were the king's sons.

"Why are you telling us?" asked the elder, whose name was Ansa. "We are just warriors like the rest."

"You are the king's sons, and men listen to you," said the subchief.

"So we are and so they do," said Ansa with a wry grin. "Are we princes of the blood now, just like civilized folk?"

"No," said the older warrior bluntly. "If King Hael were dead, you would be the plain warriors you claim to be. But while he hovers between life and death men are confused and they look for you to take his place."

"That is honest, at least," said the younger brother, Kairn. "I, for one, have no ambition to be a prince, but if everyone wants my permission to ride for home, they have it. There is nothing more we can do here."

"Then we need not wait," said Ansa. "Let's go and give the Thezans the bad news." He wheeled his cabo and the rest did the same.

Trailed by the squadron of warriors, they rode from the hill onto the inland plateau, until they came to a sprawling encampment. It lay along a stream and was dotted with tents of hide and cloth. Once, great herds of cabos had been kept nearby, but as the forage gave out they had been moved to the hills farther inland, reducing the instant responsiveness of the unique, mounted army. The air was foul with the stench of long occupation and swarmed with buzzing insects.

"No wonder there is so much sickness," said Ansa. An accomplished warrior despite his few years, he had high cheekbones and a broad forehead, betraying his half-Shasinn ancestry. "This place has become a wallow for toonoos. Father would not have tolerated this."

A strange lassitude had come over the vast plains army. After the lightning campaign that had taken it in a vast crescent to liberate half a continent from Gasam's tyranny, they had stopped here at the coast like a machine whose spring had run down. Without King Hael's leadership, they were reverting to their former habits as nomadic warriors, capable only of sporadic effort. They had not yet fallen apart into warring tribes but that, too, was just a matter of time.

"If Father does not recover, I do not know what will happen," said Kairn.

"I do," said Ansa. "It will be every tribe against all others, just like in the old days. Some will welcome it."

"Don't talk like that," his brother said in a low voice. "Morale is bad enough as it is."

"It's Father's fault," Ansa replied. "He made himself a king and never paid any attention to succession. He should have listened to Queen Shazad. She tried to tell him . . ."

"She has no children," Kairn pointed out.

"She's made some sort of arrangement," Ansa

said. "A royal cousin or some such. The point is, a kingdom falls apart if there is no orderly transfer of the crown. Father forged a kingdom in a matter of a few years and ran over half the world with it, but it could not survive him and he knew it."

"I think," Kairn said slowly, pondering the matter, "that Father was never convinced that kingdoms are a good idea. He did what he had to do to bring peace to the plains, then to curb Gasam, but he had seen in other lands how degenerate dynasties and their nations can grow. We've both seen that as well."

"Aye," the elder said grudgingly. "He still thinks the Shasinn had the best life in the world, before Gasam ensorceled them. I wonder if he would have thought so if he had ever been anything but a junior warrior among them. To a young warrior, new to his weapons, the world looks simple and good."

His younger brother grinned and poked him in the ribs. "Are we such weary old fighters, then?"

Ansa laughed. "By the spirits of running water, I feel like it! We did more riding and fighting in a few months last year than most men ever see in a lifetime." He shook his head, still dazzled at the wonder of it.

"Men will sing of it forever," Kairn averred.

They rode along the stream until they came to an enclosure surrounded by a cloth windbreak. In its center was a broad awning. Beneath the awning and standing around the enclosure were a double score of men who were of a breed different from the riders. They were tall men, tough and muscular. Most wore armor of reptile hide. The little party of leaders dismounted and went beneath the awning, where a small group of Thezan officers sat cross-legged on the ground.

"We must leave," Jochim told them bluntly.

"Will you be back?" said a middle-aged Thezan. His helmet was the grotesque, fanged snout of a swamp dragon.

"If the king lives, I daresay we will," Jochim answered.

"There is nothing else we can do," said Kairn, ashamed to be abandoning these people who had become their allies. "We are out of forage, the men are sick, and many think the Mezpans have a northern army invading our homeland even now."

The Thezan leader was stone-faced but he radiated despair. "If it is what you must do, then go. It was no small thing to destroy Gasam's army. You were not to know that the Mezpans were the greater threat."

"There we disagree," said Ansa. "Gasam wrecked the kingdoms of the south, which had always kept Mezpa at bay. When he was defeated in turn, it was as if a breach had broken a dam and the Mezpans came pouring in. You have a chance now. We have armed you with steel weapons. Gasam would have exterminated you while the Mezpans watched and waited their chance."

"As you will," said the Thezan.

"What will you do now?" Kairn asked.

"We will go to the hills and hold out there. We have learned the folly of opposing the Mezpans on the field. Their armies and their fire weapons will not serve them so well in the eastern hill country, where the land is broken and the brush is thick. Our king has established a capital in exile out there. He thanks you for the new weapons."

"May they serve you well," said Jochim. "We ride now. We can put many miles behind us before dark."

The subchiefs rode through the camp shouting,

sounding horns and whistles. Drums began to sound, too, and the great camp began to break up as tents came down and pack animals were loaded. It was a sight that always impressed strangers. Within minutes a camp that looked semipermanent was packed and moving north. Hael had drilled his warriors in this maneuver as assiduously as in any battlefield tactic. Movement was the essence of his style of warfare and he knew that no amount of speed on the field would make up for slowness in getting into action. The sons of King Hael gathered their mounts as the others prepared to march.

"I am not going home," said Ansa.

"Neither am I," Kairn told him. "I still think the key to breaking Mezpa is those rebels I met in the forest. I will go join them, see what sort of fire I can kindle under Deathmoon's rump to distract him from his northeastern and southwestern ambitions."

"And see your healing woman, no doubt."

"That, too. Don't you miss your Lady Fyana?"

"I do indeed," his brother confirmed. "But as much as I would like to go to the Canyon and see her and Father, I have another task."

"What is that?" asked Kairn, mystified. He had assumed his brother would journey to the Canyon.

"I go to see Queen Shazad. With Father and Gasam in limbo, she is the only monarch of real power left in the world. Deathmoon is just the head of a council. If Father will not take a long view, somebody must. I have to try to talk her into a long-range policy of containing the Mezpans before they overrun us all."

"Excellent," Kairn said admiringly. "Will you ride back along our invasion route?"

"No, the land is devastated and a plainsman riding alone might be welcome only as a target. I'll ride to one of the ports south of here and take a ship to Neva. This time of year the passage will be faster than overland and I'll see some new sights. I'll need only a single cabo for that. You can take my others."

"I thank you. I'll stay with the army for a way north of here. When I split off, I'll take only the cabo I'm riding and a pack animal. I'll give the rest to Jochim to take home for us."

Ansa shrugged. "They may be grandsires before we see home again. If you reach the hills before I do, tell Mother I have not forgotten her."

"You do the same. You seem gloomy, considering you have the prospect of a little adventure after such lengthy inaction."

Ansa grinned again. "The world is a dangerous place, as we both know, little brother. We may next meet in the spirit world, which Father assures us is an interesting place."

"When you reach Mezpa," Kairn said, wanting to lighten the mood, "send word home by the royal messenger corps. I will try to get word there as well, somehow."

"I'll do that." Ansa looked around them. Where just minutes before there had been a huge camp, now there was only a stretch of barren ground, scattered with the sort of refuse a camp always leaves behind. In a year the grass would be high and green and only the circles of blackened stones where campfires had been would reveal that men had ever been there. "There is nothing to keep us here, little brother. Best we say farewell now."

"Aye." Kairn did not want to say more. His throat felt too thickened for words. He took his brother's hand and held it for a few seconds. Then both wheeled their mounts and the two brothers rode from the former camp, one to the north and one to the south.

It had been a long time since Ansa had last ridden alone. In the past year he had been with the great plains army, just one warrior among many. And he had had his brother with him much of the time. It would take some getting used to, but he was already getting back the enjoyable sensation of perfect freedom that a good mount, fine weapons and a wide horizon gave a man. In this he differed from the plainsmen and hill people among which he had been raised. They were tribesmen and felt very unsettled when separated from their fellows for any length of time. He supposed it was his father's blood that accounted for it. Hael had been a wanderer from his youth, and even as king he had a tendency to take off on long, solitary journeys without telling anybody.

As he rode, Ansa sang and whistled old tunes. He kept an eye out for game, but he saw none. The great host had denuded the landscape of wild game for many miles in all directions. When evening came, he camped by a small stream and ate from his store of preserved rations. The cabo munched contentedly on a bush that had somehow escaped cropping the last time the army's cabos had been pastured in the area. The stars were bright and the sounds of the night animals and insects were restful. His small fire produced the only light on the broad plateau and the wind carried the salt smell of the nearby sea. He slept well.

The next day he came to an escarpment overlooking a small port. He kept his cabo below the skyline and crept up to the ridge with his treasured telescope. It had been a gift from Queen Shazad at the beginning of the epic ride against Gasam. Smaller than a nautical telescope, it packed easily into his saddlebags and he knew from experience that it could save a man's life when everything depended upon keeping distance between him and his enemies.

He extended the instrument and studied the port below. The little telescope had a tiny field of view, so he had to quarter the town slowly so as not to miss anything important. The town was typical of the coast. It had a few buildings of massive stone: a temple and what were probably government headquarters and warehouses. The rest was of wood raised on stilts against the frequent floods. There was not much use in building permanent structures of wood, which would be carried away every few years in the tremendous storms that swept the coast periodically. Instead, most of the lesser buildings were made of light but resilient bamboo, cane and reeds.

He saw people moving among the buildings with no great urgency. Most wore the fairly skimpy loincloths, kilts and light tunics common to the coast, but Ansa thought he detected figures dressed in long-sleeved tunics and trousers in solid colors. These were not native. He raised the glass and scanned the harbor.

Among the numerous fishing craft and small cargo vessels was a larger, bargelike ship. He trained the telescope on its masthead. A banner hung limply there, but he watched it patiently. Presently a light breeze stirred it, enough for him to see that it carried the colors of Mezpa.

He crawled back from the crest of the ridge and shut the telescope with a click. So much for using this port to take ship for Neva. If the Mezpan presence was established this far south, he would be ill advised to stop anywhere near. He went to where he had picketed the cabo and remounted.

For four more days he rode south, then he swung eastward once more until he came to a port. This time there was no high ground overlooking the town, so perforce he had to ride in. He did so warily, ready to wheel and run at the slightest threat.

The town was far larger than the one he had scanned through his telescope. It had an earthwork and timber palisade and a massive gate through which Ansa rode. He gave his name to the gate guard, who told him that the town was called Mudflat.

"Have any Mezpan vessels called here?" he asked.

"No. We hear that they are north of here," the guard said, scratching at his ribs beneath his armor of laced bamboo slats. "No doubt they'll send someone down here to demand our submission." He looked ruefully over the shabby, neglected palisade. "No doubt they'll get it without much argument, too."

Ansa rode into the town and saw that it was moderately prosperous, sitting as it did on a medium-sized river and serving the farm villages in the higher ground to the east. The riverfront collected produce barged or rafted downriver and trans-shipped goods from the harbor where the river met the sea. An artificial seawall of great antiquity broke the force of the waves and gave the harbor some shelter from the great storms.

In the center of the town was a huge, abandoned temple. It looked as if the townsmen had quarried it for centuries for building stone, but the bulk of it remained. He surmised that Mudflat stood on the site of a far older city, and that the builders of that city had probably built the breakwater as well.

The people in the streets looked at him curiously. He did not know whether any plainsmen had ridden this far south during the campaign, nor whether Gasam's black-shield warriors had been through. The town showed no obvious signs of destruction and slaughter, so he surmised that Gasam had missed it.

At the waterfront he found a number of vessels readying for travel to the south and west. He nudged the cabo to a wharf where a capacious cargo vessel lay moored, taking on a cargo of grain. He dismounted and tethered the beast to one of the bollards that moored the ship.

"Where is the master?" he asked a sailor who was directing slaves in the stowage of the grain sacks. The sweating man pointed to a portly individual who stood in the stern of the vessel, going over bills of lading with an ink-stained clerk. Ansa went back and addressed the man.

"Shipmaster, I need passage to Neva. Do you sail there?"

The shipman's eyes widened. "Neva! You'll find no ship sailing that far from this port. *Seasnake* sails all the way southwest to Cape Flood."

"Do any of these other ships sail farther?" Ansa asked.

"No. They all stop well short of there." He added proudly, "*Seasnake* is the widest-faring ship to sail out of Mudflat."

"Then I'll take ship with you, if you're agreeable to carrying passengers."

"Gladly, if you can pay. But I can't carry your animal. No ship here has accommodation for any but small livestock."

Sadly Ansa patted the beast's graceful, arching neck. "I plan to sell him. When do you sail?"

"We are almost finished loading. We will go on the morning ebb, just after moonset."

They dickered for a while about the fare. Ansa only did so for the sake of form, and because the shipman obviously enjoyed it. He had collected an adequate store of loot on the campaign and had been living off the land for most of the last year. He left his gear aboard the ship and, carrying only his weapons and leading his cabo, he went in search of a livestock market.

It was still dark when they sailed the next morning. The moon was lowering its scarred face below the hilltops to the west when the *Seasnake* cast loose. Ansa had never sailed upon the sea before, and he watched with interest as they drifted outward. The sailors manned long sweeps, but he quickly saw that they were using them only to maneuver among the anchored vessels and around the end of the breakwater. The subtle but great power of the tide itself was carrying them out.

When they were well beyond the breakwater, the shipman, whose name was Tallis, sang out orders and the seamen began to chant as they hauled rhythmically upon ropes. The long yard rose up the single mast until it slanted with one end thirty feet above the fantail and the other almost touching the bow. With a deep rumble the triangular sail filled with wind and the ship surged powerfully forward.

The sky was reddening in the direction where the bowsprit pointed and Ansa noted the fact. "We are sailing due east."

"Aye," the shipman said. He leaned on the tiller, a wide grin splitting his face, relishing his control of the power of his ship. "We sail east for another hour before swinging to the south. That is to clear the headlands that thrust well out to sea south of here.

No sense ending your days aground on jagged rocks, is there?"

"No, I would as soon avoid that."

"You are a rider. Is this your first time at sea?"

"Aye. I like it well, so far."

"Good, good. So long as the wind holds fair it is a pleasant experience, even for a landsman. If it turns foul, seat yourself on deck and tie yourself down to a cleat. Do not try to walk about with the deck pitching, you've not the legs for it. And don't cut yourself loose just because we go under for a bit. We never stay down long enough to drown a man."

"Does the ship really go underwater?" he asked, wondering whether this was some joke seamen played upon landsmen.

"It will feel like it. The great waves can cover us, but as long as the holds stay watertight, we breach water in just a few seconds. But as soon as it's calm enough, grab a bucket and start bailing, for we'll need it." The man roared with laughter, as if the prospect of foundering and drowning were enormously amusing.

The sun broke over the watery eastern horizon with a splendor Ansa had never known even on the great plains of his homeland. He looked back along their wake and stifled a gasp. The land was no more than a dark line astern of them. Suddenly the fact that they were isolated amid limitless water became a reality to him. It was an unsettling sensation, as was the sudden realization that there was nothing but water *under* them. It was like hanging in empty space.

He fought down the unwonted attack of nerves. It ill suited one who had been the personal prisoner of Queen Larissa, slated for a horrible death, to be afraid of mere water. The deck beneath his feet was hard and solid, even if it did move continually up and down.

He walked along the deck and familiarized himself with the vessel, noting how the ropes, which made a confusing web when he first saw them, had each its own function. In a short time he worked out the meaning of each, and the rigging of the ship made a complete, sensible picture. The sailors were constantly hauling on one rope, loosening another, changing the angle of the sail or the height of the yard. It reminded him of a musician tuning the strings of his instrument, never satisfied that it was in perfect tune. The sailors seemed never to be satisfied that they were making the best use of the wind.

The vessel was about a score of paces long. He had seen far larger vessels during his brief stay in Neva, but it still seemed strange to him to see anything so large moving independently.

The sailors themselves were a mixed lot. He had learned that seafarers were cosmopolitan, always traveling and with no real home save their vessels, whatever their land of origin may have been. Two of them were tiny men, black as a starless sky. Another was huge, probably twice Ansa's own bulk, pale-skinned and with red hair not only on his head and face but all over his body. Between these extremes were a half score others ranging in color from white to deep brown and with hair and eyes similarly varied. Their language was the language of the sea, which was full of words spoken nowhere else.

Soon they hauled the yard about and the helmsman who had taken over from the skipper leaned against the tiller and the ship swung its sharp beak southward. The breeze freshened and soon the ship was moving through the swells like a spirited cabo, barely restrained by its reins. Ansa felt so strong a sense of exhilaration that he almost forgot the seriousness of his mission. The sea, he learned, was intoxicating.

For many days they sailed south and west. They put in at one little port after another. They loaded and off-loaded cargo at market demand and frequently took on fresh provisions, especially water.

Once, they sailed into a large harbor, its entrance defended by a pair of fortresses built upon twin capes. The city within was large and had once been wealthy. Its name was Crusa and it was great no more. Almost two years before, Gasam's barbaric army had stormed it from the landward side and the inhabitants who survived were hungry and haunted. All the strong young men had been killed. Fair women and young children had been carried off as slaves.

"A great pity," said Shipmaster Tallis. "This used to be a fine town for a revel. That man Gasam has ruined much of the world. I suppose we owe you plainsmen our thanks for ridding us of him."

The townspeople had little to trade, for the place had been picked clean. The ship did not linger, but continued its journey southward. Six days after putting in at the ruined city, they arrived at Cape Flood. It was the southernmost point of the continent, and after the cape the coastline curved to the north and west.

At Cape Flood Ansa put ashore at the town built along the coast. Ships did not tarry long there, for the town of the cape had no true harbor, just an indentation in the coast with a series of wharves and a line of warehouses. Few skippers chose to cruise both coasts, but sailed south to the cape and then turned back homeward.

He felt uneasy for a long time, being ashore and afoot. He was accustomed to the saddle and had a plainsman's dislike of walking, but he had spent enough time among his mother's hill kin that his feet were not totally unfit for walking. They were hunters who ranged widely into places where all game would be frightened away by mounted men.

The terrain of the cape was steep and mountainous, thickly jungled down to the narrow coastal bench. There were no westward-faring ships in port and it did not take long for Ansa to exhaust the amusement possibilities of the little port town. He had little taste for the rough, crude company, and to them he was an alien. He decided to do some exploring in this remote zone.

In the cool morning of his fourth day ashore he took up his bow and arrows, his sword and knife, and with his bundle of provisions over one shoulder he left town and turned his steps toward the hills.

There was no wall, for the town had little worth protecting and there were no hostile people dwelling inland. A few score paces north of the beach the buildings dwindled out and the land ascended sharply. The sandy soil gave way to thick grass and brush, and then the trees closed in. He found a well-marked path and followed it.

Almost immediately, the sound of the surf's constant pounding ceased. The thick-plaited branches overhead closed off most of the light from the rising sun. Soft forest sounds came to his ears: a gentle buzzing of insects and the more raucous sounds of birds. His father, who could talk endlessly of the ways of animals, said that the birds of the jungled lands had such bright plumage and such awful voices because they would otherwise have trouble attracting mates in the dense foliage. Plains birds could be seen for miles in flight and their quiet, melodious voices could be heard for a similar distance.

Ansa was not new to the hot, forested lands. He had traveled in Sono and Gran, ancient lands of heat and jungle. But this was different. Those had been lands long settled, where a thousand generations of men had hacked at the growth to keep it back from their fields. They had cleared the jungle to build great cities, and in time those cities had crumbled and the jungle had resumed its domination, only to be cut back so that newer cities could be built. This place looked as if human beings had never set foot in it.

The path he was on was well marked, but as far as he could see it was a game path. None of the people he had spoken to at the cape town had ever fared inland. They were all transients from elsewhere: company factors, beached sailors, outlaws waiting out their exile until they could return home. None were native to this place. They knew of no natives and had no interest in the land beyond the beach.

Within just a few minutes' walk along the path, he felt his spirits lifting. It was good to be on his own in a strange land, undisturbed by men he could not trust. The sea, at least, was endlessly diverting.

He knew that Cape Flood was claimed as a part of the Kingdom of Sono, but that meant little. Usually there was an official and a small garrison in the town to collect duties, but none had been there since Gasam's invasion. This was a land apart, a wilderness unclaimed because no one really wanted to claim it. It was too wild, too unproductive. No great river broke the mountain wall leading to fertile lands inland. No valuable minerals had been discovered, not even natives to prey upon for slaves.

In the branches overhead he saw tiny faces staring

down at him. There were hundreds of breeds of man-of-the-trees, and this was one he had never seen. Their long, bushy tails were white with narrow rings of black and green. Their bodies had short green fur, and the skin of their naked, wizened faces was pink. Some chattered at him indignantly while others looked on with solemn interest.

He kept walking, and abruptly, as if there were an invisible wall cutting through the branches overhead, the green man-of-the-trees ceased and a larger, blue variety hooted at him. These had bifurcated tails with a pair of fingerlike appendages at their tips. He saw one pick a fruit with this subsidiary "hand" and nibble at it while using its true hands to groom a neighbor.

By noon he was far into the hills and the land was growing ever higher and steeper. He came to many swift-flowing streams but none were too wide for him to cross. The path forked many times but he did not worry about getting lost. Whatever route he took, he had but to head downhill to find the sea once more. Even if he lost a path, he could always walk along any of the streams.

He had seen innumerable animals but all of them were small. The largest were a family of slender-legged hoofed creatures no more than half his bulk. Their elegantly arched necks were topped with long heads sporting eight or ten short, tightly curled horns. They ate by extending their black tongues, each half as long as his arm, wrapping them around the base of a branch and drawing them back in, efficiently stripping off every leaf. The leaves they chewed meditatively until he came too close. Then their ears fluttered and they bounded off into the bush, their white tails twisting in excited circles.

He was about to step over a fallen log when it

moved. So peaceful had the morning been that he felt as if his throat had been seized by a great hand, shutting off his breath. Heart pounding and scalp prickling, he watched the "log" crawl off to his right. It was an immense serpent, the scales and markings of its sides mimicking perfectly the bark of the nearby trees. It seemed to go on forever before its blunt tail slithered past him.

Mentally he cursed himself. He of all people should know how deceptive appearances could be. He had let the quiet forest and its small, harmless fauna lull him into thinking that this was a safe place. Something like that snake could have dropped upon him from the trees. There might be something huge and hungry eyeing him with calculation at any time.

He chose a clearing to pause and eat. The clear area was large enough to give him a good view in all directions. He sat on a rough, flat-topped stone and uncapped his water flask. The dried meat and hard bread were sustaining, but it took a lot of water to get them down, and by the time he was finished his flask was almost empty. He made a mental note to refill it at first opportunity. Water as swift-flowing as that he had been crossing all morning was almost certainly clean.

He was repacking his rations when something about the shape of the clearing took his attention. He had assumed that it was an ordinary clearing, perhaps burned out by a lightning strike. But now it seemed to him that it was oddly regular: a rectangle with two long sides and two shorter, slanting sides. He rose from the stone where he had been sitting and walked around the whole clearing. The sides were not razor-sharp, and the corners were not precisely angled, but still it seemed too regular to be natural.

Within the clearing was only low, scrubby growth and stringy grass. On all sides were tall trees swarming with life: birds and bats, reptiles and man-of-the-trees. Even as he watched, a gliding lizard sailed overhead, the web stretched between its elongated ribs fully extended, its flat tail paddling furiously. A predatory bat dived toward it but the scaly glider put on an extra burst of speed and was among the branches just ahead of the bat's snatching claws. With a clatter of braking wingbeats and a disappointed squeal the bat stopped at the edge of the trees and flew away.

Having nothing better to do, Ansa got up and started to investigate. Immediately, he noticed that the stone upon which he had been seated was also suspiciously regular in shape. Although much weathered and pitted, he saw that it had once been an oblong with squared sides. Squinting his eyes a little, he could see that it was covered with carving, although the marks were so far deteriorated that he could not tell whether they had been pictures, writing or mere abstract decoration.

He had assumed that the clearing was caused by fire in years past, but now he noticed that there were no stumps of large trees such as grew all around, but numerous seedlings that had died or remained stunted because of thin soil. He picked up a flat stone and scraped at the dirt until he had exposed a small stretch of flat stone carved with curling, intertwining designs. A few more such excavations revealed that the whole area was paved with great stones many paces long and joined at right angles with great precision.

It occurred to him that, since the ground sloped

away on all sides from the clearing, he might be atop a great building or platform long since reclaimed by the jungle. The world was full of such places: the mysterious relics of civilizations long vanished. He had seen them in deserts, grasslands and forests, along the great rivers. It meant, his father had explained, that the world was very ancient and had been more populous than now. It was in such a ruin, one of the oldest, that his father had discovered the great trove of steel that had made his kingdom rich, powerful and far-famed.

What sort of folk, he wondered, had raised their temples and palaces in such a place? For that matter, what sort of place had this been in that long-ago time? These were not questions that bothered most tribesmen of his acquaintance. They lived very much in this world, and thought that things now were as they always had been. But Ansa had been raised on his father's tales, and the king had insisted that his sons read the works of learned men.

Thus it was that Ansa knew that a land that was now an overgrown, humid jungle might long ago have been a snow-covered waste. The arid desert of today perhaps had been fertile farmland once, and before that a sea bottom. The contour of the land itself changed, albeit slowly. Once, on a long trek over the mountains, his father had halted the column and dismounted. Scrambling up a stony slope, he had dug with his knife at a thin stratum of whitish deposit that ran parallel to the darker layers like stripes woven into cloth.

He had come down to show his mystified sons a handful of curling mollusc shells and explained that this mountaintop had once been the bottom of a warm, shallow sea. To the other tribesmen this was further confirmation, if any was needed, that King

Hael was mad. His sons had slowly come to accept his outrageous pronouncements as true, although they, too, knew he was mad.

For reasons unknown to him great civilizations rose, flourished, declined and fell. The historians he had read differed in their reasons for this. He knew from experience that powerful kingdoms could be devastated by war. Some held that plagues periodically ravaged the world. Others said that simple exhaustion of the farmland was the usual reason that civilizations died.

This last was hard for Ansa to accept. A nomad at heart, he had the true nomad's contempt for farmers. Even his father, who was incredibly tolerant in most things, had difficulty in hiding his distaste for people who spent their days stooped over like fourfooted beasts, toiling at the grudging earth to produce the weak, savorless foodstuffs of the settled lands. How was such a life in any way superior to mere slavery? Yet those writers had insisted that agriculture was an important thing, and there could be no great populations without it. Why it was necessary to have a great many slavelike drones escaped Ansa. He preferred a numerous and varied wildlife, and great herds of domesticated beasts.

He decided the clearing would be a good place to camp. He had no desire to go back to the town for a day or two, and he had never much liked sleeping with trees overhead. All sorts of unpleasant things could drop from the branches onto a sleeping man, while the open sky seldom dropped anything worse than rain.

His possessions were wrapped in a square of heavy, oil-treated cloth. This he unwrapped. One side he pegged to the ground by two loops sewn to the corners. The opposite side he set upon the great stone and weighted with rocks. Satisfied that the rude shelter would do to keep the worst of the weather off him, he took up his bow and went hunting.

The branches were full of man-of-the-trees, but he had never felt comfortable with the idea of eating them. They looked too human. In his travels in the south he had found that people bore no compunction about eating the little beasts, but then some of those people had been eaters of humans as well. In any case, other game was abundant enough to obviate the necessity of eating them. Late in the afternoon he saw a small herd of toonoos. The fat little scavengers looked much like those he knew, save that their dappled brown–green hides closely matched the forest floor they roamed. He brought one down with an arrow and took it back to his campsite to clean and skin. Before beginning this task he kindled a fire. By the time he had the beast quartered he had a bed of coals suitable for cooking.

He sat in the twilight, smelling the savory smoke coming from his fire. For a moment it occurred to him to stay in this place, but he quickly set aside the thought as foolish. He only felt so because the land was both wild and peaceful, in distinct contrast to his recent life and surroundings. He knew he could not be here long before the land revealed its inevitable evil side. And he had responsibilities. He had to confer with Queen Shazad. He had to know whether his father would recover. He had to get back to Fyana.

So much had happened since he had last seen her. He had been a young, untried warrior when they met. Since then he had fought his way over half the world, against men and the forces of nature. He had grown tired of fighting, but he knew that was only temporary. A few days in this quiet forest and he would be itching for action again.

As it was, his forest idyll lasted only two days. By the time he had cleaned the last toonoo bone of flesh, the lack of human company was urging him downhill, toward the cape. He could not stay in one place. He had to be moving. There were two new ships in the port when he walked down to the shore. One of them, he found, was about to head west.

It was a black-hulled craft with an odd black sail. Its skipper was a large, rough-looking man and his crew was equally rugged of mien. This hardly surprised Ansa. He had noticed that men of delicate look and temperament did not seek their living upon the sea.

"Who might you be?" asked the skipper as Ansa walked the pier where the black vessel was unloading.

"My name is Ansa. I seek passage west."

"We go west. How far are you bound?" The skipper's tunic was of stained, dark brown leather, frosted with a rime of dried salt. Sheathed to his bronze-studded belt was a wide-bladed knife as long as a man's forearm.

"To Neva. The port of Kasin."

"We may not go that far. It's been many a season since I last rounded the lighthouse of Perwin."

"As far west as you go, then. There will always be another ship."

"If you're lucky. To be sure, come aboard. I've carried many a landsman as freight. I trust you can pay your way?"

"I can, but I've no objection to working as well."

At this the shipmaster laughed, a deep, belly-shaking rumble. "A landsman working my ship! It would turn the spirits of the deep against me. No, you shall ride as cargo, my friend."

"As you will," Ansa said, annoyed but lacking any option. He needed a ship westward and who knew when another might appear? He carried his gear aboard and stowed it on the forward deck near the bow. Then he sat and watched as the crewmen and shore workers stowed the last of their cargo. Some of it looked like the bales his last ship had unloaded. There was not a great deal of it.

The ship was much like the one he had taken south but somewhat longer and narrower. The arms racks carried a larger complement of weapons, from which he surmised that this ship sailed in more dangerous waters. He had heard that, since Gasam's disruptions of the south, piracy had grown rampant. The crew was as varied as the other. More of these men bore the features of the southern coasts and islands of Chiwa: stocky, strongly built men wearing distorting plugs in lips and earlobes, their bodies carved with patterns of ritual scars.

They set sail that afternoon, catching a strong easterly wind that filled the black sail and drove them powerfully westward. Ansa felt exhilaration as the spray shot high from the bow and showered him with its salty coolness. Within an hour Cape Flood was below the horizon and they were upon the open sea, with the mainland far to starboard and the broad breast of the ocean interrupted only by the irregular dots of rocky islands.

The next morning, having nothing better to do, Ansa went over his weapons, checking for any slightest speck of rust. He kept them heavily greased, knowing that the salty moisture of the sea was far more destructive than the inland air. Like the others, he had stripped to a breechclout and a headcloth to shield his crown from the fierce sun. As he sat cross-legged with his sword, his dagger and his light fighting-axe before him, the skipper came up and eyed the weapons with interest.

"You are well armed, young Ansa." The skipper, whose name was Utho, had adopted an air of bluff good-fellowship toward his passenger. It did nothing to alter Ansa's sense of unease about the man.

"I've just come from a great war. Having arms and knowing how to use them was the only way to come out alive." He gave his knife another stroke with his small whetstone. It was two palms long and slightly curved, its single edge keen enough to shave with, its spine thick, bestowing strength and adding power to a slash.

"One of King Hael's men, eh? You surely don't look like one of Gasam's." He pointed at the glittering metal that lay around Ansa. "I can remember when so much steel was a treasure beyond most men's dreams. Men would have banded together to kill you for the knife alone. With that sword I could have retired from the sea and bought an estate and slaves to work it."

"Fortunately," Ansa said, "steel is plentiful these days." He gave the edge another stroke and smiled up at the shipman. "So I can sleep secure, knowing that no one will slit my throat for the sake of my weapons."

"Aye," Utho said uneasily. "That is true. Times are better now." They both looked up at a shout from the masthead.

"Sail to port!" The man's outstretched hand pointed to a speck of red so far away Ansa would not have known it for a sail. He took his telescope from his bag and extended it. He saw that the red object was, indeed, a sail. It was square and below it was a twin-hulled vessel.

"What do you see through your instrument?" Utho asked.

"A ship, but I don't know what kind." Ansa handed the tube to the skipper. "Here, look for yourself."

Utho scanned for a few moments to find the vessel, then he worked the tube to focus the image. "A Chiwan. From Sancri, I'll warrant. That's one of the islands. Been prosperous, these last few years. Not paying any taxes to the king of Chiwa, you see. And Gasam never got to the far southern islands." He folded the telescope and handed it back. "A fine instrument. My thanks."

Ansa nodded, making no comment. Within an hour the other ship was within hailing distance and the skippers began calling back and forth, exchanging news. Ansa could not understand the heavy dialect they spoke. The Chiwan vessel came about as Utho ordered his own sail lowered. Both ships lost way and began drifting together.

Ansa walked up to Utho. "What is happening now?"

The skipper grinned. "I asked them if they had any hava root. Chiwans always carry it. Told them some of the men are coming down with the spotted sickness. Hava root clears it up."

"None of the men look sick to me," Ansa said.

"They're not to know that, are they? Now, you just stay out of the way, landsman. These are seamen's matters."

Ansa backed away from the rail, not liking the tone of this. He knew something was about to happen, and he knew he was grievously outnumbered aboard a vessel he did not know how to operate. A

line was cast from the twin-hulled vessel and made
fast to a rail as the sides of the two ships touched.
The Chiwan vessel, despite its twin hulls, carried a
smaller crew, perhaps a score of men. They wore
colorful kilts and necklaces of beads and feathers.

The smiling crew of Utho's ship laughed and
waved and then, the moment the ships touched, they
stormed over the rail, wielding weapons they had
held concealed beneath the edge of the bulwark.
Their smiles and hails changed in an instant to
howls as they hacked the other sailors down.

Ansa had been expecting trouble, but this abrupt
savagery caught him off guard. He retreated to the
extreme bow of the ship and drew his long sword.
Having disposed of the other crew, he expected the
men to attack him next. He vowed they would not
have as easy a time with him as they were having
with the unsuspecting crew opposite. Most of them
were killed in the first rush, but a few dropped to
their knees and clasped their hands behind their
backs in a gesture of surrender.

As Ansa had expected, the gesture was futile. The
surrendering men were dragged to the rail. While
their arms were securely held, one of the seamen,
with a practiced routine, placed a knee in the middle
of each man's back, took a handful of hair and
jerked his head back, and with a quick sweep of the
knife slit his throat. Arms released, each man was
hurled into the sea, still gurgling and spouting
blood.

Ansa had seen a great deal of violent death, but
the cold brutality of this murder at sea left him ap-
palled. In a matter of minutes all the crewmen of the
other vessel floated in the water, but only for moments. As if by magic, the sea was cleft by the fins
of sharks and the scaly, serrated backs of predatory

reptiles, then it was churned to pink froth as the meat-eaters tore at the corpses and at each other.

Utho came walking toward Ansa, wiping his broad knife with a scrap of cloth. "Put up your sword, landsman," he said, his eyes twinkling with amusement.

"Why should I do that? I am to be next, am I not?" He gripped the sword tightly and sighted upon the place where he intended to commence carving on Utho. "I promise you, I won't go as easy as they did."

Utho sheathed his blade. "Aye, I'm sure you would furnish some lively amusement, but we have what we wanted. Now, you're not a part of the crew, so you're not entitled to a share. But we want no trouble from you, either." Several of the crewmen now stood behind their captain, eyeing Ansa warily. Now he understood.

"You're not fighters. You're not warriors of any sort. Murder is your style. You want no truck with a fighting man, do you? I didn't think I was taking ship with pirates."

"Who is a pirate?" said Utho with wounded innocence. "We are simple sailormen, making a living on the hard sea. If a little easy prey comes our way, should we insult the gods by refusing it?" He loosed his belly-shaking laugh. "If men have goods worth taking, it is their fault if they cannot protect them." He turned to his men. "Come, let's see what we have."

As the cutthroats turned away, Ansa sheathed his sword. He knew he was in for some sleepless nights, but these carrion bats were not cause for much worry. He hoped they would find strong drink in the other vessel's cargo. If they got drunk, he would kill them all and take his chances making his way back to shore. Perhaps he would keep one alive to work the vessel.

He stayed watchful all that night, nodding off from time to time but always snapping wide awake at any irregular noise in his vicinity. It was no special hardship for him. He had lived much of his life in the saddle, tending herds that were always in danger from predators, or on long hunts where beast and man poised an eternal threat. In the last year and more he had been on wartime status, on endless scouting patrols and standing sentry duty, where wakefulness was a literal matter of life and death. He had long cultivated the art of sleeping in brief snatches, one eye open, ears poised, weapon in hand.

There had been no strong drink aboard the foreign vessel. The sailors had transferred the cargo to their own ship and then smashed holes in the bottoms of the other ship's hulls. They raised their sail and continued their journey, with the ill-fated craft settling in the water behind them. Ansa knew that it would be just one more ship that never returned home. He knew there were scores, perhaps hundreds, such every year. He wondered how many were victims of piracy rather than the elements. With all evidence disposed of, Utho and his men could resume their pose as innocent merchantmen, at no slightest risk of retribution. And who would listen to the accusation of an outlandish plainsman?

Three more restless nights brought them to an island large enough to be mistaken for the mainland by an inexperienced traveler. They cruised past its low southern extremity and Ansa watched with interest as the ridge in its center climbed until, hours later, they came even with the northern end of the island, where the ridge terminated in the hulking cone of a volcano. A thin column of smoke drifted from its crest. The crest itself was, incongruously, rimmed with snow.

He had seen volcanoes before, deep within the Poisoned Lands and in the Canyon country, but to see one rising abruptly from the sea was bizarre. The juxtaposition at sea-level tropics and a snowy mountaintop struck him with a sudden, disorienting sense resembling vertigo, as if the natural order had been overturned.

The shoreline looked unpromising, with rocky cliffs plunging a hundred feet or more to the breakers below. Birds, bats and flying reptiles dotted the air between sea and cliff face, light flashing from bright feather and jewellike scale as they passed back and forth between their feeding grounds and their nests in the ledges and caves of the cliffs.

To his surprise, Ansa saw two small ships sailing from what appeared to be a narrow crack in the cliffs. Utho's ship headed for the same crack. Had he not seen the ships emerging, he would have thought the steersman had become suicidal, for it looked to his untrained eye as if they were sailing straight to disaster on the rocks beneath the cliffs. He gripped the rail and gritted his teeth as they lurched toward the cliff, then his tension eased as they entered the crack in the wall and he saw it was considerably wider than it had appeared to be from a distance.

"Smoke Island," Utho said, coming up beside Ansa. "Finest harbor in the islands. None better on the mainland, in fact. A ship can ride out the worst storm in this harbor." The shipman had been behaving toward him as if nothing had happened, as if the slaughter of a shipful of men were nothing but the most trifling incident of an uneventful voyage.

"Will there be many ships there, this time of year?" Ansa asked.

"Oh, aye. There's a fine town and good water, and the farmers inland raise plenty of provisions. There are a score or more of ships hear anytime of year."

"Good. I'll find another for the balance of my journey."

"I wish you would reconsider. You seem to be taking to the sea well enough. I've heard of how you plainsmen can shoot those big bows of yours. A real warrior who could pick off a steersman from a cable's-length distance would be a valuable addition to the crew."

"I think not," Ansa said, his temper flaming.

"Very well," Utho said reasonably, "a double share, then. But you have to be part of the boarding party."

"I am no pirate!"

Utho looked disgusted. "You people are raiders, are you not? What is the difference? When valuables are there for the taking, men of spirit take them. Who cares about the fools who do not know how to protect themselves?"

"I never killed a man who was not trying to kill me. Everyone my people fight have fair warning of what is coming."

"Riders!" snorted Utho, turning away. "They always think they are too good for any work that can't be done from the back of a cabo!"

Ansa had no interest in setting the man straight. He just wanted to get off the ship as soon as possible. This looked like a good place for it, at least. The lagoon they entered was almost circular, surrounded by gently sloping ground green with vegetation. A town of multistoried buildings clustered along the southern rim of the circle, and he saw at least fifteen ships riding at anchor within the lagoon and a few others tied up at piers. Surely there must be some less loathsome vessel headed toward Neva.

Utho's crew ran out oars and maneuvered the ship toward a pier where another craft was casting off. As soon as the ship was fast to the wooden walkway, Ansa leapt ashore, carrying all his belongings and not bothering with farewells.

He felt intense relief at being off the ship and there was a spring in his step even though the pier seemed to sway beneath his feet like the deck of the ship. If any nation claimed the island, there seemed to be no officials around questioning solitary travelers.

The waterfront featured many establishments catering to ships and their crews. There were sailmakers and shipwrights, chandlers and victuallers. There were also brothels, taverns and inns. He decided that an inn farther inland would be a safer and more agreeable place, so he made his way uphill, toward the landward side of the town.

Ahead, over the rooftops of the town, the smoking mountain hulked ominously. It gave him a sense of unease, even though it was evident that the mountain had not erupted for centuries. That did not mean that it would not blow up at any moment. He passed through an area of market stalls and paused to have a look at the goods on sale.

He was surprised to see valuables from many lands. There were jewels and instruments, bolts of luxury cloths and even books. A weapons shop displayed a large number of the new steel weapons and he saw a beautiful Shasinn spear such as the one his father always carried. He had seen many such as a captive among the Shasinn, and he wondered how one happened to make its way here.

He left the market with a greater sense of unease

than the volcano had given him. It suggested that the
port was a pirate haven, where they disposed of their
ill-gotten loot before sailing on to more civilized
places. His unease did not prevent him from picking
up a handful of steel arrowheads. However they came
to this place, he was sure to need them.

Near the edge of the settlement, he found an inn
that catered to the less nautical sort of travelers. It
was clean, with walls of whitewashed stone and a
roof of flat slates. The room he was led to was on an
upper floor, with a window that opened upon a vista
of orderly, cultivated fields that ascended the slope
of the volcano. Best of all, it had a door that could
be bolted from the inside. Having settled his bill, he
bolted the door, undressed, lay down on the narrow
bed and slept the rest of the day.

He was awakened by someone knocking on the
door, announcing that dinner was ready. He roused
himself and looked around for a basin. There was
none in the room, but he remembered seeing a small
fountain at the bottom of the stair. He dressed and
armed himself, then unbolted the door and went out
to the landing and the stair that led down the outer
wall.

The basin was set into the wall of the inn, and water poured into it from a pitcher held by a sculp-
tured hand that protruded from the side of the
building, as if someone were reaching out through
the wall to pour. He bent over and splashed his face
and then jerked back in surprise. The water was hot.
It was not painfully hot, but it had caught him by
surprise. He had braced himself for frigid water.
Over his astonishment, he finished his ablutions and
went inside.

The common room of the inn was low-ceilinged,
but it was bright in the daytime because about half

of the roof was open to the sky. Beneath the skylight thus formed was a pool to catch rainwater and the tables were arranged around the pool. The sun was almost down but there was still plenty of light, and a servant was arranging torches around the pool.

He took his seat on a bench and saw that a man seated across from him was looking him over with some wonder. The other was a middle-aged man, with a graying beard and clothing Ansa recognized as Nevan. Since the man was staring, Ansa stared back.

"Please forgive me, young man," the other said. "A plainsman is the last wonder I expected to encounter in this place. I am Scholar Ambleis, of the Royal Academy of Kasin." He held out a fine-boned hand and Ansa took it.

"Ansa, a warrior of Hael the Steel King."

"I surmised you were of that nation. I had the privilege of meeting King Hael at a court reception when he came to aid us against the barbarian Gasam. Like all my countrymen, I bear the greatest gratitude toward your king and his warriors."

"An enemy like Gasam makes friends of the rest of the world." He had grown cynical about the gratitude of one nation toward another. It seemed that it seldom survived the immediate mutual danger.

"How true, how true. How do you come to be so far from your native plains?" The man seemed honestly interested, and Ansa knew that scholars could be curious almost by profession.

"I need to confer with your queen on my king's behalf." A serving girl set a cup before him and filled it from a pitcher of purple liquid. The stream of wine gave off a savory fragrance. He took up the cup and sipped. It was sweet, with a pungent undertaste.

It tasted strong, and he reminded himself to eat something before he drank too much of this.

"Ah, you are a royal official? It did seem to me that you sound, shall we say, more cultured than the other plains warriors I have conversed with."

"You spoke with the warriors when we were in Kasin?"

"At every opportunity. I am a scholar of nature and I wished to learn of the flora and fauna and weather of their native lands." He took a long drink from his own wine cup. "Unfortunately I had great difficulty in understanding their speech. You, on the other hand, speak excellent Nevan."

Ansa knew that he was in for an interrogation and he was right. At every opportunity he tried to steer the conversation to subjects of more interest to himself, with some minor success. Over the fish course he learned something of Smoke Island.

"At various times both Chiwa and Neva have claimed this place. While both nations were preoccupied with Gasam and the Islanders it grew virtually independent. As a result, it is nearly lawless. Did you see the market?"

"I did," Ansa said. He described the events he had witnessed at sea and Ambleis nodded solemnly.

"That sort of behavior has grown rampant. Never fear, though. My queen is busy reestablishing order and Smoke Island will soon be secured under Nevan authority. It was once a famous resort, you know."

"Resort?" Ansa said, unfamiliar with the word.

"Oh, yes. It is famous for its hot springs. The wealthy used to come here to partake of the curative waters."

"That hot fountain outside!" Ansa said. "I wondered about that."

"Exactly. Is it not marvelous? You see, the rain-

water that falls inland percolates through the porous
layers of stone and is heated as it passes through the
volcanic mountain. Then, when it reemerges here on
the seaward side . . ." and the man was off on a
lengthy description of his favorite subject.

Ansa ate his fill and drank all the wine he wanted,
knowing that he had a secure place to sleep. With
dinner over he followed the scholar's directions to
one of the bathhouses. There he soaked for two
hours or more in pools of progressively hotter water,
scrubbed by attendants and feeling the bone-deep
weariness leave him along with many weeks' accu-
mulation of dirt, sweat and sea salt. He could not
vouch for the water's curative qualities since he was
not sick, but they certainly made him feel better.

Washed and dressed in his carefully hoarded clean
clothing, he felt able to take on the world. He even
considered looking up Utho and killing him, but dis-
carded the thought as impracticable. The times allowed such men to flourish, and there were countless
others to take his place. He would accomplish nothing save to get himself mobbed in a town that catered to the likes of Utho and his crew. With no
prospect of action, and knowing better than to wander alone in a strange city at night, he returned to his
room, bolted the door and soundly slept the night
away.

The next day he explored the town and looked
over the ships in the harbor. The scholar from Neva
had explained that the strange, circular lagoon was
actually the caldera of an older volcano, now sunk to
sea level and filled with water. Several captains were
bound for Neva and willing to take passengers, but
he had no way of knowing whether they were as bad
as Utho or even worse. A man certainly could not
tell by looking, for sailors, as a breed, looked villain-

ous. They lived a rough life amid a dangerous environment and could hardly look otherwise. With so many to choose from, he felt no need for haste.

The next day he did some exploring in the countryside. There were cultivated fields of grain and other produce, of vineyards and orchards. There was very little wildlife, and he learned that the island had been cultivated for so long that nearly all of it was farmland, with very little haven for wild beasts. Thus it was beautiful but not at all exciting. He knew he would go mad in a short time amid such surroundings, which civilized people professed to find ideal, which he knew to mean safe.

On the third day he was about to make a choice of vessel for the balance of his voyage when he heard a commotion along the waterfront. Everybody was rushing to the waterfront and staring toward the harbor entrance, so Ansa looked that way himself.

In stately procession three large warships cruised into the harbor, the sunlight flashing upon their banks of oars as the polished wooden sweeps rose, dipped and rose again with machinelike precision. The ships were brilliant with paint and gilding, their rams sheathed in bronze wrought into the semblance of monsters' heads. Across the water of the bay came the pounding of the timekeepers' drums, but no other sound came from the intimidating ships.

Forming a line abreast, the three ships came toward the shore as if they intended to ram the island and sink it. Then all the oars dipped into the water and held there, raising a great spray as the ships lost way and came to a stop within a few strides of the piers. The crowd cheered raggedly at the masterful maneuver, but there was apprehension as well. They seemed to know that this could portend something bad.

The center ship lowered its massive boarding bridge that swung out like a crane from the towering mast. Its bronze spike, designed to bite into an enemy's deck and fasten the ships together, sank instead into the wood of the pier. An officer in cape and gilded armor strode down the bridge, followed by a double file of marines bearing steel-tipped spears and belted short swords.

The officer carried a scroll in one hand, and the sunlight flashed from his helmet as he walked down the pier to the waterfront and climbed onto a platform that was usually employed for holding auctions. The crowd gathered around the platform as he unrolled his scroll.

"Her Majesty Queen Shazad of Neva," he began, "hereby takes possession of her maritime province, Smoke Island, the rightful possession of the kings of Neva for more than a thousand years." There was some grumbling from the crowd, which he ignored. "Her Majesty most graciously extends her amnesty toward any of her subjects who have committed nefarious acts upon the great waters during the times of troubles brought about by the outlaw barbarian Gasam. Now that her rightful sovereignty over this island, and these waters, has been restored, the customary penalties are back in force, to wit: Anyone apprehended in acts of piracy is to be hanged immediately, without trial."

He pointed at a three-storied building that stood derelict upon the waterfront. "I hereby reestablish the Royal Port Authority. All shipmasters now in port are to report there forthwith to pay their duties. Any who try to depart before obtaining royal leave shall be rammed and sunk. That is all. Long live the queen!"

There were no cheers this time as the crowd dispersed, looking dejected. The gilded man did not look at all disappointed by their reaction as he came down from the platform. Already, more marines were coming ashore and men dressed in royal livery were striding toward the reopened customs building, followed by slaves bearing chests and furniture. Ansa walked up to the speaker and the man's eyes widened at the sight of him.

"By all the gods, a plainsman! Surely King Hael's forces do not ride across water."

"I took ship from the coast near Mezpa. I need to confer with Queen Shazad on matters touching our two nations."

"Say you so?" The man raised his eyebrows skeptically beneath the bronze rim of his scarlet-plumed helmet. "And your name?"

"Ansa."

"Come with me." The man whirled abruptly, making his green cloak flare out behind him. He walked back toward his ship with Ansa following. "I am Commodore Elkon, late of the fleet securing the old Chiwan port of Halis. A cutter came with orders for us to rejoin the main fleet at Kasin, after first stopping here to show the flag and get the taxes flowing again." They went onto the bridge and crossed to the warship. "This is the flagship of my flotilla, the *Shatterer*." His voice took on the affectionate sound mariners always had when speaking of their ships.

The sparkling deck of the ship was lined with marines and sailors standing to arms. Either they were taking no chances or they were always under tight discipline. Ansa followed the captain to a cabin in the rear. It was well appointed, with glass windows and fine furniture, but the beams overhead were so low that he had to duck his head. Elkon opened a chest and took from it a thin book bound in beautifully worked leather. He sat behind a desk and studied it.

"As it happens, I have here a listing of the foreign dignitaries entitled to call upon the royal navy for transportation when on diplomatic missions. What was your name again?"

"Ansa." He was impressed by this degree of organization.

"Ansa, Ansa, let me see . . . this list was brought up-to-date just three months ago . . ." His eyebrows went up again and he looked up at his guest. "Ansa, elder son of King Hael?"

"That is I," he said, in what he hoped sounded like official tones.

"Would you have credentials or other identification?" Then he waved a hand in dismissal. "No matter. It says here that Ansa is known personally by Her Majesty. If you are Ansa, she will receive you royally. If not, she will hang you as an imposter. Certainly you are welcome to passage. Bring your belongings aboard at once. We shall have plenty of cabin space as soon as we've moved all these officials off."

Ansa could hardly believe his luck. "When do we sail?"

"We go at first light tomorrow. Our orders are to waste no time whatever in joining the fleet. Some sort of activity is afoot." He looked up again, speaking in a low voice. "I don't suppose your mission has anything to do with this?"

Ansa answered conspiratorially. "I am not at liberty to say."

"Just so. Say no more, say no more. We'll deliver you to court safe and sound, Prince Ansa."

It still seemed odd to be so addressed. His warrior companions would have hooted with laughter to hear it. He rushed back to his inn and gathered up his belongings. He took his leave of Ambleis, who beamed when he heard the news.

"Wonderful! Civilized order returns! Now I will be able to submit to the academy my paper on the effects of subsurface thermal water upon cultivation of the common winefruit."

"It will make your reputation," Ansa assured him.

The next morning he was on his way to Kasin with a swift warship beneath his feet.

FOUR

There were, thought Ilas of Nar, definite advantages to be had from serving Queen Shazad. Her open purse and priority access to her shipyards, for example. *Seasnake* was a sloop of war, lean and swift. She was only a few years old and had recently been renovated, so her paint was bright, her sides newly tarred, her sail unfurled for the first time when he sailed from Kasin. The master of the shipyard had been infuriated when he walked in demanding the vessel, but a message from the queen had silenced him swiftly.

It had gone likewise with the provisioning. He had requisitioned the best of victuals and had insisted on opening personally each wine jar to ensure that its contents were the finest. Then he had taken the vessel to a servicing area up the coast and had altered her appearance so that she would not be identified as a ship of the Nevan navy. Thus altered, she was, in fact, exactly the sort of ship favored by pirates.

Ilas had quickly abandoned the idea of traveling to Gasam's islands in the guise of an ordinary merchant. He would go as a pirate. It was more believable and they would accord him greater respect. When he picked up his crew, all men long known to him, they were mystified by his sudden prosperity. He would not tell them too much, but he dared not tell them too little. He explained that he had bribed a naval official to condemn the vessel as unfit for service and sell it to him for a pittance. They knew that much could be accomplished with bribery and blackmail and were satisfied.

He had not had to use Queen Shazad's methods of persuasion to entice the crew to take part in a hazardous voyage. The naval press gangs were rounding up seamen for the mobilization of the fleet and men were all too anxious to take any other sort of work. Pirating was no more dangerous and the rewards could be lavish.

He was musing over the vagaries of fortune when Tagas, his mate, came to join him in the waist, where he leaned on the crimson-painted rail. The ship moved along soundlessly, the strong southerly wind filling their taut yellow sail so that it swelled like the belly of a pregnant woman. The crew lounged at ease, with nothing to do until a change of wind should call for some rope-hauling.

"Safe waters now, Captain," Tagas said. "Time to begin the work we set sail for." He leaned on the rail beside Ilas, gripping it with big, scarred hands. His left hand was missing its smallest finger and half of the finger adjacent. Both wrists were banded with wide, bronze bracelets that stained his wrists green.

"Though I'd have thought south was a better direction."

Ilas heard him out. Discipline on a pirate vessel was not like that on a naval ship or even a merchantman. Pirates spoke their minds and had little regard for rank. His right to set their course, plan their operations and command in action was unquestioned, as was his full third share of the loot. In other things pirates believed in democracy to the point of anarchy.

"For one thing," Ilas explained, "the winds this time of year are not right for it. More importantly, there is too much competition down there. The coastal towns have been picked over like a carcass that has seen too many carrion bats. On top of that, Queen Shazad has reestablished her coast guard in formerly Chiwan waters these last two seasons. I fear that the fine days of chaos in the south are drawing to a close."

Tagas nodded. "While the north has been growing fat of late. And now, with the fleet assembling at Kasin, there will be little patrolling in these waters."

"Exactly."

"But that may be only for this season, Chief."

"It goes without saying. A man can make enough to retire on in a season. And what pirate takes heed of the future? We are not merchants, after all. We go along from season to season, taking our prey as it comes to us, relaxing in port during the storm time."

Tagas grinned and chuckled, a deep rasping sound from somewhere in his corded throat. "Aye, aye!" Then, more seriously: "But do you think it is such a good idea, going to the Storm Islands? Those folk are hard to predict, and surely they must be rich already."

"No one is ever too rich," Ilas pointed out. Then

he leaned toward the mate and spoke in a lower voice. "I have it privily, on the very best authority, that this gathering of the fleet is in preparation for an invasion of those islands. This may be our last chance to share in that wealth of theirs."

"Truly? Neva has come to grief ere now, taking on those savages. They'll have no King Hael sailing with them."

"Very true. But what is it to us if she meets with disaster? Anything that weakens the fleet strengthens us. And one cannot guess the future. There may be no Gasam leading the Islanders as well. There could be fine pickings for us in those islands if Gasam's forces are shattered. They are handsome folk, and their women and children would bring the highest prices as slaves."

"And we would be the first there! You have a good mind for this work, Captain," Tagas said approvingly.

"It is why I am captain," Ilas said complacently. Indeed, he was well pleased with his situation. He had picked an excellent pack of cutthroats, good seamen all, and he had never had so fine a ship. It was only his right as a nobleman, but it was his observation that matters of right carried little weight in the world. He relished the freedom of the seas and his instincts were always predatory.

Most of all, the prospect of gaining land and title inflamed him. His family had been landed gentry for generations. He liked to give himself the airs of a great lord, for he felt that it was his rightful heritage to be one. To be a great lord in fact, with the patents of nobility and the estate to go with the title, was a prospect so fine as to be physically painful.

He trusted no one, but he did not think that Queen Shazad would deal treacherously with him.

Reputation held her to be stern, even ruthless when need be, but never cruel or arbitrary. She always kept her word, it was said. Of course, there had been no witnesses to their negotiations, and she could always disown him, but he thought not. His dealings with men and women were of the broadest sort, especially with the most evil specimens of both. It was his experience that few could play at being publicly upright while acting treacherously in private. Always, the inner corruption surfaced in public dealings. Shazad had been monarch for many years, and no such inner evil was manifest.

Larissa was another matter, and he felt no shame that the thought of her caused his bowels to quake. Ilas was aware that he was not a good man, but at least he was a man. Larissa and Gasam, he suspected, were not truly human. They were like demons from the underworld, given life and flesh, beauty and power. They dealt with their fellowmen not as with lesser beings, in the usual order of royalty, nobility, commons and slaves, but rather as members of a different species entirely.

Only a madman could regard such creatures without fear. Whatever his moral failings, Ilas of Nar was not mad.

One of the sailors, a man from a semicivilized nation far to the north, knew of a town, not much more than a large village, that lay near the coast on a middling-sized river. *Seasnake*, with her shallow draft, could approach the place by way of the river undetected, for the stream took a sharp bend just downstream of the town. The sailor had been a slave there for a time and longed to see it sacked. It was agreed that this town should be their first victim.

With the former slave in the bow taking soundings, *Seasnake* entered the river by moonlight. The oars were muffled, the oarlocks wrapped in coarse cloth. Silent as a ghost, the predatory vessel made its way through the misty night. The men waited nervously, eyes peeled for sign of night fishermen, who might raise an alarm. But there seemed to be none about and their luck held as they neared the village. Where the river formed a bight just below the village, they quietly grounded the ram and the raiding party jumped onto the soft earth of the riverbank.

Stealthily, Ilas in the lead, the former slave showing the way, they crossed a low, wooded knoll and then the village sprawled along the riverbank before their eyes. A glow of mist-diffused moonlight bathed the settlement in ghostly radiance. Thin smoke ascended from low-banked fires, forming a flat layer of heavier mist over the rooftops.

There had once been a log palisade around the town, built in unsettled times, but during the years of peace it had fallen into disrepair and there was no sign of a watchman. Grinning at this additional favor from the gods, they crept toward the sleeping town. It was yet three hours until sunrise, the time when sleep is deepest, when people awakened need minutes to sort dream from reality.

In single file they passed through a gap in the old palisade, their feet making no sound on the rotted wood that cushioned the ground. Not a voice was raised, not an animal stirred. Quickly they made their way to the center of the village. As in most small towns it formed an open assembly and market area.

They were north of the land where tiled roofs predominated. Here most were of thatch. Ilas selected a large house and pointed to its roof. One of the sailors found a few smoldering coals beneath a rack for smoking fish and thrust an oil-soaked torch against them. In seconds it was ablaze and others fired the torches they had brought from it.

The thatch was old and took flame quickly. In less than a minute it sent a tower of fire far into the night sky and the pirates raised a banshee howling, shattering the peace of the night. Cries of alarm arose from every house and people began to stumble out, groggy and rubbing at their eyes. Women shrieked, children cried in terror and bewilderment.

A few men emerged from their houses bearing arms, and these were cut down ruthlessly. Shouting and waving their weapons, the pirates herded the rest into the center of the village. Any act of defiance was instantly and drastically punished. Soon, except for the wailing children, all stood mute and sullen, stunned by the sudden, inexplicable savagery that had invaded their lives.

"Sort them," Ilas ordered. "We take only the best stock." Quickly the pirates culled the crowd of villagers, separating the comeliest women and the sturdiest children and marching them down to the river, where the ship was being maneuvered against the bank and its gangplank dropped ashore.

A knot of men stood to one side, finally believing the reality of what was happening. One of them shouted something inarticulate and reached for the arm of a woman who was being dragged away. The pirate who dragged the woman thrust his spear through the man's throat and he collapsed, blood pumping in a rhythmic stream onto the ground. The other men set up a clamor and seemed on the verge of open rebellion.

"Kill them," Ilas ordered. "They are no good to us."

The pirates were greatly outnumbered, but they were fully armed and the village men were all but naked. Sword and axe fell, spears thrust, clubs smashed. In the confined space there was no place to flee, and bare hands were futile against weapons of metal. In a very few minutes more than a hundred men lay dead on the ground, which was rapidly growing muddy from all the spilled blood. The surviving villagers, mostly elderly or otherwise unfit, were thoroughly cowed.

With the villagers taken care of, the pirates dashed into the houses, searching for valuables. The village was not wealthy, but they knew the penchant of such people for hoarding, and soon began to apply torture to the householders, eliciting the locations of several caches. The most enthusiastic torturer was the man who had been a slave in the village. He personally cut the throat of the headman after a lengthy interrogation.

"Shall we kill the rest?" Tagas asked, as the first light of morning revealed the scene of carnage and devastation.

Ilas surveyed the crowd of the old, the crippled, the blind, together with the children too young to bother with. "No, it will take too much time. We've stayed here too long as it is. We have what we came for. Back to the ship!"

Setting fire to the houses as they left, in order to keep the survivors occupied for a while, the pirates reboarded and drew up their gangplank. A few minutes of rowing along with the current saw them back out on the open sea. They hoisted the yard and once again the broad sail filled with the southerly wind.

"A good night's work," Ilas said, surveying their new slaves and the loot. "A few more such villages, and we will be ready to set sail for the islands."

The men, put in a good mood by the action and the excitement of spilling the blood of others, disported themselves for a while with the women. Finally, sated at last, most of them dozed on the deck or in the open, central hold. The constant sobbing of the women made, to Ilas's ears, a not entirely unpleasant counterpoint to the rushing sound of the ram as it cut the waves. The children were frightened but quiet. They had already learned the folly of attracting the attention of the pirates.

Ilas, braced for the ordeal of confronting the Shasinn and their formidable queen, was shocked when *Seasnake* rounded the headland and he saw the three foreign ships riding at anchor. He knew instantly that they were part of the same fleet as the strange ship that had been towed into the port of Kasin. What might this signify?

His mind worked, seeking for advantages and hidden dangers. He felt as if the deck had been cut from beneath his feet. The meaning of this thing was unfathomable. But there was no help for it. The only way he was going to learn anything was by going in and finding out.

The sailors were equally alarmed. Ilas addressed them as they slowly worked the ship toward land. "You all saw the strange ship in Kasin Harbor. It looks as if there are more of them. While we are here you will keep your mouths shut and your ears open. Don't mention the other ship. You are just pirates with business to transact, ready for some revelry if there is any to be had in such a port."

He eyed the strange ships hungrily, eager to know their secrets. What might a man of the proper spirit accomplish with such a vessel. They were made for long voyages, that was clear, and he calculated that the largest of the three must hold five times the cargo of the most capacious ship he had ever seen before.

"These are bigger ships than the one in Kasin Harbor, Captain," Tagas said. "What would you wager we've found the flagship?"

"My very thought." He rubbed his lean, stubbled chin. "I would give much for a look aboard her and the others. We must be careful, though. Doubtless Queen Larissa has her own plans for the strangers, and for all we know they have already been cooked and eaten."

Tagas nodded glumly. All the pirates were hard men, but the Islanders were capable of any conceivable behavior. They drew the line at absolutely nothing.

"Bear yourselves meekly," Ilas warned them. "Until I can negotiate some sort of protection for us, these savages will kill you without hesitation for the most trifling offense." The men glared sullenly at him, deeming this an unwise port at which to call.

"Not many war canoes onshore," Tagas noted.

Ilas could see only six of the small, deadly craft. There were no larger ships at all, except for the strangers. The bulk of Gasam's war fleet had been caught in port when King Hael and the Nevans had united to drive the Islanders out. The remnants of his army had evacuated aboard some transports, but none of these were in evidence.

As they drew up to the long wharf, a party of three warriors awaited them. One of them, a long-armed man with a scarred, middle-aged face, pointed at Ilas with his spear.

"Are you the captain?"

"I am," Ilas said.

"Come with me. The rest stay on board."

"Not much help for it," Ilas said to Tagas. "Rest

easy here. I will straighten things out with the queen, if she is here." He knew that they would desert him at the first sign of hostility. He also knew that they would never make it as far as the harbor mouth. A single canoe full of Shasinn warriors was more than adequate to massacre this pack of rogues, he knew, and probably not suffer a loss themselves.

With his escort of three, he walked to the shore and up the slope to the sprawling wooden structure. They passed through a small army of warriors who chattered among themselves in the island dialect. The few who deigned to notice him showed only lordly contempt. He knew that there was nothing personal in this. It was the way they regarded all lesser people, which was to say anyone who was not Shasinn.

With that thought he realized that only Shasinn warriors were present. None of the other island tribes were represented. Where were the rest? This lot must be the royal bodyguard. He was sure of that because he could now see Queen Larissa herself, lounging on the verandah of her little palace. He had never seen her, but he knew her by reputation. When he reached the verandah, he knelt swiftly, abasing himself.

"You are a bold one," she said. "Sailing here in a single warship of Nevan make. Is there some reason why I should allow you to live?"

This was ominous, even from such a source. "In times like these a warship is a safer vessel than an ordinary merchant ship, Your Majesty. It serves notice that one is not easily to be taken. As for its Nevan manufacture, the shipyard officers of that nation are not immune to the desire for profit. I had an opportunity to acquire a superior fighting ship and I took it."

"It looks like a good one," she said, lounging in a filmy gown, sipping something from a golden beaker. She looked, he thought, more like a high-priced harlot than a queen. "Not much cargo space, though."

"I have always preferred high-value cargoes of low bulk," he said, his knees aching from prolonged kneeling. He did not try to straighten in the slightest, all too conscious of the spears poised at his back.

"And a ship like that is just the thing for acquiring cargo without the process of exchanging one set of goods for another, is it not?"

"If Your Majesty has heard scurrilous rumors about me . . ."

"I have no idea who you are," she snapped, "nor have I any interest. But you needn't be shy, I have never seen the point of paying for something one is strong enough to take. You are a raider, are you not? What have you brought?"

"I have a cargo of first-rate slaves, Your Majesty."

She fanned at her face, driving away the small insects that plagued the coast early in the dry season. "What need have we of slaves?"

"Everyone needs slaves, my queen," he said. "Especially a race of warriors. There is work to be done that is beneath warriors. Young men get up to endless mischief trifling with the daughters of elder warriors. If there are comely slave girls at their disposal, such friction is reduced."

She smiled. "How good of you to come here just to relieve me of domestic worries. Oh, get up. You shall live, just so you keep me amused. Show me your wares."

He rose and relaxed very slightly. "Shall I have them brought up here?"

"No, I need the exercise and I want to see your ship. Attend me." She came down the steps of the verandah and he fell in beside her, impressed with her springy stride. She was as beautiful as rumored, but Ilas had long since schooled himself to ignore the physical charms of women and the posturings of men, save as they revealed the weaknesses within. They descended the slope, with the queen's bodyguard falling in behind them.

At the ship he had the prisoners paraded before them. Larissa ignored the children, examining a few of the comelier women. But he could see that her mind was elsewhere. His own attention strayed to the strange ships. There was little sign of activity about them. A few men worked listlessly on deck or in the rigging, performing the incessant chores that have to be tended to, even when ships ride at anchor.

"They seem a fit lot," she said. "I'll buy them, if your price is not too outrageous. Perhaps we can establish a regular trade."

Ilas stifled a smile. It was as he had thought. For years the huge warrior population of these islands had been partially sustained by the plunder of the mainland. The queen was feeling the need of a labor force. But what of the king?

"I have only one ship. But you are the great queen of the islands. If you were to give me more vessels, and men to crew them, I know where splendid laborers are to be found at little risk."

"We shall speak further of this." She saw his gaze wander to the strange ships. "Interesting, are they not? Have you ever seen such ships?"

"Only one."

She jerked around, astonished. "Where?"

"In the great harbor of Kasin, Your Majesty.

Shortly before I departed there, a vessel like one of these was towed in by a coastal guard ship. It had been severely damaged."

"Shazad has one?" Her face flamed and her voice was hoarse. Ilas was alarmed. He had spoken too abruptly. In such a mood this savage queen might kill any who stood near.

"A small one," he soothed. "Its crew were in very poor condition."

Larissa hissed, seeming to take little comfort in the smallness of the vessel and the decrepitude of its crew. "What has been learned from them?" she asked, reining in her anger.

"Nothing that leaked out into the city before we left. I saw shipwrights swarming over the craft and artists making drawings of every detail of it. Whether the crewmen were even able to speak, I do not know."

She turned and stared at him for a full minute, saying nothing. From scalp to boot soles she looked him over, her cold eyes seeming to search beneath his skin. Hard man that he was, Ilas felt his innards tremble. The warriors nearby seemed to catch their queen's mood, going from relaxed ease to slit-eyed tension in an instant.

Something she saw seemed to satisfy Larissa, and the bowstring-taut wariness in her eased. The warriors returned to their habitual state of casual alertness.

"Come with me," she said. He was not about to dispute any suggestions she might make, so he complied.

She did not return to the palace, but began to walk along the shore. The beach was broad and shaped like a crescent, dotted here and there with small structures, most of them sheds for the war canoes and their gear. Others were huts where, presumably, the warriors slept and took shelter from inclement weather.

On a slightly higher patch of ground stood a wallless, thatch-roofed shelter, supported by pillars of intricately carved and lovingly polished flamewood. Its furnishings—chairs, lounges, woven carpets—were sparse but of exquisite workmanship. They were not manufactures of the islands. Even as they reached it a pack of slave women arrived, panting after their run from the little palace. They set about plumping pillows and dusting furniture, filling cups from pitchers and taking up feather fans. The queen collapsed with boneless grace onto one of the lounges.

"I love this place," she said. "It catches the cool sea breezes in the afternoon. Sit." She gave the peremptory command as if it were the most gracious of offers. He sat cross-legged on a hassock of fragrant leather. He would have preferred a chair, but to place one's head higher than a sovereign's was to invite displeasure. He took a proffered cup but waited for the queen to sip at her own before sampling the wine. It was, as might be expected, the finest.

"An experienced courtier, I see. That isn't common among pirates."

It alarmed him that he was making himself so transparent to her. The best course here would be to use the absolute minimum of duplicity.

"Many a man of high birth is cast from his proper station through misfortune or treachery. What is a nobleman of spirit to do? Work with his hands? Unthinkable. The soldier's life is honorable, but without the support of the great to secure a proper command, I would have to serve as a common foot soldier, at best a cabo trooper, under the authority of my inferiors. Better to seek my fortune upon the seas. Plunder is honorable. My crewmen are scum, but better to command scum than toady to a lesser man."

She laughed; a rich, full expression of genuine pleasure. "How good it is to hear honest thought, honestly spoken. I know well the pleasures of lordship and have very little use for modesty, false or real. I am tempted to take you up on your offer to outfit you with a flotilla, but I have many captains, and they would resent my appointing an interloper."

"If these are the men who fight your wars and carry out your raids, there need not be friction. Slaving is a profession few choose to follow. My crews need not be your own people."

She nodded abstractedly. "This bears thinking on. Tell me"—her attention seemed to veer in another direction—"is Neva at ease? Or does Queen Shazad beat the war drums?"

"The land has been tranquil for many months," he said, "but just before we sailed the naval shipyards swarmed with workers and the bosuns were rousting the sailors out of the dockside taverns."

"It is early for that," she said.

"Early enough to excite some comment."

She hissed again. It was a sound he was beginning to associate with her feelings toward Queen Shazad. "Is she coming here?"

He spread his hands expressively. "These things are of course never made public until the fleet is ready to sail. Sometimes there is no official announcement until it is well out to sea. But most are of the opinion that the fleet will go south, to seize ports lost to Chiwa many generations ago. Neva never renounced its claim and the land is in anarchy."

"You mean to say that, if *you* were sovereign, you would choose Chiwa as your prey, rather than these islands?"

"I cannot speak for Shazad, but it stands to reason. She could take the whole land of Chiwa without much difficulty. But the islands? When your warriors have defeated Nevan armies repeatedly? I cannot see those advisors who surround her countenancing such a thing."

"They are a timid lot," she agreed. "But I will not rest easy until that woman is dead."

He wondered that she would admit anything in the world caused her unease.

"I had her at my feet in chains once, many years ago. It amused me to have a royal princess for a slave. I should have killed her the instant she was identified among the prisoners. Ah, well, it is a futile thought. She has been an amusing enemy, at any rate, and you are probably right. No Nevan army can hope to prevail against us in our homeland. I would almost welcome the sight of her sails appearing on the horizon."

"I am not overly familiar with these islands, Your Majesty, but it seems to me that they make poor prospects for an amphibious invasion. Your warriors could defeat a landing at almost any point."

"Yes, yes—" Her mind seemed to wander again, then snapped back. "Tell me, is there any reliable news on the condition of King Hael? We've had no contact with the mainland for months."

"We hear that he lingers between life and death in the Canyon. Whether this is the truth or airy fantasy I cannot say. I incline to disbelieve anything that partakes of the magical. And the plainsmen might well wish to conceal the fact if he is truly dead." He was not about to address the similar rumors surrounding King Gasam. "The war in the southeast tapered off and we have heard little from that quarter. With the new sailing season reliable intelligence should be coming in soon."

"Interesting you should speak in terms of 'reliable intelligence,'" she said. His heart stopped. "I have need of persons skilled in gathering it." His heart resumed its activity, and he hoped he had not betrayed his sudden dread.

"I deal in appropriated treasure and human livestock," he said, "but I have found that information is a commodity much in demand. It is the ideal cargo: It can be acquired sometimes without cost, its bulk is nonexistent, it is easily transportable and it is more valuable than steel, in the right market."

Once again she laughed. If this queen was horrid in most things, he thought, hearing her laugh was one of the world's great pleasures. He wanted to make her laugh again.

"I like you, mariner. You must attend me while your ship is in port."

"It shall be my great pleasure," he said with heartfelt sincerity.

"Now I must attend to other matters. Return to your ship and tell your men they have freedom of the port. You may take for your use any of the buildings you wish. Many are empty just now. As long as the men comport themselves carefully they shall be under my protection."

"Among your warriors," he assured her, "they will exert themselves to be agreeable."

"Then attend me in the morning, on the verandah of the palace. You have my leave." She held out her hand and he took it, bending to press his lips to the backs of her fingers and holding it perhaps a few seconds too long. She did not seem to think it an impertinence and he backed away bowing with the grace of a trained courtier.

He walked back to his ship feeling both dazzled and exultant. He had accomplished a major part of his task already, and with the greatest ease, although at some hazard. But most of all he was stunned by the woman. Being close to her was like standing near some vast, intense flame, fearful of its heat but enthralled by its beauty. Her lightning flashes of menace were truly heart-stopping, but her warmth was something men would kill and die for.

He had always sneered at the belief that the high-born were somehow touched by divine spirit. He was of high birth himself, and he knew that nobility and royalty could be as base, as treacherous and evil, as anyone else. He knew that Queen Shazad was a strong and clever woman, but a woman for all that.

But Larissa was truly different. Could it be true that these Islanders, Larissa and Gasam and Hael, were something more than human? She had shaken him as few things had ever done in his life. And he wanted more.

Tagas grinned when he returned to the ship. "I knew you were well, Captain. These rogues feared you were being taken to execution when the queen of these savages led you off." The others nodded, wearing grimaces of worry.

"She but wished to confer," he said. "We will be here some little time. You are all under the queen's protection, so you may go ashore and disport yourselves but stay out of trouble. Tagas, find us a good-sized shed for quarters and to store our gear. No use leaving it exposed to the weather while we abide here."

"But, Captain," said one of the men, "we all want

a bit of rest and sport, but we have already sold our cargo. Why linger here?"

"The queen and I have business to transact. It will be greatly to our profit, I assure you, and we'll not have to be around these Shasinn overmuch."

"That's good to hear," said someone. "I'd sooner swim in a school of sea-lizards than live among these blood-mad barbarians for long."

"Aye," chorused the others. How typical of them, Ilas thought contemptuously. They were always eager to slaughter helpless people, but they quailed in the presence of genuine warriors. He felt a stab of envy. What must life be like for Gasam and Larissa, whom these matchless warriors worshipped as gods?

The next morning, after sleeping on the ship, Ilas went ashore to examine the small warehouse shed his men had appropriated for their use. They all lay on the floor, still stuporous with drunken sleep. Some of them lay on the ship's folded sail. Others lay on the bare boards. It was to avoid their snoring and general slovenliness that he had slept on the vessel.

He had spent the previous evening seeking information about the strange ships, and about the mysterious absence of the queen's war fleet. He had had little success. The warriors were not interested in speaking to strangers, and the slaves were fearful of saying anything. It was not as if they sought to conceal anything, merely that they were reticent as a matter of survival.

In the dimness of the hut he heard someone groan. It was not an unexpected sound after a night of debauchery, but something in the tone disturbed him. He made his way over the recumbent forms to the groaner and found the man curled into a ball, his arms wrapped around his belly. Seizing a shoulder, he rolled the sufferer onto his back. With a gasp, Ilas jerked back, wiping his palm upon his breeches.

The man's face was swollen and covered with purple blotches, his breath fetid. In a corner of the hut another man groaned. Ilas felt a nameless dread steal over him.

FIVE

Shatterer cruised around the promontory whereon stood the huge Perwin lighthouse and into the great harbor of Kasin. The waters within the bay were busy with ships, both merchant and naval, being fitted out for the season. The very air smelled of paint and new cordage. In a broad area set aside for naval training the rowing crews drilled endlessly, sharpening skills dulled by the long, easy months ashore. The polished oars flashed in the sunlight, rising and falling with machinelike regularity. Commodore Elkon came to stand beside him in the bow.

"Is it not magnificent?" he said. "There is no sight in the world to match that of a fleet preparing for war." He looked like a man gazing upon the woman he loves.

"I've never seen such a thing," Ansa admitted. "I

was in Kasin only briefly, and then to organize a land campaign. It is a rare spectacle, indeed."

"I will go ashore as soon as we drop anchor. Have your gear ready and the men will load it in my boat. I will report to Her Majesty as soon as I am ashore. Accompany me and we shall see if you are who you claim to be."

Shatterer and the little flotilla of lesser ships that sailed in her wake added only incrementally to the fleet assembling in the harbor. There were capital ships and cruisers, swift sloops for reconnaissance and carrying dispatches, and innumerable transports for supplies and the hordes of foot soldiers who would do the hard, bloody work of conquest. Bright sails and colorful banners leavened with gaiety a scene of ominous, martial brutality.

There was no space at the docks, so *Shatterer* was rowed to the broad anchorage where more than a hundred ships rested. The commodore's boat was lowered over the side and Ansa dropped into it as nimbly as any of the sailors, and somewhat more so than Elkon, who was hampered by his cumbersome dress armor. With a creak of oars they sped toward the docks.

"We are in luck," Elkon said. "Queen Shazad reviews the fleet this morning." He pointed to a marble stand beneath a purple canopy where a glittering assemblage viewed the goings-on in the harbor. The early light gleamed from helmets of gilded bronze and glowed more softly amid the colorful gowns of the queen's ladies and the livery of the palace slaves.

The boat tied up at one of the crowded piers and Elkon sprang up the stone steps, closely followed by Ansa. In the bustle of the ongoing preparations, even so unusual a sight as a plainsman went unremarked. Besides the swarming workmen, crowds of idlers

stood everywhere, exercising their immemorial pre-
rogative of subjecting everything to comment and
criticism.

Elkon knelt at the foot of the reviewing stand,
then stood and climbed its steps. At the top he knelt
once more, this time at the feet of his sovereign.
Ansa, one step behind him, did likewise. An atten-
dant leaned over and whispered something into
Shazad's ear.

"Welcome home, Commodore Elkon," she said.
Ansa guessed that the servant had reminded her of
Elkon's name. Even a sovereign as thorough as she
could not be expected to remember the names of all
her officers.

"Long life and victory to Your Majesty!" he intoned. Then he held out a wooden casket. "I give
you the submission of the southerly ports and islands, returned once more to Your Majesty's domin-
ion."

The queen accepted the casket amid the cheers
and applause of her courtiers. "I thank you, commodore, and I will hear your full report at this afternoon's admiralty assembly." Then she noticed Ansa.
"I see you have brought us a visitor."

"This young man joined us at Smoke Island, my
queen. He claims to be . . ."

She held up a hand, stopping him. "I know him.
Prince . . . ah, Kairn, is it?"

"Ansa, Your Majesty. I am Kairn's elder brother."

"Forgive me. You were here so briefly and things
were so hectic. We had no time to socialize. That we
shall rectify. Come sit beside me." She turned to a
servant. "Bring a chair for the son of my good friend
Hael the Steel King."

A beautiful but haggard-looking lady rose. "Give

the prince my chair, Majesty. I fear I must return to the palace."

Shazad was alarmed. "Are you ill?"

"I fear so. It came suddenly. I can barely see." The woman had gone pale as death.

Shazad clapped her hands. "A carriage for Lady Penduma. Send runners ahead. Have the physician in attendance ready in her chambers when she arrives!" All was bustling activity, then serenity reappeared as if by magic. The woman was whisked away and it was as if she had not been there. Ansa took the emptied seat as a chamberlain leaned close to the queen.

"Lady Penduma breakfasted with Your Majesty this morning," he murmured. "Might this be another poisoning attempt?"

Shazad thought for a moment, then shook her head. "We ate from the same dishes and drank from the same flask. It is an illness, no more." Then she turned to Ansa, smiling. "We had not expected you, Prince Ansa. I hope you bring us good news of your father?"

"I suspect your own information of him is fresher than mine," he said. "I sailed here from the southeastern coast."

"And however did you end up in a place like Smoke Island?" she asked. The queen was as beautiful as he remembered, but he had never seen her in the glare of full daylight. The marks of the years and the burdens of office were plain, but they did not mar her as they would have a lesser woman.

"It was necessary that I confer with you," he said. "I felt that a sea journey would be swifter and safer than riding here alone. Swifter it was, I think. Safer, I am not so sure. I came from . . ."

She patted his knee. "We shall confer later. You

have come far and must rest and refresh yourself. Watch the fleet preparations with us and then we shall return to the palace for an informal luncheon. We have plenty of time for discussion."

"As you wish, my queen." He knew this was not flightiness. She did not want to discuss serious matters in front of this mob. The suggestion of poison chilled him. Even the great Queen Shazad was not safe in the midst of her courtiers.

Servants set iced wines and delicacies before him and the court ladies made a great fuss over their visiting prince. He knew that they would have treated him with icy disdain had the queen not received him so warmly.

They watched and applauded as one ship after another cruised past the reviewing stand, dipping its colors in salute, the marines presenting arms in a flash of bronze and steel. The sight heartened Ansa. Here was military might to stem the expanding power of Mezpa, the only truly powerful kingdom left in the west, after the disasters of the latest round of wars. He wanted to ask the queen what her plans were, what she was going to do with this massive fleet, but he knew better than to broach the subject in this place.

In the afternoon they returned to the palace. The luncheon passed amid expressions of affection but no serious discussion.

"I must attend my admiralty assembly now," Shazad told him. "I trust you will find your quarters comfortable. If you wish, please go to the stables and choose some cabos for your use. I know how uneasy you must feel, getting around on foot."

"That is very kind of you," he said, feeling exactly that way.

"This evening we shall speak of more serious things. There is much of importance going on."

"And I have important matters to report," he assured her.

"This evening, then."

The quarters assigned to him were lavish beyond his imagining. On his only previous visit he had slept in the camp with the rest of the plainsmen, seeing only a few of the formal areas of the palace. Here he had a bedchamber larger than his father's campaigning tent, receiving rooms, even a room devoted to nothing but the bath. He availed himself of the latter and then went to find the royal stables.

The grooms, forewarned, had a score of magnificent animals ready for his inspection. He separated five and rode each, settling upon three for his use. They were superbly trained, less fractious than the plains-bred cabos he was used to. He suspected they might not have the endurance of his own animals, and he was unsure whether he would trust them in battle, but the sheer pleasure of riding after so long afoot or afloat overcame any reservations he felt.

He went back to the palace, feeling slightly sore from the saddle, for the first time in years. In his quarters, from long habit, he went over his weapons, making sure that they were in perfect condition. While thus engaged, a palace servant came to tell him the queen awaited his pleasure. He followed the man to a small sitting room, one wall of which was open to a broad terrace. Queen Shazad sat by a small table and gestured gracefully to a chair by her side.

"Prince Ansa, what a pleasure it is to see you." She extended her hand and he took it.

"Your Majesty, I am not used to being addressed as Prince. If you would just call me Ansa . . ."

"Only in private," she said. "If you do not stand upon all your privileges, people here will not accord you the proper respect. They seize upon every perceived weakness."

"I shall remember that."

"Do so. Now, I wish I could be casual, and entertain you as I would like to, but I fear that I must ration my time. Great preparations are afoot and I must be everywhere, it seems. You said that your mission was urgent."

"It is. After the lightning campaign Gasam was crushed. Even though my father was terribly wounded, we thought our victory was nearly complete. We were wrong."

"I know," she said, musing, then: "But we may be thinking of different things. What is your situation in the southeast?"

"At the moment, none at all. Our army has been forced to returned home."

She stared at him for a long moment, then sighed, suddenly weary. "Tell me about it."

So he told her of the long, dragged-out campaign against the Mezpan invasion. He told of the vast, antlike armies of that land and their mastery of the new fire weapon, and how the plainsmen feared that a second prong of the attack was even then aimed at their homeland.

"There was no choice," he said at last. "Our army is entirely mounted, and we had stripped the land of forage. There was no way we could keep the field. The Mezpans travel on foot, carrying the supplies they need in wagon trains. They wear no armor and their weapons are light, so they march almost as fast as Gasam's Shasinn. They are too clever to come against us on an open plain, where we can ride rings around them."

"This sounds ominous," she said.

"Ominous! It is deadly! The Mezpans will crush every nation in their path, one at a time. They are not flashy conquerors like Gasam. Mezpa is like a great dragon that devours all before it, slowly and methodically." He did not like her look, so he went on in a lighter vein.

"But I have seen your great fleet. We plainsmen are the masters of mounted warfare. Combined with your infantry and navy, as when we fought Gasam, we can crush the Mezpans between us."

She was silent for a long time and he did not think it a good sign.

"I appreciate your alarm," she said at length. "And I agree that, very soon, we must consider an alliance against these upstarts. But this season I lead my war machine elsewhere."

"What?" he said. "Do you go to occupy Chiwa?" He sifted through the map in his head. "That would not be an unwise move. You can at least fortify the mountain passes leading to Sono and Gran, which Mezpa will soon swallow up. But I think a concerted attack on both our parts—"

"No!" she said. "I'm sorry, but my plans are laid. That fleet you saw me reviewing is preparing to invade the Storm Islands. I am going to destroy Gasam and Larissa, and end the threat from that part of the world for good."

He was stunned. "But . . . but, they are all but destroyed already. I saw my father's spear pierce Gasam's body! Larissa is a monster, I know her personally, but she cannot control those Islanders by herself. The islands will not threaten you for a generation, if ever. But the Mezpans . . ."

"No. My word on this is final. I must destroy them. When that is done, we will discuss an alliance against Mezpa. I recognize the threat, but do you not see? They are far too remote. My people will not stand for a war in a far land against an enemy they have barely heard of. I would face civil war right here!"

"Once, the Islanders were a remote threat, too," he reminded her.

"I remember all too well. It took an invasion by Gasam to wake us to the threat. Then I saw my father humiliated in two great battles. Sometimes that is what is required to wake people up. But there is, as yet, no palpable threat from Mezpa."

"I will not stop trying to persuade you."

She smiled faintly. "I do not expect you to. But there is more. Did you see the strange ships in the harbor?"

He shrugged. "I saw more ships than I knew existed in the world. I am a landsman. They all look strange to me."

"Then listen to this." She told him of the arrival of the battered ship, and of the others the coastal guard had found and towed or escorted in: five alien vessels in all.

"We still do not know what this means, but the main part of that fleet is still missing. My master mariners tell me that the winds of the season may have carried some of them as far as the Storm Islands."

"But they are from an unknown land," he said. "One very far away. How can they affect things here, just a few shiploads of them?"

Her eyes had a faraway look. "I do not know. But many years ago, two men came into my life. One was your father. The other was Gasam. Two nobodies, savages from an obscure island. Between them, they turned upside down a world that had been stable for centuries. I will never again underestimate the danger of obscure people from faraway lands."

That evening Shazad was in her study, dictating letters, when the master of the Physicians' Academy craved audience. She admitted him immediately and the expression on his face frightened her. He was a very fat old man with wiry gray hair, dressed in a black gown and flat, black hat.

"Very good of Your Majesty to receive me," he puffed, sinking into the chair she led him to. "I assure you, I would not have imposed had not the most urgent necessity impelled me."

"I know," she said impatiently. "What is it?"

"Majesty, there is an unknown disease in the city."

Her heart sank. "A plague?"

He nodded ponderously. "I fear so. It began a few days ago, in the neighborhoods near the docks. People began to complain of dizziness and disorientation, raging headaches, terrible skin lesions in some cases, many other symptoms. A number have died already, and many more are expected to. I fear this is only the beginning. My queen, you and your people have been much at the waterfront lately."

"Penduma," she breathed, her face paling.

"Your Majesty?"

"The chief of my ladies-in-waiting. Lady Penduma. This morning she fell ill and had to return to the palace."

"I should see her at once," he said, lurching to his feet.

"Come with me." She led the way to a nearby suite of rooms. The servant women were amazed to see the queen barging in unannounced and they dropped to their knees. Shazad saw the tears streaking their faces and her alarm deepened by the second. She rushed to the bedroom and gasped when she saw what lay on the bed.

Just that morning, Penduma had been a beautiful, full-fleshed woman. Now she looked like skin draped over a skeleton. The flesh of her face had fallen in, leaving the bones of the skull visible, with her huge, staring eyes grotesquely prominent. Their whites had turned deep yellow and clearly saw nothing. Her once-lustrous hair lay like dried straw upon the pillow. Oozing red sores covered her arms and hands.

The attending physician sprang from his bedside chair. "Come no nearer! You must leave, my queen! I have never seen anything like this before."

"I have," grunted the master. "It is the dockside sickness."

With a last, horrified look, Shazad whirled and left the room, forcing herself not to run. The master came to her side.

"Your Majesty, it pains me to say this, but you would do well to isolate all the servants who have attended her, kill them and burn their bodies. You may yet contain the sickness here in the palace."

"The physician as well?"

He sighed. "Him, too."

She whirled to face him. "Master Physician, the time for that is past. This lady dressed my hair and handled my food this very morning. If the sickness is here, we have all been exposed."

"There is still a chance," he urged. "Your father . . ."

"My father was a hard man, but he was not a fool, and neither am I! Now, let us sit down and discuss this like rational people."

They returned to her chambers and she called for wine. Then she gave her chamberlain orders to report on all sickness within the palace. Mystified, the man went off to do her bidding.

"Now tell me," she said. "How did this come about?"

"The origins of disease are always mysterious, Majesty," he said. "But I can scarcely believe that the simultaneous arrival of the strangers and the plague is coincidental."

She glared at him. "I was assured that there was no contagion aboard."

"And there was not. In fact, the foreign mariners are in the best of health, fully recovered from their ordeal."

"Then how can this be?"

"Your Majesty," he said with a great air of futility, "there is so much we do not know about disease. I am of the school which holds that demons and spirits have nothing to do with bodily illness, although they may affect the mental sort. Some think the tiny animalcules we can see through lenses are the culprits."

"I have read all this," she said. "What of it?"

"It has long been known that persons may be carriers of disease while not suffering from the disease themselves. When men come from a far land, one with which no people here have ever had contact . . ." He shrugged and spread his hands. "Who knows? There is a disease suffered only by a single tribe in Chiwa. In your great-grandfather's time a sickness struck Neva that affected only persons who had red hair and brown eyes. A disease that makes the children of one race mildly ill may kill adults of another breed. These men may bear a host of illnesses and be utterly unaware of them. Better we had killed them on sight and burned their ships at sea."

"A little late for that," she said, drinking deeply from her beaker. "Oh, this could not have come at a worse time! My whole fleet is assembled in the harbor! My armies are gathered in their camps outside the walls!"

"Circumstances could not be more terrible for the spread of a pestilence," he agreed somberly.

"We must take steps," she said. She clapped her hands and ordered her entire messenger corps assembled. "It may be too late, but we must try *something!* A series of quarantines, spread the camps farther apart, keep sailing vessels within the harbor . . . Physician, I want a list of steps to be taken immediately!"

"Yes, Your Majesty. But be realistic: As soon as word of plague spreads, the healthy will flee the city to escape it, carrying the sickness all over the nation."

She sank into her chair with a groan. "Now I *hope* those other ships reached the Storm Islands!"

Ansa awakened to strange sounds and smells, and to a sense of dread. He rose from his unwontedly soft bed and went to the balcony opening off one of his sitting rooms. It overlooked the city, and everywhere he looked he saw columns of smoke ascending to the sky. Some signified the morning sacrifices in the temples, but there were many smells besides those of incense. All manner of herbs were being burned, along with less agreeable things.

He heard bells ringing, and the thunder of gongs. There was a braying of horns and conchs, and there was nothing joyous in the sound. The orderly, cheerful city of only a day before was transformed into the semblance of a madhouse.

A servant came in and bowed. "Prince Ansa, Her

Majesty urges you to go nowhere today, to have contact with no one save the palace servants, and with them only at a distance. They will bring you anything you require."

"What?" Ansa said, outraged. "Am I a prisoner?"

"By no means, sir," said the servant. "The whole city is under quarantine. Plague walks among us."

"Oh, no," he said, abruptly remembering the woman who had yielded him her chair the morning before. "That lady . . . Penduma, was it?"

"She is dead, sir. The first in the palace to contract the sickness. There were more than a hundred cases here this morning."

"Very well. I will stay here, but I would speak with the queen at her earliest convenience."

The servant bowed again. "She will be so informed. Your breakfast has been laid out on the terrace."

He went in search of the terrace. From the hallways outside he heard sobbing and frightened whispers. He found a lavish spread on an elegant table, complete with fresh flowers, as if nothing were untoward. He sat and ate with little appetite, hearing the disturbing sounds from the city below. From somewhere just outside the walls, a vast cloud of smoke ascended. A mass pyre, he guessed, where the bodies of the dead were to be cremated.

This was frightening in a way he had never experienced before. Twice in his young life he had experienced the spread of deadly pestilence, when the folk had died by the thousands, and none could do anything except wait for it to pass. The herb-women and spirit-speakers were helpless and even his father could only shrug, saying that some things were matters of nature, controllable by neither man nor spirits. The only thing one could do was hope to be passed over by the dread visitation.

But this! Always before, he had heard of the approach of the new disease, for rumor flew ahead of even the swiftest contagion. People grew somber, knowing that soon the sickness would be among them. Not this time. On the long voyage to Neva they had heard nothing, not even in the port at which they had called only two days previously. How could so many contract the disease and die in a single day and night? The most virulent plagues he had ever heard of took days to kill.

Grimly he considered his chances. Should he take one of the animals that had been put at his disposal, saddle up and ride from this place? The prospect was sorely tempting. He might yet escape the infection. But where might he ride? He would take the northeast road through Omia to the mountains, thence down onto the great plains of his homeland.

He sipped at a goblet of tart fruit juice. By going that way, he might be spreading the plague to his own people But that could not be, he thought. If he contracted the disease, he would be dead or recovered long before he reached home. Surely he could not pass it on after that. But did he know that?

One thing seemed certain: His mission here had failed. The queen was determined to destroy her island enemies and had no interest in containing Mezpa. Her need to be rid of Gasam and Larissa had become an obsession, overwhelming more realistic goals.

He knew the story; his father had told it many times over the years. Shazad's father had suffered catastrophic defeat in the harbor battle, losing much of Neva's war fleet in the process. Shazad had been captured, and Larissa had used her as a slave for months before Ansa's father and the plains army had liberated the city and the captive princess as well.

Ansa had seen firsthand how Gasam and Larissa treated prisoners and slaves who excited their more twisted interests. He could imagine how the old humiliation must have gnawed inside Shazad for all the years since. Overtly she held that she was undertaking the coming campaign to make her kingdom safe. In reality she wanted revenge. She would not recognize another enemy until she had her two old foes at her mercy.

But what of her expedition now? Surely it could not begin with plague raging. This would take some more thought. Perhaps, if the sea campaign should have to be abandoned, a more modest but crucial expedition by land might seem more reasonable to her.

Then he was struck by the futility of all such speculations Anything could happen in time of plague. Within days he might be dead, or Shazad might be dead. People, he knew, became irrational, even hysterical, when pestilence stalked the land. They would follow wild men who promised intervention by the gods. They rose up and threw off their traditional rulers, as if political change could somehow stem the spread of infection. Sitting peacefully in this great, solid palace, he could be in a deadly precarious situation.

His breakfast finished, he went back into his rooms and gathered his few belongings together in one place. He wanted to be able to grab them and run at a moment's notice, should necessity so dictate.

He found that, from the balcony opening off his bedchamber, he could see the yellow-tiled roofs of the stables down a slope to his left. One of the palace's innumerable terraces was immediately below his balcony, and beyond that a sloping lawn decorated with statuary and shrubs curiously trimmed. He could spring to the terrace beneath, be over the balustrade and down to the stables in a matter of minutes. Having determined this, he went back in and transferred his bundle of belongings, setting it casually next to the balcony.

Restless, he went back to his own terrace. The remains of his meal had already been cleared away by servants who came and went as silently as ghosts. From somewhere he could hear the music of harp and flute, as if this were an ordinary day. It struck him that those must be precisely Shazad's orders: that all must carry on according to routine, the weight of custom suppressing any tendency to panic.

In several sloping streets of the city below he saw solemn processions of people, some bearing on their shoulders elongated litters. The dead were being taken for burial. More precisely, he corrected himself, for cremation. How many?

"Four hundred," said a voice behind him, as if reading his thoughts. He turned to see Shazad coming onto the terrace from his suite. "Four hundred this morning, give or take a score. Probably a thousand by nightfall." She went to the balustrade, not looking at him but gazing over her grievously ailing city. "We have to burn them, and that distresses the people almost as much as the pestilence itself. We are a folk of ancient custom, Ansa. We are very attached to our rituals, and none are so sacred as the obsequies for the dead. It is a process that takes six days, with regulated stages of mourning and burial amid much pomp even for the poor. Now their dead must be peremptorily burned like so much trash."

"Will there be trouble over this?" he asked.

"There will be nothing but trouble for a long time to come." She turned and faced him. "Already my counselors are recommending I leave the city."

"Don't do it," he advised. "They just want to take over in your absence."

The corners of her mouth crooked upward a fraction of an inch. "Your father schooled you well. Yes, I know all their tricks and maneuvers. But they are right to be concerned. In the past, insurrection and civil war have often followed in the wake of a great dying."

"Perhaps it is not so serious," he said, without much hope. "It may kill a few hundred and be gone as swiftly as it came."

"By all the gods, I hope so." She shook her head. "It is only at times like this that I call upon the gods at all. In my youth I was much addicted to forbidden religious practices. I performed the rites of gods banned from Neva for a thousand years. Sorcery and black magic intrigued me."

He wondered why she was telling him this. He decided that she just needed to talk with someone, and it had to be someone who was not a part of her world yet was near being her equal. If he was what she needed, he would strive to be agreeable. He had not yet abandoned all hope of persuading her to help contain Mezpa.

"When you are very young and spoiled and irresponsible, orgiastic practices have a great appeal. I was a puppet for a string of evil priests and fraudulent wizards." She contemplated the scene before her. "I've hanged most of them since coming to my senses. But there are more of them, and they are busy today. All sorts of mystical troublemakers will be getting rich off this curse."

"Post a proclamation," he advised. "Summary execution for any who promise protection from the plague through appeal to these evil gods."

"I already have, for what good it will do. Desperate people pay little attention to cautionary words. If only there were some way to fight this thing! My physicians are all but certain that the strangers from the south brought the sickness, but they have no idea how it is spread. Through water? By the breath? By contact?"

"How can they be certain that the newcomers brought it?" he asked.

"First, to believe otherwise strains the limits of coincidence. More importantly, the sickness first appeared in two places: the waterfront and the palace. These are the first two places where the newcomers set foot. There are many inland districts of the city where the plague has yet to appear."

"Then there is a chance of containing it?"

She shook her head. "None. They have been here for many days and people have traveled freely since. It is just taking longer to appear in some areas."

A royal messenger ran onto the terrace and cast himself down on one knee, extending a copper message tube to the queen. She accepted it, opened one end and read the rolled-up paper it contained. With a sigh she let it fall to the polished stone. "It is as I had feared. The illness has appeared in three villages within ten miles. In one place the first case was four days ago. Someone must have traveled there from the docks the very day the strangers arrived. It is loose and it will devastate my kingdom."

"Not just yours," he reminded her. "There was never a plague yet that respected man-made borders."

She laughed hollowly, a humorless sound. "Since

it will spread from here, everyone will call it the Nevan plague or Shazad's curse. I will get the blame."

"Where are these newcomers?" he asked.

"A few are on their ships, but some are in a house I provided for them. They are healthy but may not remain that way, if they are as vulnerable to our diseases as we are to theirs."

"They may not live long enough to catch them," Ansa pointed out, "if the people come to hold them responsible for the plague. You should post guards to protect them."

She thought for a while. "I am tempted to leave them unprotected. If the people blame them, it may relieve the pressure on me. It was their doing, after all, albeit unwitting."

He began to protest. "You cannot . . ."

"Oh, I shall protect them," she said. "It would be a violation of the ancient laws of hospitality to abandon my guests. It is just that the prospect is tempting."

For days the disease raged in the capital. By the third day the funeral processions were inadequate for carrying out the dead and carts were pressed into service. As the queen had predicted there were assaults on the strange ships and on those of the foreign sailors who took refuge in the city. But the attacks were desultory and easily repulsed. The people were as yet too weakened and fearful for concerted mob behavior.

SIX

The slave was a repulsive sight, his limbs wasted, his skin so ulcerated that it was sloughing off in sheets. His breath wheezed out between gums that had been lined with teeth just the day before. Three days previously he had been a robust young man. Now he looked like a barely animated corpse.

"How many are like this?" Larissa asked.

"Nearly one-third," her steward answered. "They are dying like this all over this island, and the sickness is in the other islands as well."

She did not go too close to the dying slave. It was not so much that she feared contagion, but all her life she had detested ugliness in any form, and she had never seen anything as ugly as this wretched creature.

"Kill him," she said. "Kill all who fall ill of this sickness. It may not help, but if they cannot be saved, there is no sense keeping them even a day in this condition."

"It shall be done," the steward said, bowing.

She turned and left the little cluster of slave huts. Followed by her bodyguard, she began to make her way toward the palace when one of her boys called out and pointed.

"Commander Pendu returns!" the young warrior said, his finger indicating the red banner waving from the point lookout station.

"Let's go greet them," she said. It would be something to lighten her mood, anyway. It was not that she put any value on the lives of slaves but the sight was disgusting. And why were they dying?

By the time she reached the beach the whole, great fleet of war canoes were being paddled toward shore at full speed. Lining the rails of their ships, the foreigners watched the spectacle with some awe. Ilas of Nar, with the half score of his men still on their feet, watched dejectedly from the shore.

The paddles flashed and churned water to foam in time with the rhythmic, deep-voiced chanting of the warriors. The paddlers plied their blades standing, putting all the strength of their superb young bodies into each stroke. The warriors standing between the files of paddlers shook their spears and shields in time to the chant, the sunlight gleaming from their weapons, feather plumes nodding, paint on face and body making a riot of color, the beautiful pelts of island beasts adding barbaric splendor to a sight that was stirring to the blood of the most jaded.

Larissa yearned for the days when the fleet returned with every canoe draped with the severed heads of enemies, piled with plunder. Those good days, she vowed inwardly, would come again. Perhaps this wonderful sight was a sign that their fortunes were about to take a favorable turn at last.

With a final shout the paddles came up and the canoes beached, almost as one. The commander leapt to the sand and the others stormed after him, raising a shout to terrify the bravest, waving their weapons, running up the dune atop which stood their queen. With a final shout and leap, the entire swarming force of warriors dropped to one knee, grounding their spears and their black shields.

Pendu stopped with his forehead almost touching Larissa's toes. "My queen," he shouted, "your islands are now restored to order. We your faithful warriors await our king's word to go forth and slay his enemies!"

She leaned forward and placed a palm upon his dark gold hair, now faintly streaked with gray. "Rise, my captain. Rise, all of you, and accept the thanks of your king and queen. Stand in readiness. Soon we return to the mainland!"

The men rose with a thunderous cheer, turned and walked toward their encampments. Pendu walked beside Larissa and they conferred privately.

"How did it go?" she asked.

"Well, indeed. Truly there was little rebellion, just restlessness and the pull of old tribal divisions. We put a stop to some intertribal raiding, killed a few malcontents and set things to order. It was a good training exercise for men whose skills are getting rusty and to break in the young warriors."

"Excellent. Tell me, is there sickness in all the islands?"

He looked at her with concern. "Here, too? Yes. As we were mopping up in the southerly islands we began to hear of sickness. When we came back north, we found it at all the islands we had visited. Is it connected with the foreigners? Did they bring it?"

"I think so, but tell me this: Have any of the island folk fallen to the plague?"

"Just the Gullah of the most southerly islands, and they are of half-mainland blood." The Gullah were the least esteemed of all the island peoples, never allowed to take part in the great raids and invasions, used only for occupation duty, because their blood was not pure.

"Otherwise, only the foreign slaves have fallen victim?"

"Yes, my queen. Is it the same here?"

"Exactly. The slaves are dying in droves. The southern foreigners are untouched. But not a single Shasinn has so much as a runny nose, and the other tribes seem equally immune."

"Huh! Disease is a strange thing. But other races are weaker than we."

"True, and this may well work to our advantage. You saw that glum-faced mariner down by the shore? That pretty little cutter is his."

"I saw him."

"He is just a pirate and he may be spying for Queen Shazad, but that is no matter. Half his crew is down with the illness, but I have a use for him. Send a man and tell him to attend upon me within an hour. I have a mission for that swift little ship of his and he has enough men to work it."

"It shall be done. My queen, what of the king?"

She smiled. "Better and better. At last, the wound is healing and he can talk above a whisper. He even laughs aloud now, when I promise to feed him the blood of his enemies."

Pendu grinned fiercely. "Splendid! Will he lead us again soon, do you think?"

"I know it," she said with equally fierce conviction. "It is the time of the Shasinn again! This plague tells me so, for it kills the foreigners and leaves us as strong as ever."

"Aha!" Pendu said. "So that is why you want the pirate and his fast ship. You want him to go to the mainland and tell you if the plague has spread there."

"Exactly. It is almost sure to be, because he told me that a ship from the new continent put in at Kasin just before he left, and his crew probably had the sickness before they arrived here. Some of them came down with it the very day after they dropped anchor. They spent that night among our slaves, but I do not think even this plague strikes so quickly. And if the mainlanders do not have the plague yet"— she shrugged, smiling—"then he can just take it to them."

Pendu laughed with her as they climbed the steps to the palace. He spoke a few words to a junior warrior and the young man ran down toward the beach, where Ilas of Nar still stood with folded arms. Then they passed inside. Two of Gasam's warrior women flanked the door to the king's chamber, inclining their heads slightly toward the queen as she entered.

"Has the sickness not affected the king's women?" Pendu asked.

"About half have fallen ill," she said, "but only with a fever. None of them have those horrible skin lesions and none have died. I think they will recover." She did not like her husband's female bodyguard, but she respected their loyalty.

The sight that greeted the queen shocked her almost speechless. Gasam was sitting up in bed, grinning at her. She almost threw herself onto him as she had done for so many years, but at the last moment she restrained herself, sitting on the bed and embracing him.

"My king! I just told Pendu that you were mending, but you are ten times better just since sunrise!"

"Aye, I am coming back, I can feel it!" His voice was deep and strong. He held out a hand, and Pendu, dropping his spear to the floor, grasped it in both of his own.

"Welcome back, my king! Your warriors are whipped into shape and ready to march!"

"Not so fast!" Larissa protested, laughing. "First he must be on his feet!"

Now Gasam laughed, wincing at the pain it caused him, then he laughed again, louder. "It is not too soon to prepare, though!"

"Listen, my love. I have important news." Swiftly she told him what was known about the plague.

His eyes went dreamy with wonder. "A pestilence that kills others but leaves us strong! Truly the gods love me! Listen, little queen: I may not be in fighting trim yet, but in two days' time, I shall be on my feet, out on the verandah, where my people can see me. Assemble them from all over my domains. Each day, I want to address a larger crowd until my whole force of warriors is assembled. By that time, I shall be ready to lead them into battle, even if I must be carried in a chair!"

"It shall be done!" she said, hugging him. "We shall conquer, and we shall wade knee-deep in blood!"

"If this sickness does not kill off our enemies first. That would take all the fun out of conquest."

"There is always the new continent to the south, my king," said Pendu. "Let us retake the mainland, even if it is occupied by nothing but rotting

corpses. Then we can go on to fight healthy foreigners in the south."

"So we shall," said Gasam, stroking Larissa's back.
"My people, the world is good again."

The queen received Ilas of Nar on the verandah.
The man was despondent, but so far he had not
fallen to the illness.

"I have a mission for you," she said. "Have you
enough sound men to work your ship?"

"To sail it, yes," he said, "but not to raid or—"

"I have no need of such," she said. "I only need
information."

"My queen, we have discussed my supplying you
with slaves, but we have not—"

"Forget that!" she said peremptorily. "I want you
to sail to the mainland and ascertain a single thing:
Does the plague rage there?"

"I think it must," he said. "My men had it when
we arrived." He put on a bold face, but he was filled
with dread. Each morning he awoke expecting to
feel the symptoms of the awful disease.

"But I must know!" she insisted. Something in her
tone pierced his dread and jolted his accustomed
shrewdness back into operation.

"You have plans that make this intelligence essen-
tial?"

"If so, I am not about to discuss them with a mere
pirate. Just keep in mind what I require of you."

He sat back on his haunches, feeling more at ease
than he had in a long time. "My queen, let us be realistic. Each of us is a human being looking out for
his own interests. You wish information. I am being
asked to take exceptional risks to get it for you."

She snorted. "You need merely make an easy voyage to the mainland in the best sailing weather. Per-

haps a few days of cruising southward. Return the moment you hear of pestilence. If it is there, it is everywhere."

"But I have only a skeleton crew, and many of them may come down with the illness before we even reach land. I might contract it myself."

"If that happens, you have few worries, indeed." She brooded for a minute, just for effect. "Very well, I am rich in gold. Choose your reward. But you shall not collect it until you return with reliable information."

"Actually I am prepared to wait far longer than that." This was a crucial move, and his heart thudded with the danger of the moment. But the mortal fear of the disease made lesser risks seem more endurable.

She looked at him sharply. "What do you mean?"

"Your intentions are hardly mysterious, my queen," Ilas said. "You want to return to the mainland to regain your lost territories. That is why you must know if they are weakened by sickness."

"And if so, you wish to take advantage of the fact?"

"Yes, my queen. Such an opportunity does not fall to one's lot often."

"And what reward do you expect to earn?" She leaned back in her padded lounge chair, enjoying the little play of wills and greed.

"When you are once again mistress of the world, you will have broad lands to divide among your supporters. Warriors are seldom good administrators of estates. They must always be going off to win new conquests for their king. When you have Neva once again in your grip, give me lands of my own, and serfs to work the land, and titles to pass on to my posterity."

She chuckled. "That is a great deal for a little voyage in pleasant weather, and a little information."

He gestured expressively. "In my life I have learned this about intelligence: Timing is everything. A few words, of little or no worth in ordinary times, may mean everything when the time is right."

"Word of a plague is not worth lands and estates."

"Who is to say? And what are these things to you and the godlike Gasam? The world is your plaything, and somebody must administer it, a thing for which the two of you have scant patience. And, I need hardly say, my service to you will not end with this one task. As your liege man, my services belong to you for life."

"No doubt." She smiled again. "I almost like you, pirate, but I cannot as yet trust you."

As if she ever would, he thought. "Would Your Majesty's attitude be sweetened by some further intelligence, information which will be of great value in your preparations?"

"It might," she said.

He took a deep breath, knowing there could be no turning back. "Know, then, that even now Queen Shazad is assembling her fleet and her armies and her auxiliaries and for all I know her foreign allies."

Calculation flashed across her face like lightning below the horizon. "She plans to invade these islands?"

"Most certainly. The official story is that she wants to move south into Chiwa, to reclaim old Nevan lands and Nevan ports, but only a fool would believe that. What other prize is there for her worth taking but these islands? Where else is the wealth of a looted world to be found? Where else . . ." He let it trail off deliberately, leaving the most dangerous words unspoken.

"Where else am I?" said the queen. "Where else to find my husband? Where else can she get her revenge?"

"My thoughts exactly, Your Majesty." He had played his hand. Now he had to see if it had earned him rewards beyond imagining, or death.

"You waited a long time to tell me this," she said grimly. Her very tone caused her guards to shift uneasily, their hands fingering the wooden handgrips of their long, elegant spears.

He shrugged, knowing he was within a hair's breadth of death. "It was not to my advantage before. Things have changed."

She was silent for a while, her slender fingers bunching the silken fabric beneath her bare thigh. Then: "Go. Find out for me what I need to know. If all is well, and if you continue to serve me faithfully, you shall have all you ask."

He rose and bowed, then he walked down the slope toward his ship. He barely felt the sand beneath his boots. He had rolled the dice for the highest stakes and he had won. Not won, he reminded himself, but turned fortune back in his own favor. Until his conference with Queen Larissa he had not yet decided to change sides. But then, heretofore he had had nothing of his own to bring to the bargaining table. And he had been demoralized by the sickness among his crew. With the queen's modest proposal, he saw a chance to raise the stakes. His life was forfeit, but what of that? He was guilty of capital crimes past counting, and he could only be put to death once.

He did not think of himself as a traitor. Shazad was no more his queen than was Larissa. Shazad thought to use him for her own purposes, trusting not in his word and loyalty, but in her own power to punish. That had been the way of it most of his life. He, a nobleman, was nothing but a pawn to be used like a whipped animal. He was no more a Nevan than he was an Islander. He would lend his support to the winning side and take his rewards when the loot was shared out. That was how it had always been. Every noble family began with a man who did favors for a conqueror and received land in return. After that, the land was passed down by inheritance, until another conqueror appeared to wipe out ancient tenure and divide the estates among his own supporters.

When he reached the shed where his remaining men lounged in sullen stupor, he began prodding them to their feet. "Get up, you lazy rogues! We've a voyage to accomplish."

"A voyage?" Tagas said. "Where?" The mate had been ill for a few days, with a high fever and a skin rash, but he had recovered quickly. Some of the others had suffered similarly. Two, like Ilas himself, had remained untouched by the illness.

"To the mainland. There are enough of us to work the ship and it will be good to get away from this place of savages and dying men."

"What of our shipmates?" one man asked.

"They'll be tended to," Ilas said. "Either they die or they recover. In neither case will we be of any use to them. Come on, there's rich reward to be had and little risk this time. No raiding, no fighting, just a little sight-seeing."

They grumbled but they gathered their belongings smartly. In truth, it did them good to have something to do. With nothing but the immediacy of death to brood upon, their mood had grown more sour by the day. As they got the ship ready for sea their mood lightened, and by the time they upped anchor they were positively cheerful. As they rowed to the harbor mouth they were singing, and then they hoisted their sail to catch the offshore breeze.

Queen Larissa watched the little ship sail away and then turned her attention to the delegation of men who stood upon the verandah.

"Ah, Lord Sachu," she said, giving him her most radiant smile, "it grieves me that you must leave us, but I quite understand that you must continue your voyage of discovery for your queen. I do hope that your stay among us has been pleasant?"

"You have been most gracious, Your Majesty. I only grieve that I had no chance to meet your husband the king." He was as courtly as always, but his hand worked nervously at his sword hilt. He had been jolted by the sight of the warrior horde in their canoes and was now anxious to be away.

"Then I will not detain you longer. You have the letters and presents I have sent for your queen?"

"They are safely stowed, Your Majesty. Queen Isel will find the gifts as dazzling as we all did." He almost fidgeted. "Ah, Your Majesty, this sickness . . ."

She put on a look of concern. "I trust your crews have not come down with it?"

"No, no! None of us have been affected. I do hope you do not think that we brought this curse here."

"It is no curse, it just kills slaves. Think nothing of it. It is an illness that affects the lesser peoples. It ravages them every few years. It improves them, I think, by killing the weak." The lie came easily to her. She did not want Sachu and his men to know what deadly carriers they were. "Do you think the charts I supplied you with are adequate?"

"More than adequate, Your Majesty."

"Excellent. Kasin is the greatest port along the coast, but do not fail to call at the smaller northern harbors. They hold much of interest and profit." She wanted the pestilence spread as widely as possible before her ravaging armies.

With many courtly bows and assurances, the explorers took their leave. Larissa was well pleased with her handling of them. As far as establishing relations with the new continent, she felt that she was letting this Queen Isel the Ninth know who the real power was in this part of the world. The plague they had brought seemed to be an added bonus. If it was all she hoped, perhaps by the next time the foreigners came so far north she and Gasam would be the sole power worth dealing with.

Day by day the great war canoes came paddling in, bearing their fearsome loads of warriors. All the warrior peoples of the islands were there, none of them touched by the sickness that killed fully one-third of the foreign slaves within fifteen days of its first appearance.

Losing the slaves was an annoyance, but there were always more of them to be rounded up on the mainland. The major problem caused by the plague was that it was getting difficult to keep the hordes of warriors fed. They had made great inroads into the domestic beasts, and soon it might become necessary to begin slaughtering the herds of kagga for food. The very thought was unbearable to the Shasinn, whose herds were their major source of pride and status.

It should not come to that, Larissa thought. They would be setting out soon. True to his word, Gasam had appeared on the verandah on the second day after she found him sitting up. He was weak and shaky, but he stood on his own feet and everyone saw him. The warriors had cheered in an ecstasy of hero worship. It went on for hour after hour, so fervently that powerful warriors passed out from sheer exhaustion. In time Gasam had to sit in a chair, but still they came up the hill, regiment after regiment of them, so that everyone could get a close look at the king, absent from among them for so long. Even now the new arrivals made straight for the palace to assure themselves that the king was, indeed, returned from the dead.

Thirty days after the foreigners had left, the last of the war bands had arrived. Daily the king grew stronger, until he was walking among his troops, leaning on his steel spear. By his side was Larissa, holding the miniature spear made to replace the one she had hurled through the body of King Hael. And on the thirtieth day *Seasnake* returned, with Ilas of Nar standing in the prow. Larissa and Gasam were sitting on the verandah when Ilas climbed the knoll to report, and his eyes widened at the sight of the king. He had concluded that the man was dead and the fact was being concealed.

"Well?" Larissa asked.

"They are dying in droves on the mainland. I could have looted a dozen towns with no effort, had I wished. Many folk have fled the towns, seeking refuge in the countryside, but there is no refuge to be found there. All is chaos. Civil order has broken down with the panic."

"Yet you resisted the temptation to loot," Larissa observed.

"This is paltry. I have pledged myself to you in expectation of greater things."

"But the plague has not touched you?" she asked.

"No, and no more of my crew contracted the sickness. I had to kill two who wanted to stay on the mainland and loot, though."

Gasam laughed, a deep, throaty sound. "You are a

man of rare determination, pirate. That is an un-common thing in a foreigner."

The man was like a great, predatory cat at rest. The signs of his recent illness—the emaciation, the paleness—did not detract from his dangerous aura. Ilas saw nothing to be gained from prevarication.

"I am no longer a pirate, my king. I am your faith-ful follower, the commander of one of your war-ships."

"Even so," Gasam said. "Tell me, Captain Ilas, is the time a good one for invading the mainland?" His eyes gave away nothing.

"Another turning of the moon would be better," Ilas said. "It would give the pestilence that much longer to work. Also, while panic can be useful, it can turn in an instant to ferocity. In a month's time most of those who are to die will be dead. The sur-vivors will be sunk in gloom. The sense of doom can work for you. Armies that would have fought, cities that would have resisted, will fall before you without resistance."

"Wise words," Gasam commended.

Thus encouraged, Ilas pointed to the rows of ca-noes drawn up along the shore. "These canoes, my king; surely you do not intend to embark your full force upon them? They are fine for raiding in the is-lands but they are small for such a voyage. I know that in your later campaigns you used them to avoid the Nevan warships, but at that time the bulk of your forces were already well established on land."

"You observe truly," Gasam said. "My large trans-port vessels sail here even now. They have been har-bored on the lee sides of the larger islands. I plan to fill them with warriors and tow more in the canoes."

"An excellent plan," Ilas said.

"You have our leave," Larissa said. "We may call

upon you later, for a more detailed report of your findings."

"I live to serve Your Majesties." Ilas rose and withdrew, exulting inwardly.

"He has proven to be a valuable servant," Larissa said. "I am glad now that I spared him."

"A stone can kill as surely as a fine Shasinn spear," Gasam observed. "No weapon is too base to be employed when one sets out to conquer."

"He is right about the time as well," she said. "Another month would give you time to recover fully."

He shook his head. "I would like to wait longer, too, but we cannot. The men are here, the canoes are here, the ships will be here soon. Another month and they will be hungry and dispirited. They are gobbling up the land already. Our luck has turned again, little queen. Let us seize it now, while the men are full of spirit and the gods frown upon the foreigners. I will go as I am. After all, it is not as if I were fighting in the front rank again. I will direct and observe. That I can do sitting in a chair."

She wound an arm around his waist. "You are right. Those who wait for everything to be perfect never act at all. Let us go and reconquer what is ours by right."

That afternoon the first of the big transport ships rounded the cape and came into the harbor. Two days later the last of them had assembled and that night Gasam addressed his warriors, standing atop a tall platform so that all could see him. In the lurid light of high-flaming fires he glowed like the bronze statue of a god.

"My warriors!" he cried, his voice as powerful, as resonant, as of old. "We have waited here long enough. Your king is once more ready to lead you!" The roar of the army was tumultuous.

"Once again, it is the time of the warrior people of the islands! It is time for the mainlanders to grovel at our feet, to own us as their masters. I shall humble the insolence of Shazad of Neva. I shall retake Chiwa and Sono. I shall crush the Mezpans, who are as ants and who fight with foolish, smoking tubes. And, if he still lives, I shall tear the heart from Hael the Traitor and eat it!"

The army cried wildly and began to stamp, beating the insides of their black shields with their spear butts, chanting, "Ga-sam! Ga-sam! Ga-sam!" over and over again, until the earth shook with the fervor of their devotion. Gasam raised his spear and gradually the tumult died down.

"Onto the ships!" Gasam cried. "We sail when the sun first pales the horizon!"

Whooping with joy, the men stormed down to the wharves and began clambering aboard the transports, pushing out the canoes and lashing them to the sterns of the larger vessels. The light of innumerable torches reflecting from polished weapons made it into a scene of strange beauty.

"It is good, my queen," Gasam said, hugging Larissa to him. "The spirit of my veteran warriors is restored, and the younger ones have never known defeat."

"It is good, my husband," she said, returning his embrace. Only a tiny unease marred her joy. Gasam was not fully recovered, and what of Hael? She would have parted with half her treasure to know whether the Steel King was alive or dead.

SEVEN

Queen Shazad was pale and haggard. Her steel-spined bearing did not fail her, but her cosmeticians labored mightily to erase the signs of care from her face. From close up, though, Ansa could see the deep lines and the dark circles beneath her eyes. She had shed weight as well, and he knew that an ordinary woman would have been wringing her hands in fruitless anxiety.

"It is unprecedented!" she said, letting her feelings show for a change. For some reason, she had chosen Ansa as the only person to whom she would unburden herself. Everyone else she spoke to sternly, sometimes roaring orders and sending her minions away cowering in terror. But at least once every day she visited with Ansa and unburdened herself.

"Fully one-third of my subjects may die before this plague abates, and that will not be the end of it! Fields lie unworked, beasts are untended. Those who survive the illness may starve. And now there are the riots." She sank into a chair and buried her face in her hands. The riots had begun days before, when crackpot religious leaders and would-be revolutionaries egged on the hysterical mobs of the city to attack whomever the rabble-rousers wanted to see destroyed. Practitioners of unpopular religious sects were mobbed, blamed for bringing the plague down upon the people.

To make things worse, certain groups seemed to be immune from the plague. A small community of artisans whose origins were in a mountain province and who differed from the Nevan norm both in race and in language suffered not a single case of illness. Naturally they were attacked and slaughtered.

"You must take the strongest measures, Your Majesty," Ansa urged. "Now is no time for leniency."

She laughed, a false, hollow sound. "Leniency is the last thing on my mind. But people are now past even such things as fear of hanging. They are as good as insane, and will remain so until this curse is gone from us."

Ansa had worries of his own, although he saw no reason to burden the queen with them. He worried about his own people. How long before the plague reached them? Was it possible that the mountain barrier could prevent it from doing so? He had spoken with some of the queen's physicians and they had no answers for him. The best that could be hoped, they told him, was that anyone who carried the sickness would die during the journey or recover and no longer be contagious by the time the long journey ended. It was a thin hope and left him unsatisfied.

"What about the preparations for war?" he asked her.

"At a standstill. There are no longer enough rowers for the fleet, the healthy soldiery would mutiny if I ordered them to march anywhere, and the priests say that the omens are all bad." She gave her false laugh again. "For that I cannot blame them. Any priest who claimed to see a good omen would be torn apart by the mob." She sat back in the chair and Ansa was shocked to see tears streaking the makeup of her still-beautiful face.

"Ever since my father began to fail, I prided myself on my strength and control. I purged my military and my administration of corruption—well, most of it, anyway. With your father's help I drove Gasam and his Islanders out of my territory and kept them away. Now, in the face of this thing, I can do nothing but hope for a wind from the sea, to drive the smoke and stench of the plague pits out of the city."

Within a few more days the royal physicians reported that there were no new cases, although those already ill were still dying. Of those who contracted the plague later in its course, a far larger percentage recovered. At least half of the population had not contracted the disease or diseases (for the physicians suspected that there were several different illnesses at work), but the losses were nonetheless devastating. The most catastrophic war never slew so many people, and certainly not so swiftly. In the space of less than two months Shazad's kingdom had been utterly ravaged. In her distress the queen all but forgot about her spy, Ilas of Nar.

The court was in a somber mood, each person present dressed in sumptuous but dark mourning clothes. Their faces were whitened with cosmetics, minute blue dots making tear tracks down their cheeks. The music played by the harpists and flutists was equally mournful. Yet there was relief in every face, for they all knew that they were among the spared. They breathed a little easier than in previous days and, for the present, the catastrophe was someone else's.

The queen sat in state, striving to return her business to some sort of normalcy, hearing petitions and receiving foreign dignitaries. Above all, she wanted to drag her naval preparations back on course, somehow rouse her sailors and soldiers from their apathy and send them at the enemy, before the inexorably advancing season should prohibit naval operations.

Beside her sat Ansa, bored and fretting. This mission to Neva, for which he had held such hopes, was proving to be an utter failure. He was doing neither his own people nor Shazad any good, idling away his days here as the queen's guest, riding her cabos, attending state dinners while, for all he knew, plague raged in his homeland.

All to the east was a mystery. The famous messenger corps that linked Neva with the rest of the world was stilled while any might bear contagion from one land to another. Ansa had no way of knowing whether Mezpa had invaded the plains, whether the spread of plague had brought all activity there to a standstill. Most of all, he did not know whether his father lived or was dead. If Hael was dead, the desolation of the world was complete. Only his unique ability to lead men and to foresee the maneuvers of his enemies could both weld together many nations into an alliance and lead them to victory. The future, to Ansa, looked bleak. It looked yet bleaker when the messenger ran into the throne room.

The man wore the red leathers and plumes of the

internal messenger corps, whose riders did not cross the borders of Neva. Like all such, he did not have to observe protocol when coming into his sovereign's presence. With a bang he thrust the doors open and charged down the length of the room at a dead run to cast himself facedown on the steps of the dais. Two grave magistrates had to jump aside nimbly to avoid contact with his dusty, mud-bespattered leather garments.

"Your Majesty!" the man cried. "Urgent dispatches from the north!" He held out a message tube of gilt bronze.

Shazad looked stricken as a page took the tube from the messenger. The boy knelt gracefully by the throne and handed her the tube.

"I will read this," she said, "but give me the gist of it quickly. I take it that the news is bad. Has a new plague broken out?"

"Majesty," the man said, all but trembling, "the Islanders are back! They have invaded the north in full strength, storming ashore in ships and great war canoes!" A collective gasp ran the length of the throne room. Mouths dropped open and eyes widened.

"And, my queen," the messenger continued, "King Gasam has been seen among his warriors, with his monster queen by his side!"

Shazad looked as if a dagger had been slipped between her ribs. Her face, devoid of the makeup the others wore, went all but transparent. She truly looked, Ansa thought, as if she could collapse, dead at the foot of her throne. He leaned toward her, knowing that the fate of the world could be balancing upon a knife edge here.

"Shazad," he said in an urgent whisper, "if you don't take action this very second, our whole world is lost!"

For a few moments it looked as if she had not heard him. The whole court was absolutely still, none daring so much as to breathe, fearing what the queen might do. Slowly the color began to return to her face. First she looked almost normal, then she began to flush, then her face turned scarlet and she sprang to her feet, hurling the message tube to the floor, flattening it and causing all present to wince at the sharp clang of metal on stone.

"That monster dares!" she shouted. "In defiance of all civilized behavior and the wrath of all the gods, he dares to come back to my kingdom and threaten us while we are in mourning! I have had enough!" Her eyes glared near-insanity as she leveled an arm, pointing at the crowd of her courtiers. "You! All of you! Out of those mourning garments! Out of them now!" The last word was almost a scream.

"I want every man in armor or in uniform! Every woman, dress for a festive leave-taking! I'll want you all down at the harbor to see our army and our fleet on their way to crush the savages once and for all!"

She whirled and pointed at a knot of priests. "I want all the requiem services stopped. Deck the temples with flowers and sing the hymns of good fortune. I want the plague pits covered now! We will erect a suitable memorial later."

"B-but, Your Majesty," sputtered a priest. "It is not yet the proper time! The rituals must be observed!"

"Later," she yelled. "The time for mourning is past. The time for action is at hand. Our gods have tested us and punished us for our decadence. Now they hurl the final challenge at us and we must not be found wanting! My people shall not wear mourning, and neither shall their queen. Get me out of this!" Frantically she began to tear at the laces of her bodice. The courtiers gasped in shock, then fled the throne room.

With the help of her ladies, Shazad tore the black gown from her body. The courtiers need not have feared for her modesty. Her white undergarments were more voluminous and elaborate than the formal attire of most women. "Go fetch me a gown suitable for haranguing my troops. Something with cloth of gold." Her ladies scurried to do her bidding. From outside, they could hear orders being shouted. The machinery of war was back in operation.

Shazad fell back into her throne. "Very good," she muttered. "It could not be better." So forcefully had she been bellowing that her lips were flecked with blood. Ansa wondered if she had taken leave of her senses.

"Let me take part, Your Majesty," he urged.

She turned to look at him. Her eyes were shockingly bloodshot. She had not feigned her rage. A page brought a goblet of chilled wine and she drank deeply. She turned to him again.

"Of course you shall." Her voice was hoarse. "I give you command of a wing of my scouts. I know it's a paltry command for a prince, but you are a foreigner and, besides, I have a very special mission for you."

"I will ride with the common troopers if you wish," he assured her.

"Nothing like that. It comes to me now that my spy has not returned from the islands. Either he is dead or he turned coat, most probably the latter. It means little now. What I wished to know is amply demonstrated now. But I need some prisoners for interrogation. I have to know whether they are at full strength, or whether the plague has struck them as well. Perhaps they are fleeing devastation in their home islands and are desperate."

"Do not pin your hopes on that, Shazad," he cautioned.

"Nor shall I. But I must know, one way or another. If they have not yet come in contact with the foreigners, Gasam's army will be devastated by the plague within days. I know it is another optimistic wish, but it must be taken into account."

He stooped and picked up the smashed message tube, slipping its crumpled scroll from within it. "Perhaps it is time to read this dispatch, Your Majesty."

"Of course." She took a deep breath and restored her calm. To Ansa, she looked better than she had since he had arrived. Her course was set and she would see it to its conclusion. Whatever might befall, whether glorious victory or death, she was content.

She began to scan the missive and mutter. " 'Strong force came ashore along a wide front of beach north of Floria . . .' By the gods, poor Floria. The unhappiest and most ill fated of my cities . . . 'a number of semi-independent war parties scouring the countryside, taking many captives, driving the rest into the city . . .' Listen to this, Ansa: 'King Gasam himself was seen by many, seated atop a high litter borne on the shoulders of spearmen, his loathsome queen seated beside him. The people of this district saw much of these two in years past, so there is no question that it is he.' "

"He is truly alive," Ansa said, shaking his head. "Is it impossible for the man to die? Yet he is being carried. He must not be fully recovered."

"That is something, anyway. We know he is mortal."

Outside, as the day progressed, they heard the mourning drums of the temples grow silent, to be replaced with trumpets of celebration.

In the days that followed, Shazad seemed to be everywhere. She went personally to the camps outside the city and herded her men through the city streets to the harbor, where they were embarked upon the transport vessels. Under her lashing tongue, the rowers churned the water of the harbor to white foam as training was resumed.

The city collectively came to life as people understood that the plague was past and they would live. They had suffered ghastly losses, but the power of the fact was blunted by a sort of exhilaration as people felt that they would now live forever. The sudden, unexpected invasion of the Islanders stirred the populace to rage. It seemed to them treacherous and uncalled-for, conveniently forgetting that they had been in full invasion preparations themselves when the plague struck.

Her generals and admirals, her captains and commodores, were not so sanguine.

"Every one of my regiments is sorely under-strength, Your Majesty," said a grizzled general. "You cannot throw such numbers against an enemy and expect them to perform as they would in normal times."

"I am quite aware of that, General," she said. "But the Islanders have taken the decision out of my hands. They are on my territory, and they are moving south. I must go north and fight them. Each regiment must fight as if it is at full strength. Spirit and valor must make up for the lack of numbers."

"As you say, Majesty," the general replied, bowing. His voice was exceedingly dubious.

"We were preparing for an invasion of the islands," said an admiral on another day. "But now they are already off the islands, upon our own territory. This is no longer properly a naval war. You should march your troops north by land, in the customary fashion, with the fleet transporting supplies and screening the land forces from flank attack by sea."

"No, my father tried those old tactics against Gasam years ago and they did not work. My war machine will go north as a single unit, except for scouts, and we will fall upon them all at once. This matter will be decided with a single battle. I will not have another dragged-out, indecisive war."

"As Your Majesty commands," the admiral said, bowing.

Ansa saw little of this. The day after the queen resumed her war preparations, he rode out to the camp of the mounted troops and assumed his new command. Following the directions of a succession of mounted officers, he found the camp of his scouts and reported to their commander. The man was a member of the border nobility. He seemed competent but he wore the harried look of officers everywhere whose units are preparing to move out.

"I had heard that a plains prince was with us." He looked Ansa over as he took his hand. "You're a rider, no question of that. And your weapons are fine." He took the orders Ansa handed him and read them. "So you're to have command of a wing of scouts, eh? A prisoner-taking sortie? I must assume you know your business."

"I do," Ansa told him. "I will need hard-riding men."

"My men are all hard-riding. These are scouts, not troopers of the household guard."

"The men I want should be the closest thing to bandits you have."

Now the officer grinned. "You know your business at that. I have just the men you need. Come with me." The two left the commander's tent and mounted their animals. They rode past the orderly campfires of the riders to a small camp a little way outside the main encampment.

"These men aren't just close to being bandits," the commander told him. "They *are* bandits. They are light riders from up on the Omian border. It's useless to demand they pay taxes, so the queen allows them exemption in return for service in war. This they accede to gladly, because, for them, it is a fine excuse for looting. They are as villainous a lot as you could ask for, and you'll have to ride them with a heavy rein, and with whip and spur, but they will ride anywhere. They can live off the land and they never tire."

The camp held little more than a light squadron, about a score of small, ragged, ill-kempt men who rode stunted but strong-looking cabos. They rose from their fire when the two riders approached.

"Men, this is your new commander," said the Nevan. "He is Prince Ansa of the Plains, and he will take you north upon an important mission. Mount up so he can inspect you."

The men sprang into their saddles and formed a ragged line. Ansa rode down the line, inspecting each closely. They were not prepossessing. Each wore a hide vest, baggy trousers and a fur cap despite the heat of the day. There was not a scrap of armor among them, which was all to the good as far as Ansa was concerned. Their principal weapon was a slender lance. Except for this, most carried only long, curved knives. Thonged to each saddle was a small, round shield rimmed with dangling black fur. It was obvious that bathing was not among their more frequent practices.

To Ansa's eye, their dirt and rags were irrelevant. What he saw pleased him. Their animals, while not groomed and curried like the regular army's mounts, were well cared for. Their saddles and weapons were immaculate. He inspected each spear point and blade. All were of shaving keenness. He detected no signs of infirmity among the cabos they rode, nor among the small herd of remounts.

"I like them," Ansa reported when he had finished.

"That is good," said the commander, "because they are all yours now." He wore a look of relief, as if this was one diminution of his command he did not regret. He saluted and rode back to his tent.

Ansa saw the men evaluating him with their eyes. "We will get to know one another as we ride," he told them. "For now, strike camp. We go north."

The men smiled like scavenging stripers as they went about the exceedingly brief task. They had not a single tent to strike, nor had they any need of pack animals. Few of them even bothered with saddlebags, each man merely rolling his few belongings into a single blanket that served him as cloak in foul weather, tying the bundle across his saddle. One kicked some dirt over the fire and they were ready to ride. This, too, pleased Ansa. This was the sort of soldiering to which he was accustomed.

They rode north at an easy canter, sparing the mounts. There was no urgency. It would be days yet before the fleet sailed. They would be in Gasam's territory long before the navy arrived. They stayed off the fine, paved road, and the hooves of the cabos made little noise against the soft earth.

"Who is the senior man?" Ansa asked.

A man rode up alongside him. "I am. My name is Uluk, and I am a headman among Long Valley people." He looked much like the others: dark-faced with narrow brown eyes. His long mustache and scraggly beard were sparse and black. His Nevan was spoken with a heavy accent. "I saw your father defeat the Omians once, years ago. It was a fine battle."

"Which side were you on?" Ansa asked.

Uluk gave a high-pitched laugh, echoed by the others. "We watched from a safe distance! When it was over, we rode down to reap our harvest, and it was a good one. I have felt kindly disposed toward your people ever since."

"That is good to know," Ansa said. "I shall put you in the way of even more loot, but this time you will have to take more part in the action."

"That is good," Uluk said. "We like action, so long as there is wealth to be taken."

"I will lead you to it, but our first duty is to take prisoners. We must know some things about these Islanders."

"Good, good!" Uluk said. "We are very good at getting prisoners to talk. Many speak freely, just knowing that we might question them."

"I do not doubt it, but these Islanders are not like the people you are accustomed to fighting. It will be no use trying to take the Shasinn prisoner. They are too proud and fierce, and they do not fear death at all. But there are other island tribes. I shall show you which ones to go for."

"How soon must the queen have this knowledge?" Uluk asked.

"Before the armies engage."

"That is plenty of time. Let us not rush, then."

"I thought you would be more eager," Ansa chided.

"But the longer they are up north," Uluk answered reasonably, "the more loot they will collect and the more we will take from them!" Shouting and laughing, the others agreed.

Ansa laughed as well. "We shall see when we get there."

It felt good to be riding hard once more. He was raised in the saddle, and he felt half-alive when he had to live afoot, no matter how luxurious his surroundings. They put the miles behind them and did not stop to make camp until the moon was well up. The men tended their beasts, rolled into their blankets and snored. They did not trouble themselves with fire.

The next morning, after a hasty meal of dried milk and meat, washed down with water from their flasks, they rode on. That morning Ansa spied a small, fat curlhorn grazing placidly on a nearby knoll. It was a long cast, but he was hungry for fresh meat and decided to hazard a shot. Taking his great bow from its saddle case, he strung it while riding, took out an arrow and nocked it. With an easy surge of power, he drew and released. The men watched wide-eyed as the arrow arched, then plummeted, skewering the beast and sending it to the ground, kicking for a few moments before it stiffened and lay still.

The men shouted admiration for the splendid cast and one of them galloped to the knoll, leaned from his saddle and picked up the beast without slowing down. He came back to the column with the beast across his saddle. Drawing his knife, with a few dextrous cuts he freed the arrow from the carcass and handed it to his commander, ignoring the blood that stained his breeches.

"I think you will feed us well, Captain," said the bandit.

"As long as you give me no trouble," he answered.

That evening he called an early halt, more to spare the animals than the men. They built a fire, skinned and butchered the curlhorn, and soon had it broiling over the coals on skewers of sweet-smelling wood. Uluk came to sit by Ansa and handed him a skewer of the flesh.

"We like you better than the Nevans who have been set over us, Captain," he said, setting teeth to the savory but somewhat stringy meat. "They are mostly parade-ground soldiers, even the border lords. But you ride like us. Maybe a little better. And you do not get weary just because of a day's ride in fair weather."

"I am glad of it," Ansa said. "But do not think that because you like me, you can be slow to obey orders."

"We are not ones to curry favor," Uluk said, spitting out a bit of gristle. "Have no fear, we scarcely need orders in battle. We like to fight, and we know how to do it."

"But if I order you not to fight, that you shall obey also," Ansa warned. "And when I say break off and run, I mean it. Our mission is not to destroy the enemy by oursleves, but to gather intelligence. I'll have no man endangering us by going off glory-hunting."

"We do not care for glory. We like loot."

Ansa was beginning to get the feeling that his men were somewhat single-minded. For loot-obsessed bandits, though, they did not seem very prosperous. Perhaps times had been bad for bandits lately. Back home, his father had made life hard for bandits, indeed. As a result, his realm was probably the safest nation in the world. The Nevans had not been so successful, but their northeastern border with neighboring Omia was a difficult place, and Shazad could not be heavily blamed for failing to wipe out the likes of these men. At least she had found a use for them.

Their third day of hard riding brought them near Gasam's area of operations. They began to see people fleeing southward, most of them carrying bundles of belongings, terror dulling their eyes. These people had experienced the depredations of Gasam's Islanders before. They pointed back up the road down which they had come, proclaiming that the savage hordes pressed them close behind.

"Men in fear flee pursuers where there are none, Captain," said Uluk.

"These people have much to fear," Ansa said. "But I suspect you are right. It would be unlike Gasam to press hard against a fleeing rabble. His advance will not be slow, but neither will it be done at breakneck speed. They will come inexorably, breaking everything in their path. That is their way." He wheeled his cabo. "Come, it is time to get away from the road. We'll swing wide and keep to the hills. When we spy the Islanders, we go to ground. Then, after a bit of reconnoitering, we shall make our sweep for prisoners."

Growling assent, the men turned from the road and rode across the fields, paying no attention to the growing crops they trampled. There was no one to tend them, anyway. All the farmers had fled. They had seen few such on the road and Ansa guessed that the farmers had driven their livestock into the hills, in hope of keeping them there undiscovered until the armies had passed. It was always the way of farmers.

As usual near cultivated lands, the hills bore little timber. The constant search for fuel and building material destroyed the forests near human habitation. This made them easy to ride, but they offered little cover from observation. It was not a matter of great importance, for it was unlikely that Gasam would have a force of riders, and they could always count upon the swiftness of their animals to escape.

The next day they saw their first elements of the Islanders' attack force. Ansa and his men were screening themselves with the low hills, every mile or two sending a man to climb one to see what was ahead and to the flank. The spy would ride to just below the crest, then dismount and climb the remaining steps on foot, until he could see beyond, exposing nothing more than his head.

About midday, one of these men made his reconnoiter, then waved his lance in a circular motion, signifying "Enemy in sight." Ansa and Uluk then climbed the hill with the same stealth, going the last few yards on their bellies until they, too, could see over the crest. Following the direction of the man's pointing finger, Ansa slowly extended his telescope.

He saw four island warriors, dressed in furry kilts and little else. They were amusing themselves with two or three captives who had not been quick enough in their flight. The men had much the look of the Shasinn, but three of them were dark-haired and one was shaven-headed. None carried the unique Shasinn spear.

"Couldn't be better," Ansa said, collapsing his spyglass. "Any more in sight?"

"None," said the man who had found them. "They

were chasing those people down when I spotted them. Caught them just before you got here."

"Excellent! Uluk, we'll maneuver a little closer to them, ride down on them and take them prisoner. Remember, they are not to be killed. I want all four for questioning."

"We know how to do this, Captain," Uluk assured him.

Ansa faced him squarely. "These are not villagers, Uluk. They may not be Shasinn, but the Islanders are all warlike and skillful in the extreme."

Uluk glared sullenly. "We are not afraid!"

"That is not what I . . . oh, foul spirits take it, then. Come on. We waste time here."

The men were excited at the prospect of a little action, especially since it sounded more like sport than battle. Taking warriors alive made it more of a challenge. They readied their ropes and their weapons and rode a short way north, then they wheeled around a small hill at a gallop. They were within a hundred paces of the Islanders before they were even seen.

The bald warrior pointed and shouted something. Two men rose from the women they had been savaging and seized their weapons. Two riders surged ahead, whooping and yipping. The first cast a noose at one of the dark-haired warriors, catching him over the head and looping over a shoulder, but the man did not panic and fight the rope. Instead, he ran straight toward the rider, ducking the lowered lance and ramming his own spear deep into the rider's unshielded belly, hauling him screaming from the saddle.

The other riders roared with rage and encircled the island warriors, hemming them in and making them easy targets for the bandits' ropes. In a few, frantic minutes the warriors were fought to the ground and trussed, but another rider lay dead, and several had taken wounds.

"You see what I meant?" Ansa said when they were secured. Then, in a more moderate tone: "You all did well. They are all alive and can talk."

"We should kill them now!" said a bandit. "They slew Amani and Geosa!"

Uluk turned on the man. "Amani was a fool, to ride ahead like that and try to take one alone! No man can manage rope and lance at the same time. As for Geosa, his luck ran out. It can happen anytime, to anyone. Besides, we have no wish to kill these men, because we have much better plans for them." The rest nodded savagely.

"What do we do with these, Captain?" one of the bandits asked, pointing to the refugees the warriors had caught. Ansa rode a few paces and looked down at them. An elderly man lay dead. A younger man had a huge spear wound in his side, and blood bubbled from his lips. Two females lay moaning on the ground, stripped and bloody. One was a girl of no more than eleven.

"These will not live much longer," Uluk said.

"Captain!" A rider pointed up the valley. A file of black-shielded warriors advanced toward them at a trot. The line of warriors stretched as far back as the riders could see.

"A full regiment, at least," Ansa said. He looked back down at the forms writhing weakly on the ground. They could load their prisoners on the remounts. They had none to spare for these. And it was as Uluk had said: They would certainly die, anyway.

"No need to let them suffer further," Ansa said. "Finish them." Knives flashed and the bodies lay still. Also killed was any squeamishness he might have felt about the coming interrogation.

The prisoners were loaded on the remounts and they sped away, long before they could even hear the chanting of the advancing island regiment.

They rode until evening, their charges lashed belly-down across the backs of four cabo remounts. At first, the prisoners bore the indignity in stoic silence, but they soon found that it was more than an insult to warrior dignity. Before they had gone two or three miles the pounding of the animals' hard spines into their bellies was an agony. With each stride of the cabos, their heads were whipped back and forward, slapping their faces against the sweaty hides of the beasts. Soon they began to groan loudly.

Uluk looked back at them and laughed shrilly. "This will soften them up nicely, like meat slipped under the saddle for a long day's ride. They will be ready for the fire when we stop tonight." The other bandits echoed his laughter. Ansa steeled himself for the process. Pity, he knew, was wasted on Islanders. Once, the people of the plains had been notorious practitioners of torture, but King Hael had suppressed it. So great was the awe in which he was held that his subjects had willingly forgone the pleasure of tormenting their enemies. Even Hael, however, had recognized that sometimes, in the extremity of war, it was necessary to employ the most brutal methods to secure vital information from an enemy.

That evening irons were placed in the fire that cooked their meat. The prisoners, already half-dead from their excruciating ride, lay devoid of strength, regarding the glowing metal with eyes so dulled by pain that even fear could not gleam through.

The interrogation was not lengthy. Ansa had only

a few questions for the prisoners, and the bandits proved to be as proficient in their work as they had claimed. So weakened were the Islanders that not one of them held out for so much as an hour. In preparation, Ansa had separated them, so that they could not concoct a consistent story.

There was another reason for this separation. His father had long ago taught him that, should he ever be driven to this practice, a warrior must always be alone. Much of the warrior's mystique, Hael had said, involved maintaining face in the company of his fellows. A warrior of no more than ordinary quality might resist heroically rather than be shamed before fellow warriors. Alone, such a man could fall apart swiftly. So it proved with these men.

"This is not good," Ansa said, sitting glumly at the fire, trying to wash the foul taste from his mouth with sour wine.

"You are young yet, Captain," Uluk reassured him. "You will get used to the work soon."

"That is not what I meant," Ansa told him. "It was necessary. I do not regret it. No, what I meant is that the Islanders did not suffer from the plague, though it killed so many of their slaves. I think the queen was counting on their losses being at least as great as her own. Not that she had much choice. She had to go to war."

"Very true," Uluk said, nodding. "My own people did not die, either. Many got very sick, with knots in the belly and a terrible flux, but only a few old people died."

"Odd how it affected different breeds of men differently," Ansa mused, staring into the leaping flames. "I am half-Shasinn myself. Perhaps that is why it never touched me."

"These are spirit matters," Uluk said. "It is not a

good thing to question them. Be satisfied that you are alive while others are dead. It will be your turn all too soon."

"Wise words," Ansa said. "But I have a bad feeling about what lies ahead. And these are not spirit matters. These are the doings of men." He continued to stare into the flames for a long time.

EIGHT

Queen Larissa felt that the world was back on course once more. Their landing had been unopposed, they had taken the northern province of Neva by total surprise and their warriors were rampaging joyously while the two-footed livestock of the mainland fled in panic. They had been demoralized by the terrible plague which had only recently run its course and were in no condition to put up any sort of resistance or protect what they had.

For the warriors, it was like an intoxicating draft. Gone was all sullenness and dejection. Quick, easy victories were a great restorer of morale, she thought. For the young men who had never been to the mainland, it bestowed the proper spirit of domination. They landed, they plied their weapons and they saw their enemies driven before them like timid kagga. Soon the story would be different: They would face the organized, disciplined armies of Neva. But the habit of conquest would have been instilled, and they would not find the mainland soldiers intimidating.

"A good beginning, my husband," she said to the king. He sat beside her in their high litter, shaded by a silken canopy. It galled him to be carried about, but he was far from fully recovered, though each day he was able to spend a little more time on his feet.

"I agree," he rumbled. "But I dislike advancing so slowly. Before, we could campaign at a run, because I was in the lead and I could run all day without tiring and was always in the forefront when the time came to give battle. Now"—he waved at the lavish vehicle below him with contempt—"I must be carried on the shoulders of men like a load of fodder. Even the finest of my warriors, bearing such a load, cannot advance at more than a fast walk." The king's warriors would not allow him to be carried by slaves. All his litter-bearers were master warriors, the elite class he had created from the men who survived to retire from senior warrior status. In battle they formed his strategic reserve. Now they took turns carrying their king.

Larissa patted his hand. "Now, Gasam, how can you complain when scant weeks ago you were abed, hovering between life and death? You have spent a lifetime training your commanders and now you need not be present at every little skirmish. The men only have to have their king present for a major battle. There should be only one during this campaign, and it will be at the time and place of our choosing."

"I know you are right," he grumbled. "But it is a burr beneath my breechclout to campaign on my backside while my warriors behave as a man should."

She laughed. "You are just jealous because they are enjoying themselves. Let them have their fun. I have an idea. Why not take ship and go along the coast by water, paralleling the advance of our army? Thus they can move at their own pace and we can travel in comfort, rejoining them every evening."

He thought it over. "A good idea. Of course, they will have to move inland at some times, and then I will want to go with them, but this may make things easier. Which ship shall we take?"

"We will use the pirate's. He is idle at the moment and it is a splendid little ship, very swift and a thing of beauty as well." To her this last quality was important. Like all her people, she loved things of beauty, often to the point of ignoring other considerations. It was for this reason that the Shasinn warriors clung to their beautiful bronze spears with their inset steel edges, even though the more practical, all-steel spears had been available to them for some time. Steel was utilitarian but not beautiful.

She summoned Ilas of Nar and he came running. He knew well how precarious was his situation. Each night he agonized, wondering whether he had made the right decision in throwing in with these savages. Since his landing on the mainland, his mind was set somewhat at ease. The all but effortless advance of the horde boded well for the future. Shazad was finished, Gasam would prevail. If he played his hand cunningly, he would prosper. The Islanders were contemptuous of mainlanders, but they needed them.

Ilas was not an uneducated man. He knew that, in centuries past, great civilizations had been overrun by barbarians. After a period of dislocation, the barbarians would acquire a veneer of culture and they would need the skilled and educated people of the old ruling classes to help run the machinery of civilization. Larissa herself had been well upon that path in Chiwa. While her husband was rampaging in the east, she had been reassembling a workable kingdom on the ruins of the decadent old nation, using the remains of the Chiwan civil servant class, just as Gasam had impressed the survivors of the Chiwan armies to be his garrison troops and siege train, reserving his Islanders to be his shock force.

They would need to do the same with conquered Neva, and Ilas of Nar intended to be high in the councils of Queen Larissa. And he knew that, as Queen Shazad had advised, Larissa was the one to deal with. Gasam was a genius of sorts, but his mind had only a single interest and goal: conquest. Within the narrow limits of waging war, his brilliance was rivaled only by that of King Hael. But Larissa was a builder and a controller. She controlled all the people around her and she controlled Gasam. Between them, they were perhaps the greatest conqueror and ruler the world had ever known.

"Yes, my queen," he said, approaching the foot of the litter and bowing.

"We shall wish to be taken aboard your ship," she said. "You shall convey us along the coast, keeping even with the advance of the army."

"As my sovereigns command," he said, not liking the assignment but knowing better than to contradict her. Prolonged coastal cruising meant danger from rocks and reefs. Even in the finest sailing weather, sudden storms could drive a ship onto the shoals with devastating fury and swiftness. However, he reflected, nothing else on earth quite equaled the fury of King Gasam and his queen.

That afternoon the royal couple and their immediate retinue boarded *Seasnake*. The capacity of the little ship was severely limited, so Gasam took only a few of his women warriors, and Larissa a handful of her juniors. The rest would restrict themselves to a line of march along the shore, keeping as close to their sovereigns as possible.

The army, under the overall command of Pendu in Gasam's absence, was divided into a number of regimental groups under subcommanders. They would roam inland, looting, disrupting, smashing any organized resistance. The whole time, they would keep in close contact by runners, to regroup swiftly should any real threat show itself. It was a form of warfare in which they were well schooled and they practiced it well. It made the best use of the limited numbers of the island warriors. Gasam hated to keep his whole army concentrated, leaving behind their advance many pockets of resistance, leaving much countryside unpillaged. This fluid system guaranteed the maximum devastation, while keeping the army ready to reunite when the main enemy army showed up.

One thing Gasam had learned in his career was how slow civilized armies were. They lurched into action like huge, slow beasts. Well handled, they could muster tremendous power, but he had also learned that they were seldom well handled. He himself used such armies better than the civilized generals did. They were fine for occupying land already won by his warriors, and there was nothing like them for carrying out sieges.

The only power to match his own, he reflected sourly, was Hael's all-mounted army of plainsmen. With their matchless mobility and their powerful bows, their effectiveness was far out of proportion to their relatively small numbers.

"Hael," he muttered darkly.

"What?" Larissa was roused from a pleasant reverie induced by the purling of the water over *Seasnake's* ram as the trim little warship cut the waves.

"I was thinking of Hael, and how his army destroyed mine at our last meeting."

She refused to give way to anger. "I have thought of little else since that day."

He regarded her sidelong, beneath his brows. "You did not speak to me of this."

"I wanted you to concentrate upon recovering. Perhaps, now that you are well upon that path, we should speak of it."

"Speak on," he said, knowing that his wife used no idle words when they discussed matters of war and conquest.

"Has it occurred to you, my love, that when you fight Hael, you fight two armies?"

"Two? You have never spoken in riddles before."

"Nor do I now. It only occurred to me a little while past. Hael commands two distinct armies: one of men and one of beasts."

"The cabos," Gasam said.

"Exactly. So inseparable are the plainsmen from their animals that we are lulled into thinking of them as a single creature. And yet they are two, each with its own requirements."

"Go on."

"We had no cabos in the islands before we set out to take the mainland, so we tend not to think of them as we do our kagga. But I used them quite a bit when we were in Chiwa. I had a whole royal herd."

"And you learned to ride well," he acknowledged. Gasam had no love of riding, preferring to trust to his own feet.

"I also learned that it takes a great deal of forage to keep a cabo in good health. And they cannot be effective in warfare if they do not enjoy good health."

"How much forage?"

"More than a grown kagga, perhaps half again as much."

"Really? And yet they are not as large." Like any other Shasinn, discussion of livestock piqued his interest. In the old days they had thought of little save kagga and fighting.

"But who ever asks kagga to run all day, mile after mile?"

"A good point," he acknowledged.

"They are elegant animals, and the royal beasts are so curried and groomed that they appear almost dainty. Yet no other animal is worked as hard. Think of it: When riders go to war, a cabo must bear the weight of man and saddle, and all that man's weapons and gear. And under this load it must be as agile and swift as if it were running bareback across the plains. Its hunger is immense. To feed all this activity, it needs acreage we do not dream of."

"And your meaning?" Gasam's mind did not work quickly, but he had a herdsman's gift of concentration and followed reasoning with great acuity.

She leaned toward him, smiling. "My love, your army consists entirely of men, and what animal is so hardy as a man? Men can go anywhere, in any weather, and can travel long and far on little food and water. But Hael's army is limited by dependence on the cabo. There is much territory where they have little effectiveness because forage is lacking. They cannot campaign the year round."

She grew ever more animated. "I have studied Hael's two great campaigns in the west. On each occasion he waited until well into the wet season to advance. At last I understood why: He could go nowhere until the grass was high enough to feed his cabos! My love, from now on, if we plan our campaigning seasons and our terrain carefully, we need not fear them!"

For a long time he sat saying nothing, staring at the waves. Then, slowly, he smiled. "Yes. Yes, I think you are right. But what must we do in the months when the grass is high? Surely at least half the year is open to his campaigns."

"At that time we must go to ground," she said. "I know, it hurts our pride and does not suit our spirit, but it must be done. These light, mobile soldiers, armed with missiles, cannot take a fortified city. If we campaign in the dry season, at its end we can take a great city and fill it with our plunder and supplies. From its walls we can laugh at the plainsmen. They can only stay for a short time before all the fodder for miles around is gone and then they must leave."

"We can gather it all before they arrive," he said, warming to the thought. "Although it pains my heart to fire grasslands, we could even do that."

"If necessary," she said, knowing that he would follow her advice.

His look darkened. "It may be the only way, but it will be hard to keep up the spirits of my warriors if they have to cower behind walls."

"It will not be so forever," she said. "Only a single campaign, perhaps two. The plainsmen cannot put up with more than that. Two such fruitless campaigns, and they will never follow Hael again. If," she added, "he is even still alive."

"He is alive," Gasam said, startling her with his certainty. "I would know if he was dead."

They sailed thus down the coast, keeping even with the advance of the army, for many days. Astern of *Seasnake* a number of transports sailed, carrying plunder, every so often putting in at the small ports as they were overrun, taking on more, so that the army always had a store of provisions should they encounter scorched earth in their advance. Yet more transports plied the waters between mainland and islands, ferrying across more warriors to swell the ranks of the invading army.

One morning *Seasnake* sailed a little ahead of the advancing land force. It was a habit they had fallen into, for there was a certain difficulty to limiting a swift ship to the pace of man on foot, even when the men were as quick as Gasam's warriors. It was an easy matter to sail ahead and pause at a convenient cove, waiting for the leading elements of the land force to catch up. Should hostile ships appear, there would be ample opportunity to turn and escape. *Seasnake* could outrun any vessel in the Nevan fleet and, once ashore among their warriors, they had nothing to fear.

"Riders ashore!" cried the lookout atop the mainmast.

"Where?" Gasam called.

"That point just off the port now," said the lookout.

Gasam and his queen lounged in their padded thrones, bored and in need of diversion. He took the telescope from its chest beside him and extended it.

"What do you see?" Larissa asked him.

"Three riders . . . no, eight or ten more just rode up to them."

"The Nevan army may be just beyond!" she said. "Should I tell Ilas to lower sail? We are ahead of the army again."

"Look for yourself," he said, handing her the instrument. "These are not regulars. Not a scrap of armor on them, and you know how the Nevan riders love bright bronze. These are irregulars—light riders, probably scouts on a reconnaissance. They could be days ahead of the main force."

"We should be careful, anyway," she cautioned. Gasam's major failing, to her mind, was his refusal to take threat seriously. She scanned along the line of riders. Three were a little ahead of the others. As she scanned past, something gave her pause. She swung the glass back to the dominant three, lingering on the rider in the center.

"A few days ago some scouts were spotted," Gasam said. "They took four men prisoner, for whatever good that will do them. When the main force is near, we will know in plenty of . . . what is it?"

"Those riders . . . there is something about one of them . . ."

"Let me see." He took the glass back from her and trained it on the riders.

"The one in the middle of that group of three. He bothers me."

"He is dressed differently from the others," Gasam said, a shrug in his voice. "That is about all I can tell from this distance. I see nothing to disturb us."

"I don't know. It is as if I had seen him before. I suppose you are right. It is nothing."

"Now, here's something more interesting," Gasam said, swinging the telescope to the tip of the point. A ship was rounding the promontory: a merchantman, doubtless one that had not received word that the seas were no longer safe. The moment it hove into view, its yard dropped precipitately. But a ship could not stop in a moment like a man or a beast and it continued to drift toward the oncoming, predatory ships as its steerman frantically tried to alter course.

"Game!" Gasam shouted. "Captain, run out the oars and let's catch him!" He turned to Larissa and smiled. "If we can't have war today, let's have sport instead."

She smiled back at him, the riders already forgotten.

Ansa collapsed his telescope, put it in its leather case and replaced the case in his saddlebag. He had been keeping just ahead of the Islanders for days now, hoping to catch sight of their leaders. Only the day before had it occurred to him that they might be traveling by ship, and his theory had proven to be correct. Could there be some way he could use this knowledge to advantage? He was sure he could, but just seeing the two of them made it difficult to think straight. They had given him some hours of the purest terror he had ever experienced.

"Look at that fool," Uluk said, pointing. Concentrating on the enemy ships to the north, they had not seen the merchantman round the point behind them. They could see the panic aboard the ship as the triangular blue sail came down and the helmsman pushed hard at the tiller.

"I don't think it's Nevan," Ansa said. "Probably a foreign ship that's been trading among the southern isles. It must have come straight north, avoiding the mainland to beat the competition, or maybe they heard about the plague and wanted to avoid it. Either way, they didn't hear about the invasion."

"They know now," Uluk said, slapping his thigh and laughing as the predators bore down on the helpless vessel. Any danger that was not his own was entertainment to Uluk and the others.

"Did the pirates see us, Captain?" asked a young bandit.

"Aye, they were studying me through a glass while I did the same to them. Our presence does not upset them. It certainly hasn't put them off their sport."

The ships were closing fast. On its many churning oars, the little warship bore down on the merchantman like a longneck upon a wounded kagga. The fat ship might as well have been at anchor. Within minutes the ships were alongside, grappled together. Even without the telescope Ansa could see that the merchants attempted no futile resistance. It did not save them. Warriors stormed aboard the ship, their weapons flashing. Moments later, corpses splashed into the water and the sea was suddenly alive with fins, jagged spines and thrashing tails, all churning the water to pink froth.

Ansa whirled his mount. "It is time to ride back. I must see the queen."

"The fun is over here," Uluk said. Whooping, they rode away.

Ansa planned as he rode. Larissa, Gasam, that ship. There must be some way he could use this. Days before, he had sent a messenger with his report of what they had learned from the prisoners. Since then he had shadowed the invading army, keeping well ahead of it and twice more sending reports by swift cabo. Now it was time to go. As for the army, it was advancing, destroying as it came and moving at a predictable rate. Gasam's seaborne personal advance was the only truly interesting information he had gathered since interrogating the prisoners.

They rode back avoiding the roads and royal highways, for these were choked with refugees, fleeing afoot or in carriages or carts, humans and vehicles alike piled high with belongings. Word of the Islanders' advance had spread swiftly and, following so closely upon the plague, it engendered even greater panic than it might have in another time.

Like all other manifestations of distress, it inspired laughter in the irrepressible Uluk. "Where do they think they are going?" he asked Ansa. "Do they think they can outrun the barbarians when they are so loaded down? Where do they expect to find safety? Is starvation in a besieged city better than a quick death by spear?"

"I've seen it in other places," Ansa affirmed. "When an alien army approaches, peasants, villagers and townsmen take this urge to get out and clog the roads. The clever ones go into the hills and hide in the thick bush. The rest do as these."

"It only makes them easy to round up and slaughter." Uluk observed. "But it has never been my way to keep such folk alive any longer than necessary, so if they choose this way to die, they may do so with my blessing."

Frequently Ansa had to chastise his men as they sought to take especially tempting possessions from the refugees. They could not understand his delicacy, but he told them the queen would be displeased.

After three days of riding they found Queen Shazad's fleet anchored in the minor port of Kantun. Its harbor could only handle a few of the larger ships, the rest being anchored beyond its breakwater. It was with relief that he beheld the Nevan fleet, but with great surprise he saw that there were others as well.

"What are those?" he said, pointing to a trio of vessels anchored in the harbor.

"Ships," Uluk said, looking at him as if he had lost his mind.

"They have three masts," he said, "like the foreign ship that brought the plague!"

"Is that so?" Uluk shrugged. "I know nothing of ships."

The sentries at the city gate let them pass without argument when he showed his royal seal. A quartermaster led them to stables where their animals could be cared for, and Ansa left Uluk and the men there while he went to the harbor. His royal seal was passport and key, taking him everywhere he wanted to go, giving him access to supplies and transport. For the moment all he needed was a boat to convey him to the queen's flagship.

That ship, *Sea Queen*, rode at anchor in the harbor. The sun had set, and it blazed with lanterns, more light streaming through the glass ports of its stern castle. A naval launch with an orange lantern at its bow and a blue one at its stern rowed Ansa out to the great vessel amid a quiet that was almost uncanny in the presence of dozens of ships and thousands of men. The strict discipline of the royal navy permitted the sailors to converse only in low voices. Lookouts could raise their voices, and orders were conveyed by means of muffled bells and mellow-toned flutes. The quiet and the colored lights gave the whole scene a feeling of unreality, like something seen in a dream.

"Who comes?" whispered the deck officer as the launch pulled up by the ship.

"Royal messenger to come aboard," whispered the coxswain of the boat.

"Come aboard, royal messenger," whispered the officer. There was a low whistle, and a massive ladder, more like a hinged staircase, was lowered from the side of the ship by means of a crane. Ansa sprang onto the ladder, noting with astonishment that its treads were covered with rich carpet, and climbed swiftly to the deck, where he saluted the deck officer.

"Prince Ansa with urgent dispatches for Queen Shazad," he murmured.

The officer snapped his fingers, the sound no louder than the breaking of a small twig. As by magic, a pair of marines appeared behind him, short swords bared in the hands. Their armor was covered with oiled fabric to protect it from the sea air and muffle its clatter.

"Escort this messenger to Her Majesty," he ordered, apparently not terribly awed by Ansa's title, somewhat to his disappointment. They marched him to the stern, and he knew that the needle points of their swords were leveled at his kidneys, which would be spitted at the first sign of treachery. In wartime all courtesy was secondary to military necessity. They would treat him as a potential enemy until ordered otherwise.

At the entrance to the queen's cabin a guard tapped lightly on the door. It opened on silent hinges and an officer beckoned them in. Ansa lowered his head and passed beneath the low lintel. The interior of the cabin was bathed in a warm light, and he saw Shazad at the end of a long table. She looked up and smiled.

"Come here, Prince Ansa. Sit by me." She looked at the marines. "You may go." The men bowed, sheathing their swords. They backed out and the door closed.

As he made his way around the table Ansa noted that among those seated at it were three of the mysterious foreigners, all of them richly if exotically dressed.

"I have important information, Your Majesty," he said, sinking into the chair she patted next to her.

"And you shall tell me all about it before the night is over. First, though, allow me to introduce these gentlemen." Something in the way she spoke these words put him on his guard. Her words were fair but they disguised a low-banked rage. "My lords, this is Prince Ansa, eldest son of King Hael of the Plains, of whom you have heard so much. In token of the great friendship which obtains between our nations, Prince Ansa has consented to serve in my army as a scout upon most difficult and dangerous missions, for which his incomparable skill in the saddle suits him so well."

"Your Majesty does me too much honor," Ansa said, feeling uncomfortable and wondering where all this was leading.

"By no means. Prince Ansa, my honored guests." Again, that note of sarcasm. "Lord Sachu"—a tall, fine-looking man bowed slightly. "Lord Goss"—a man with a meager, pocked face inclined his head. "And Lord Mopsis"—this was a distinguished, white-haired man with a scholar's face.

"Gentlemen, I am honored by your acquaintance," Ansa said, as he had been schooled.

"And we by yours," said the one called Sachu. "Our queen will be most pleased that we have contacted so many persons of royal distinction." The man's tone suggested that he considered the plethora of kingdoms to be a sign of backwardness.

"We encountered the lead ships of Queen Isel's expedition in this little harbor," the queen explained. "They were under attack by the local people for obvious reasons, and we rescued them." She smiled bleakly.

"And you have our heartiest thanks for your timely aid," said Lord Sachu, his face flushing. "We did not expect hostility and therefore had our sails lowered and were at anchor when your subjects attacked us, utterly without provocation."

"It was fortunate for you that so many had fled the city," she said. "Thus it was only the weakened remnants you had to deal with. I apologize for my subjects' discourtesy, but you must expect people to behave emotionally when, after suffering the greatest plague in all of history, they see the plague-bearers appear in their harbor!" Now her hostility was open.

"Your Majesty, I protest!" Sachu said, refusing to be intimidated. "If we have been the bearers of this terrible visitation, my sorrow is boundless, but we had no way of knowing. Queen Larissa assured us that the plague was a recurring thing and of little consequence."

"Queen Larissa is the greatest liar of this or any other age, as her husband is the greatest killer who has ever lived! You know that now. She wanted you to come hither, to assure that you spread your plague to the mainland, to soften us up for their invasion!"

Now Sachu flushed scarlet. "Again, I protest! It is only your assertion that we have brought this plague!"

"Yes, Your Majesty," said the man called Mopsis. "It may be the merest coincidence that the plague attended our arrival. It is well known to scholars that a disease may be present for months before a virulent outbreak occurs, and it is also known that the positions of the stars and planets have much to do with these matters."

"Let us be calm, gentlemen," she soothed, having precipitated the rancor herself. "It ill becomes us to argue. Now, I must confer with my royal friend, Prince Ansa. I trust you will forgive us if I receive his report in our own dialect of Northern. I must have perfect accuracy and Southern is not our native tongue."

Sachu bowed again. "Matters military of course take precedence over all others. Pray proceed."

She turned to Ansa and said in Northern: "Did you understand all that?"

"Yes. It seems to me that you are being hard on them. Even if they did bring the plague, it was unwitting. We might have done the same had we gone looking for their continent. Who would ever give thought to carrying such catastrophe?"

She nodded resignedly. "You are your father's son in this. Yes, I fully understand that. Indeed, much of my anger is feigned, although I nearly perished of rage when I saw those ships here. But I learned from my father that it is always best to keep men off balance and I have kept them unsure whether I am well- or ill-disposed toward them. It will render them easier to handle. When they confirmed your report that the Islanders were untouched by the plague, my mood was not improved."

"They have been in the islands?"

"Yes. In the storms they missed the mainland entirely and an evil fate took them straight to Larissa. She has been poisoning their minds ever since. She gave them quite a show of power and wealth as well. Bad as things were, I was hoping that she was at least as badly hurt by the plague as we, but such was not to be. I fear that she and Gasam are not only strong but perhaps as strong as ever."

"How do you mean?" he asked, taking up a beaker of wine proffered by a servant.

"Your father has told you how it was in the islands in the days of his youth? The warrior fraternities, the rules and taboos?"

"Endlessly," he confirmed. "His reminiscences were the trial of my own youth."

She smiled gently. "All of us spend our childhoods thus. Anyway, the junior warriors could not own property or marry, and few of even the senior warriors had enough livestock to buy a wife, so that the elders had most of the property and women."

Ansa nodded. "Yes. He learned young that their customs concentrated all the power, wealth and women in the hands of a few old men."

"Everyone's customs do that," she said. "It also kept their population small, so that they did not overpopulate their islands. Gasam abolished the fraternities and did away with the marriage customs. He encouraged his people to breed as soon as they were old enough and gave them property from the loot he gathered. He wanted more and more warriors, and he got them."

"My father suspected that something of the sort was going on. We found just too many Shasinn in our battles. The other tribes as well."

"Truly. I have had my own spies in those islands, whenever possible. In the old days a new batch of junior warriors was enrolled every four to seven years. The boys became junior warriors at ages fifteen to twenty-two. Now they all become warriors at fifteen and a new batch is enrolled every year. They used to retire to elder status, sometimes before they were thirty years old, to make way for the new class of juniors. Now any warrior who lives past his thirtieth year becomes a master warrior. Warriors in their prime are no longer taken out of the fighting force."

"So, when we drove them from the mainland," Ansa said, "they had not only their remnant but a new force of warriors ready to take the field?"

"And a force of young men who have never known defeat. Remember, the casualties of the last war fell chiefly among the subject peoples and among the other island tribes. The Shasinn deaths were comparatively light. Now I learn that they never even caught the plague. I do hope you have brought me some good news."

"I may have." Briefly he told her about the little warship he had observed.

She sucked in a breath between her teeth. "That is the ship I gave to Ilas of Nar. The rogue has turned coat or been killed. Go on."

His mind had been working feverishly since seeing Gasam and Larissa on the ship. The new ships in the harbor had given further impetus to his thoughts.

"Majesty, they have separated themselves, both of them, from their army! This has never happened before. If we can catch that ship, we have them! Their army will fall apart without Gasam and Larissa! They are not just king and queen, not mere leaders: They are gods to their warriors!"

For a moment she looked like one who has been saved, but her countenance clouded quickly. "But they keep close to the coast."

"I saw them traveling some way ahead of the advance elements. They are arrogant and self-assured beyond all measure."

"But as soon as they see so much as one of my naval vessels, they will turn tail. That little ship I gave Ilas in my foolishness is the swiftest afloat. They will be safe in the bosom of their army before we approach within ten bow shots."

"But they attack unoffending ships for sport," he pointed out.

This made her stop and consider, stroking her chin. "An ambush? My coast guards have caught pirates that way. It will have to be a lone vessel, to keep them from becoming suspicious." She thought a while longer. "But their bodyguard will be made up entirely of Shasinn and those hideous warrior women of Gasam's. Could we get enough fighting men into a merchant vessel to overcome them? I would want at least three-to-one odds in our favor even to attempt it. No merchant vessel is as large as a Nevan warship and there are none of the big two-hulled Chiwan ships afloat these days." She pondered. "Perhaps two ships crippled and lashed together, as if they had suffered storm damage?"

"They would smell a trap," Ansa said. "I have a better idea." He looked at the visitors from an alien land. "Give me one of *their* ships."

A radiant smile spread across her face. "You *are* your father's son!" She looked at her guests from afar, still beaming. "I knew I was tormenting these men for some good reason. They'll give me little trouble now."

She switched to Southern. "Gentlemen, I am now up-to-date on the enemy's latest movements."

Sachu seemed to find her sudden benevolence at least as alarming as her wrath. "It would seem that Your Majesty is pleased with His Highness's report."

"Very much so. And now I must ask a favor of you."

"If it is within my power to grant." His face and voice were rigidly noncommittal.

"I must ask you to lend me one of your ships for my use in this campaign."

The men looked very grave. "Your Majesty," Sachu began, "you ask me to employ a vessel of Queen Isel in a war in which she has no interest. For us to take sides in this dispute would be intolerable!"

"I appreciate your position," she said. "Yet I must insist."

"And I must refuse," he said stubbornly.

"Will you make me use force?" Her tone grew icy.

"I fear Your Majesty must."

This surprised her. "Do you mean you will offer resistance?"

"By no means. That would be utter futility." He leaned forward, his fingers interlaced upon the table before him. "But all must see that we are forced unwillingly into this. There must be no question. I fully appreciate the gravity of your situation. Sometimes diplomacy must yield to military necessity. Your Majesty knows best the parameters of her own desperation."

Her respect for him went up a notch. "Your queen sent the right man to head this mission. Very well. What I do now I do unwillingly, but I am driven by necessity. I need your ship to—"

"I do not wish to know your intentions," he said.

"I understand."

"My queen," Ansa asked in Northern, "do you have men who can sail one of their vessels?"

"My mariners have been studying their ships since they first arrived. I believe they can manage a short sail up the coast."

"Then let's take the largest, and fill it with your best fighting men. As you've said, it won't be an easy fight. And we will need clothes such as these people wear."

"Your Majesty," Sachu said, "while of course I cannot give my consent to this undertaking, yet I must know how we are to be recompensed should my ship be lost. Our fleet is already much diminished."

"You shall have full run of my shipyards, both for materials and for workers. You may build yourself a new ship. Build a fleet, with my blessing, and fill it with the treasure of your choice."

Mopsis looked stunned and Lord Goss's eyes glowed, but Sachu said merely: "That is acceptable."

"Then I think we all need some rest. If you gentlemen will return to your ships, I shall send men to arrest you in the morning. Your accommodations shall be the best this city affords. You are to regard yourselves as my honored guests, despite necessary appearances."

They rose and bowed deeply. Sachu said: "Your Majesty is generous, but we will stay aboard our remaining ships. Which will you take?"

"The largest," she said. "We shall do our best to return it to you unharmed."

They left and Shazad relaxed a little. She took some wine and allowed her weariness to show. "Well, what do you think of them?" she asked.

"Lord Sachu is impressive," he said.

"He shows much experience of courts and government, and he is able to lead an exploration fleet. This Queen Isel knows how to pick men. What of the others?"

"Mopsis seems to be an amiable scholar, but I do not like the one called Goss. He said nothing but he has the face of a striper."

"He, too, is a familiar figure. My court has more

than its share of such men. I can tell that he covets Sachu's leadership and I bear in mind that he has been in Larissa's court of late."

"Do you think he had dealings with her?"

"Unless I read him wrongly he did. Double-dealing is second nature to men of that ilk. I shall watch him closely while he is my guest."

"Enough of them," Ansa said. "What about the mission I propose? Will you give me command?"

She raised her fine eyebrows. "You are ambitious."

He grinned. "As you have said twice, I am my father's son. He came to the mainland with nothing but a spear and a sword and he built a kingdom before he was my age. And this is my plan."

"I grant you that. But I have my senior commanders to consider, especially my husband. It isn't easy for a consort to live perpetually in the shadow of his wife. He thirsts for a little military glory and he has already promised, before witnesses, to deliver Larissa to me in chains. For me to put an upstart boy in command of this mission would insult him beyond bearing."

Ansa bristled. "I am an experienced warrior! I . . ."

"I understand that, and I did not mean to speak so abrasively, but you must understand my position. You saw how Lord Sachu observed the diplomatic niceties. I must do the same with my own people. How does this sound: My consort, Over-Commander Harakh, will be in overall charge of the ship and the mission. You will be the leader of the boarding party with the rank of marine captain. Harakh is too old and too senior in rank to lead a hand-to-hand fight, anyway. Is this acceptable?"

"It is," he said, knowing he would not get a better offer. His father had often cautioned him against allowing warrior pride to overrule his judgment, but it was hard to let another man take over a mission that was his own idea.

"Good. Now, let me offer you something to eat. You have had a strenuous few days." She clapped her hands and a steward appeared. She ordered food laid before them. She snapped her fingers and an officer came in. She ordered Prince Harakh and a number of her senior men summoned at once.

"Do you never sleep?" Ansa asked, marveling at her activity.

"I'll catch up on sleep when this campaign is over and I am safely home. If we're to take advantage of the intelligence you brought, I must act quickly. I shall brief my officers tonight. They can pick their crew and fighting men in the morning. I want that ship sailing to intercept Gasam and Larissa by afternoon. I know how quickly advantage is lost in war. I, above all others, know the importance of speed in fighting these people."

NINE

Larissa peeled back the bandage and examined her husband's chest. A thick ridge of scar tissue marked the place where Hael's spear had torn his body. "Lean forward," she said. He did so and she examined the similar scar where the vicious point had torn its way out. There was no sign of seepage or inflammation.

"Completely healed," she said with satisfaction, wadding up the bandage, tossing it overboard. "You can do without this now."

He smiled complacently. "I've been healed for weeks."

"Not to my satisfaction," she said.

Idly he fingered the scar on his chest. "My worst battle scar. Even worse than the one that boy gave me." Now his fingers traced the scar that ran down his face from temple to jawline, then down to the collarbone where a continuation of the same sword blow had cut the flesh and nicked the bone.

"That boy," she said, musing. Something about the words obscurely troubled her. What had she seen recently?

"Well, it's done and I am well." He got up and stretched. "I feel better than I have in years! Little queen, it is time for us to go ashore. I should be with my army. It is unfitting that we lounge at ease, allowing this ship to carry us like cargo, when my warriors are afoot." His guard, male and female, beamed worshipfully to see their king acting his old self again.

The sight and his words drove the brooding thoughts from Larissa's mind.

"So we shall," she said, clapping her hands. Ilas of Nar ran up to them.

"Yes, my queen?"

"Ilas, is there a place we can put in near here to await the ground forces?"

He pointed along the coast. "Just beyond that point of land crowned with the layer of black rock is a small cove where we can drop anchor. The way inland from there is easy, no high bluffs or swamps to impede progress."

"Excellent," she said. "Put us in there."

"As my queen commands," Ilas said. He was more than pleased at the prospect of ridding himself of his passengers. He had pinned his fortunes to the pair, but their constant presence set his nerves on edge, and their arrogant warriors and outlandish female guards grated upon him. He was accustomed to being king on his own ship. Their presence rendered him a mere functionary.

They were just rounding the point, ready to steer

into the cove, when the lookout sang out. "A ship!" he called excitedly.

"Game!" Gasam said exultantly. "What do you say, my queen? One last hunt before we go ashore? This is better sport than hunting the great cats back home."

"If you wish, my love," she said, not rising from her couch. Gasam was such a boy sometimes. Still, she could not find it in her to deny him this little pleasure, especially when he was rejoicing in his newly recovered health. These attacks on shipping were meaningless, since the world would soon belong to them, anyway. They had become reflexive, the way a predator would sometimes spring upon anything smaller than itself, the instinct totally removed from genuine hunger.

The prey vessel was rounding a smaller, more southerly point. It sailed toward them and did not lower sail.

"Now, this is odd," Gasam said, stroking his chin. "He does not seem to fear us. Perhaps he thinks us to be what we appear: a legitimate Nevan warship."

"My king," Ilas said, "that is one of the foreign vessels. Their flagship, I think."

"Yes,'" said Larissa. "So it is. Why is it sailing back north alone?"

"Perhaps," Gasam said, grinning, "they had a warm welcome from the ones who survived the plague."

"They will have little love for us now," Larissa said, "since I misled them somewhat. What shall we do with them?"

"Let's show a friendly greeting, then kill them," Gasam said happily. "This may be their last ship afloat. We've learned all we need from them. Queen Isel's fleet will just disappear, as she might well have expected. When we are done here, we shall build our own fleet and pay her a visit. Then she shall learn all she needs to know about us."

"As you will, my king," Larissa said, uneasy about the whole thing. She was not sure why. Predator and prey had been their way as long as she could remember. All other people were just slaves to serve them, livestock to die when they required. Even so, something about this situation bothered her.

They worked their way closer to the other ship, sail down and oars out, until they were close enough to see men on deck, dressed in the outlandish clothes of the strangers. They worked their way closer still.

"Every man still and quiet," said Commander Harakh in a low voice. He wore a slouch hat to hide his face from observers on the little warship. He relished his role in this adventure. It reminded him of the days of his youth. "Keep below the rails, you'll see them soon enough."

Ansa hugged the deck, pressing his cheek to the warm, tar-scented wood. Next to him lay his bow, an arrow nocked to its string, and his sword was loose in it sheath. Behind him the deck was carpeted with prone soldiers and marines. More of them waited in the hold. The sailors who worked the ship wore clothing taken from the foreign mariners. The brief voyage had been rough and at times dangerous, for the Nevan seamen were using a strange rigging for the first time. They seemed pleased with it, though, and had remarked throughout the voyage how superior it was to their own. The sailing master had filled his ears with explanations that meant nothing to Ansa, of how the rig let them sail "closer to the wind," whatever that meant, and about the great pulling power of the sails and the steadiness of the deep keel. It was operating the bewildering cobweb of ropes, blocks and pulleys that had the Nevans at their wit's end, although they seemed to be enjoying the experience, which their passengers certainly were not.

"Don't look welcoming," Harakh said. "Look puzzled and apprehensive, that's what they're expecting."

Ansa had to admit that the man had steely nerves. As Shazad had predicted, he had not liked having to share the mission with Ansa, but he was too much a soldier to complain. Even so, his attitude toward Ansa had been cool. It was of no account, he told himself. Action was about to commence. There came a faint scraping and a thump.

"Now!" shouted Harakh.

Ansa sprang to his feet, drawing his bow as he did. All was surprise and confusion on the deck below but he did not search out a target. It had been chosen for him in the planning stages of the mission. Much as he would have liked to kill Gasam, there was a more important target in the opening seconds of the fight. He spotted the helmsman at his tiller and loosed. The range was so close that the arrow passed through the man too swiftly to be seen. It scarcely slowed down and raised a tiny splash in the water beyond.

Grapples flew from the taller ship and bit into *Seasnake*'s rails. Gasam's unmistakable roar rose above the general din and a wall of black shields appeared as if by magic between the king and queen and the enemy's weapons.

With a thunder of shod feet the soldiers clambered up from the hold below and the rails were quickly lined with fighting men three deep. Arrows, stones and javelins began to fly. Ansa got off another shot, then he saw something all but unbelievable: Grossly outnumbered, standing on the lower deck, the island warriors were attacking the larger ship, and successfully! He had grown up on tales of their prowess and had seen it firsthand in years past, but this demonstration was extraordinary.

The long spears flashed luridly as the young warriors swarmed upward, climbing the grappling ropes, springing from each other's shoulders for a chance at the enemy. It seemed that every stroke of each long blade opened a neck or ran through a body. Numbly he understood that these fanatics were selling their lives dearly to give their sovereigns time to escape.

As the ranks thinned on the ship below, Ansa saw gaps appear in the shield wall and he drew his bow. For a moment he saw Gasam and he prepared to release. Abruptly a hideously scarred and painted woman hulked before him, swinging a short axe. He jerked back and the blade missed his head but it cut his bowstring. The bow snapped back violently, catching the woman in the face, toppling her screaming into the water below. Already the predators were gathering.

Now the warriors were aboard the ship, pushing the Nevans back from the rail. But there were Shasinn bodies in the water and on the enemy deck as well. Even their fury had to end soon. The grim, methodical fighting of the Nevans was taking its toll. Ansa tore his sword from its sheath as a tall young man charged him. The youth had somehow gotten aboard encumbered with his long black shield and he held his spear low for a gutting stroke.

Ansa knew the folly of fencing with such a combination, so he opted for main force. He took his hilt in both hands and whirled it in a great circle from right to left, battering the black shield aside, turning the youth half around and exposing his left flank. The blade continued its circle around his head and he swung it even harder, slashing deep into his opponent's body before the Shasinn had a chance to recover his guard. The youth did not scream, but merely grimaced as he collapsed bonelessly and waited for death.

Blood on the deck was already making footing very treacherous. Frantically Ansa scanned the deck below, where warriors and sailors were slashing at the grappling lines. Where were Gasam and Larissa? Then he saw them, hemmed in by a knot of guards of both sexes. He cursed the loss of his bow as he saw the ships beginning to drift apart. The stern of the vessel began to drift past him, and he saw the helmsman he had shot slumped over his tiller. In seconds all opportunity would be lost. It was intolerable.

Tightening the wrist thong of his sword, Ansa sprang to the rail and jumped. He landed with feet well spread, but the blood on the soles of his boots almost made him slip. He recovered quickly and a sailor stared at him, wide-eyed. Ansa hewed the man down and jumped over the body, dashing toward the knot of Islanders grouped in the bow. All the rest were concentrating upon the rail above them. No one seemed to have noticed his one-man boarding action. Swinging his sword savagely, he struck the royal party at a dead run. He had only a second or two to make his fury felt, and he intended to make that time count.

There were screams and his blade bit somebody. He saw Gasam whirl, his eyes wide with shock, bringing his great, steel spear across to meet this new threat. Spear and sword rang together and Ansa felt a cold thrill along one side of his body, then he was bulling into the royal pair. They toppled, legs scrambling, and his left arm went around a waist and he gripped with all his strength as they hit the rail and then they were falling and the water was a sudden jolt.

The creature he held writhed in his grasp and he released his sword, letting it dangle by its wrist thong as he wrapped both arms around his prey. He felt that his lungs would burst, but he held his breath and stayed underwater. The body twisted frantically and bubbles tickled the side of his face, then it jerked one last time and was still. Slowly he kicked to the surface. Something rough brushed against and his heart went cold as he remembered that the water swarmed with blood-crazed predators.

He burst to the surface and looked to see what he had. The beautiful face and water-darkened white hair told him. He held Larissa and she appeared to be dead. Then a huge, triangular fin swept past behind her and his heart thudded. The larger ship hulked near even as the smaller one was drawing away toward shore.

"Get us out of here!" he screamed, frantic to be heard over the din that continued above. "I have her and we'll be eaten!" Beside him the huge, scaly head of a marine lizard broke surface, the shredded body of a Nevan marine clenched in its toothy jaws. The water was almost pink.

Ropes dropped near them and he grasped one, wrapping it around his right arm. Then he was hauled from the water, his arm almost wrenched from its socket as he was dragged up the side of the ship, refusing to loosen his grip on Larissa. Soon an abundance of hands grasped them and they were pulled unceremoniously over the rail and landed dripping on the deck.

He reached up, grabbed the rail and hauled himself to his knees as Harakh rushed to his side. "Is Gasam dead?" he demanded.

"No, curse the luck," Harakh said.

"Then chase him!" Ansa said, almost overcome with frustration.

"Can't," Harakh said in his laconic fashion. "Look." Only then did Ansa hear the booming chant and looked to see the nearby beach lined with rank after rank of Shasinn warriors. More were pouring down a path that led between a pair of low hills a few hundred yards inland. The small warship had managed to run out a few oars and was limping toward the shore.

"They're already in water where we'd beach," Harakh explained. "Then those savages would be all over us."

Beside them Larissa began to twitch, then to writhe. She made some choking groans, and she vomited bloody water in a long, convulsive spasm. Her pale face turned red as she retched, then she gasped, pulling air into tortured lungs. She coughed for a while and in an amazingly short time, she was breathing evenly.

Harakh shook his head, clucking. "They're just not normal people." Then, to Ansa: "Best lie down and let the surgeon tend to you, son. You took some wounds."

For the first time, Ansa noticed that blood was pouring from his body to the deck. Gasam? Somebody else? Perhaps a shark had bitten him. In his fury he might not have noticed.

"If it makes you feel better," Harakh went on, "in

a lifetime of soldiering, I've seen only a few genuinely heroic feats. What you just did was one of them. It was as good as when your father went alone into Floria to rescue Shazad and kill Gasam. He got half of it done, for which I'm grateful." The words, if grudging, were nonetheless heartfelt.

"We have a family history of doing half a job," Ansa said, the pain of his wounds hitting him for the first time. He knew he was in for a bad few days. "I intended to kill or capture both of them."

"Not bad for a beginner," Harakh said drily. Then, to his men: "Well done, all of you. Now, hoist this slut to a yardarm."

"You are going to hang her?" Ansa said, surprised.

"No, richly as she deserves it. I'm just going to let Gasam know that we have her and she's alive. It will give him something to think about."

Larissa was sitting up already and men began to pass ropes beneath her arms and around her waist. "Harakh, is it? My sister queen's pet and bedmate?"

"The same," he said. "Please accept my compliments. You're the first woman I've seen who can remain beautiful while puking."

She looked to Ansa, who no longer had the strength even to kneel. Her eyes widened. "You! I left you half a world from here! I saw you a few days ago, with your riders, but I didn't recognize you. No wonder I felt uneasy then and today. The stink of Hael and his spawn carries far." He felt too weak to answer her, but his satisfaction was deep.

"I told my queen I would throw you in chains at her feet and I shall," Harakh told her.

She laughed. "Have you any idea what my husband will do to you now?"

"You mean in vivid contrast to his former benevolence?" Harakh commented. "Hoist her up, lads."

Larissa rose and Ansa saw her silhouetted against the sky and the forest of spars, trussed like a hunter's prey but her head erect.

"You can't fault their arrogance," Harakh commented.

The surgeon squatted by Ansa and assessed his wounds. "This one will need about two yards of stitches. He looks like a butcher has been at him."

"One swipe of Gasam's spear did that," Harakh said. "Halfhearted, backhanded and glancing off his sword, it still did all that damage. The boy's lucky to be alive."

The doctor felt about his hips and legs. "Prince, you took half a dozen small cuts from your own sword as you were hauled up the side. You should have let it go when you went into the water. Sentimental attachment has killed more than one man."

"I thought I might have to fight the sharks," Ansa said. Then darkness closed over him like the waters of the sea.

Gasam staggered ashore, helped by the few survivors of his guard. The junior warriors of Larissa's guard wept unashamedly while the bizarre women looked grim. Ilas of Nar and the surviving sailors were pale, as if the world had been cut from beneath their feet. The king shook his head dazedly. Ansa's sword pommel had caught him alongside the head as the boy had made his flying attack. It had been so sudden that Gasam was not truly sure what had occurred. They had broken off action and rowed the ship away from the ambush while they still had arms to man the oars. *Seasnake*'s ram was dug into the coarse sand of the beach.

"Larissa!" Gasam said. "Where is Larissa? Tell me!" They all stood silent, none willing to speak. A man came trotting up to the king and all drew back, grateful that someone of authority had arrived on the scene.

"Pendu!" cried the king. "I must find Larissa. Where is she?"

"The queen?" The general looked around at the frightened faces, then caught sight of Ilas. He beckoned and the Nevan traitor came forward. "Upon your life, man," Pendu rumbled, his voice very low, "tell me what has happened and tell me swiftly."

Ilas rendered a succinct report of the action. He had remained well to the stern throughout, taking no part in the fighting, confining himself to directing his sailors. In that capacity he had been able to observe the incident in detail.

Pendu nodded at the end of the recitation. "You're no warrior, but it is good that someone kept his head in the middle of all this foolishness."

"Larissa!" Gasam bellowed. "Where is she?"

Pendu laid a hand on his king's shoulder. "Gasam, listen to me: She is dead or she is alive. Either way, we will know soon enough."

Ilas had scrambled back aboard the ship and dashed to his cabin. Moments later he reemerged holding a large telescope, which he trained on the three-masted ship in the cove. With a wordless shout he jumped from the ship and ran to the king and his general.

"My king! Look over there!"

Gasam snatched the spyglass and directed it toward the ship. "What is . . . Larissa!"

Pendu beckoned to a young warrior and the youth took a smaller telescope from a satchel at his side. The general took it, slipped it open and set it to his eye. Instantly he saw the human form dangling bound from the yardarm. The streaming white hair left no doubt as to identity. She writhed very slowly, like a caterpillar on a strand of silk, spinning a cocoon. She raised her head and gazed shoreward.

"She lives!" Gasam shouted. He lowered the telescope and used it to point to *Seasnake*. "Get aboard! We are going to get her!" His lips were flecked with foam. Men darted toward the little ship.

"Stop!" Pendu bellowed. The men broke stride and looked around them uncertainly. They were not accustomed to contradictory orders.

Gasam whirled on him, madness in his eyes. "What do you mean?"

"It is useless, Gasam! See, they already turn about. Their sails catch the wind." Over the water they could hear the popping rumble as the heavy sails began to take the wind.

"What of that? This ship is the swiftest afloat. We can catch them!"

"You think so? How many trained rowers do you have left after that foolish battle? Half?"

Gasam looked to Ilas. "Shipmaster?"

"General Pendu is right, my king. The best rowers were killed in the fighting. Even with new men at the oars, it would take weeks of drilling to approach her old speed."

Gasam's eyes grew wild and he began to tremble. Pendu stood very close and placed both hands on his king's shoulders. "Gasam, Gasam, listen to me!" Gradually the king calmed. "Gasam, she is alive. They have her, and she is alive. Concentrate on that. They will not harm her, she is too valuable. This happened because of your foolishness."

Gasam glared at him. "You try me, old friend. No other man speaks to me thus."

"One man must. Everyone else worships you and will not tell you the truth. You took to the sea to complete your recovery, then you made a sport of attacking the enemy. You should not have done that, not with just a few untried boys and your insane women for an escort. You must have been mad not to foresee a trap like this!"

Gasam calmed and patted the side of Pendu's neck, drawing their heads together until their brows touched. "You are right, old companion. Something—the spirits, the gods, I know not what—made us mad, even my Larissa, who is as wise as any three kings. What's to do now?"

"Now is a time for negotiation. We will have their demands soon enough. Now tell me: This man who took the queen—Ilas said a single man did it. Can this be true?"

"It is. And I knew him. It was the son of Hael!"

"Hael's son!" Pendu hissed with surprise. "Kairn?"

"No, the elder one, Ansa. The one who carved my face."

Pendu looked around, saw the uncertain, alarmed looks on the faces of the men. He addressed the king in a low voice. "Gasam, you must say something to the men. Their faith is shaken, but this business of Hael's son puts a different face on things. Everyone knows that Hael is no ordinary man, as you are not. It stands to reason that a son of Hael might deal us a check without loss of honor. Tell them, and quickly."

Gasam patted Pendu on the back and drew away from him. Raising his arms skyward, he shouted: "My warriors! All of you know the ancient enmity that lies between me and Hael the Accursed! Each time we think that it is done and buried, that unnatural creature appears again in some form. Once again, Hael has challenged me with his cowardly magic! It was the son of Hael who came aboard my ship and snatched your queen from my side! Many of you saw this! I ask you, could a mortal man, trusting only to his own strength, courage and skill, do such a thing?"

The mob of warriors rumbled their rejection of such an idea. Pendu looked on with satisfaction, marveling as always at his king's skill with words and the way men were swayed by them. He sensed that Gasam somehow inspired a will in men's hearts to believe, so that even his most outlandish statements struck them with the force of eternal truths.

"Now the enemy have your queen in captivity!" There were groans of dismay from his audience. The youths of the queen's guard were in frenzies of grief. "But this is not defeat! Hael cannot best me by his magical arts! A mere mongrel son of Hael cannot prevail! For now, I must treat with our enemies. For now, we shall consolidate our gains, enjoy our conquest and increase our strength. I shall have my queen back, and we shall finish our conquest of the world. We shall destroy Hael and his spawn forever!" The men roared their approval and Pendu came to stand by his king, leaning on his ancient Shasinn spear of bronze and steel.

"That is better, my king." He smiled grimly. "Strange how Hael became a wizard of a sudden, when you yourself proved all the spirit-speakers to be frauds."

Gasam shrugged. "He is not as other men, and wizard is as good a word as any. Words are my weapons, now as always. I will have to practice using them with especial skill since now I must treat with Shazad, as if the slut were my equal."

"Have patience. How did this Ansa accomplish such a feat? I wish I had seen it."

"There was no magic. The boy was brave and I

was careless, I'll own up to it. He slipped aboard while our attention was elsewhere. I think I hurt him badly. With luck he'll die, but I seldom have good luck where Hael is involved." Gloomily he watched the foreign ship sail away with his queen, its sails stained red by the setting sun.

TEN

Shazad's face was a mask of composure. She saw the ship drop anchor in the little harbor, and she saw that its deck was covered with wounded men, lying on litters. No messenger was sent ashore, but she let out a small sigh of relief when she saw the sun gleaming from her husband's familiar dress helmet. He had changed from his disguise to full regalia for the reception. She retired to her impromptu throne room and sat, waiting to hear Harakh's report. Her courtiers and the ladies who had accompanied her on the campaign stood absolutely silent, none of them daring to make a sign until they should know whether the occasion was one for rejoicing or mourning.

The doors opened and the armored form of Harakh strode in smartly. He saluted and bowed.

"Welcome, my consort," she said. "I rejoice to see you well."

"My queen, I bring you a gift." Harakh turned and clapped his hands. A double file of marine guards entered. Between the files a slight figure walked, her steps confined by the golden chains that bound her ankles. From a neck ring of gold depended chains connected to manacles about her wrists and these were also connected by shorter chains to a loop of chain that encircled her tiny waist. At Harakh's nod the guards forced her to her knees, then to her face before Shazad's throne.

"My queen," Harakh said, "thus do I fulfill my vow."

For a moment Shazad feared she would faint. For years she had dreamed of this moment, never daring to believe that it might actually come to pass. The memory of the humiliations this woman had inflicted upon her had inflamed her thoughts every day of her life since she was a very young woman. Slowly she pushed herself up from the throne and descended the two steps to the carpeted floor. Standing beside the prostrate woman, she slipped her right foot from its black slipper, sewn close with tiny pearls. Delicately she placed her bare foot on the back of the slender neck, its warmth and the feel of the silky hair sending a strange thrill up her leg and through her body. Slowly she leaned her weight upon it, pressing the woman's face hard against the floor.

"Larissa," she intoned, using an ancient formula, "I claim you as my prisoner, to live or die at my pleasure. Thus do my gods triumph over yours." The throne room erupted in cheers and congratulations. A page held her slipper and guided it back onto her foot and she returned to her throne. At her gesture, Harakh took the slightly lower seat to her right. She could hardly take her eyes off the bound woman.

"Gasam?" she asked in a low voice.

"Got away," Harakh said uncomfortably.

"Ah, well, I suppose it was too much to hope." A sudden thought occurred to her. "Where is Prince Ansa?"

Harakh pointed to a litter carried by four stalwart sailors. "He got badly cut up, I'm afraid, but you should have seen him. It was unbelievable."

"You shall tell me all about it over dinner." She summoned the sailors and they brought the young warrior prince to her. He was terribly pale and his body was invisible beneath a mass of bandages. He smiled weakly at her.

"Sorry I didn't get Gasam," he said, the words clearly costing him.

"This is such a gift as I have never received before. It is sufficient." She looked at her steward. "Set a couch here by my throne for Prince Ansa." Servants scurried and the couch was in place within seconds. She looked back at Larissa. The woman had struggled to her knees and watched Shazad with an expression of sardonic amusement.

"She is a queen," Shazad said. "She must not sit on the floor. Bring a seat for my guest who is also my prisoner."

A padded stool was brought and set on the dais before the queen. Guards helped Larissa up the steps and seated her, so that her head was only a little above the level of Shazad's waist.

"My husband will slaughter you all," Larissa said.

"Your husband always intended that," Shazad said. "Your empty threats mean nothing. Your husband, the mighty Gasam, could not save you from capture." She had the satisfaction of seeing the unflappable Larissa blush deeply. In the Shasinn fashion the island queen wore a length of silk wrapped closely about her body from armpit to knee.

"You are not regally clad, despite your golden chains. Shall I have a gown brought for you?"

"Does it upset you that I am more beautiful naked than you are in your miles of silk and layers of paint?" Larissa smiled sweetly.

"Vanity was always your weakness, sister queen. By now you should have learned that beauty of the flesh is a trifling thing."

"Beauty is one thing, but there are others," Larissa said. "The aching of the joints, the shortness of wind, the tedious heaviness that increases year by year." She studied the backs of her unwrinkled hands complacently. "I suppose I shall feel all of those things someday."

"You are lucky you fell into my hands late in life," Shazad said heatedly. "Time was when I'd have flogged the hide off your back for insulting me."

"How you've mellowed with age."

Ansa groaned. "Can't you two find something better to talk about? For this I could have stayed home and listened to my sister scolding me."

Harakh burst into laughter, quickly silenced by the queen's glare.

"You are right," Shazad said evenly. "We have a victory to celebrate; a feast to hold. And we have some policy to discuss. The balance has changed."

Ansa could take little pleasure in the feast, despite the honors heaped upon him by the grateful queen. He managed to eat a little, and Queen Shazad insisted upon feeding him with her own hands. So greatly did the long slashes on his body pain him that he could scarcely raise his arms. Every motion made him feel as if his wounds were ripping open anew, even though he knew that he had been stitched up as strongly as a ripped sail.

Larissa formed a sort of centerpiece to the banquet, although she sat next to Shazad on the side opposite Ansa. She was dressed no more lavishly than before, although her strip of silk had been replaced with new cloth, and her scrapes and bruises lightly dusted with cosmetic powder. Her white hair gleamed in the candlelight. The other guests could not take their eyes off her. They could hardly believe that this was the legendary monster-queen. In the flattering light she appeared to be no more than twenty years old, and she looked fragile, almost tiny, sitting next to their more substantial, heavily gowned queen.

Larissa nibbled at bits of fruit and took occasional sips of wine, seeming to glory in all the attention, as her just due. No one knew quite what to make of her. When spoken to by the guests, she replied as graciously as if she were entertaining them in her own throne room.

"What do you hear of our brother monarch King Hael?" Larissa asked as a platter of sweets was set before her. She ignored them.

"He lives, and recovers," Shazad said. "So said a messenger who braved the ride from the Canyon just a month ago."

"What a pity. Well, my husband is fully recovered from a far greater wound. I suppose we shouldn't expect so much from a lesser man."

"You must have been picking your teeth with that little spear of yours," Ansa said. "It poisoned the wound."

She smiled at him. "Such a lovely boy, Shazad. The younger one, Kairn, is even comelier. Their mother must be truly beautiful, because half-breeds are usually ugly." She looked around the banquet hall. "Where are the foreigners? Surely, having lent you their ship, they should partake in the celebration."

"I took the ship by force. I have them under guard. I do not hold them responsible for the plague they brought, but many of my people feel great anger toward them. It will pass, and I will establish friendly relations with Queen Isel. But you sent them here hoping to further spread the plague. That was a new wrinkle in the history of war, if you want to call it that, one uniquely your own. Is there no treachery to which you people will not stoop?"

"Oh, treachery doesn't even enter the equation. One cannot behave dishonorably toward inferiors."

"Tell me, Larissa: Whatever possessed you and your madman of a husband to invade again, less than a year after you were so painfully expelled? Is there some sort of suicidal instinct in those islands? Even if you could defeat me, which you cannot, there is still Hael and the plains army, and beyond them this Mezpan power I have heard so much about, with their incomprehensible weapons. Don't you realize you must be slaughtered?" She sounded exasperated and genuinely curious.

"Oh, Hael isn't that dangerous. Assuming he lives to defy us again. And without Hael, who would lead those nomadic hunters? Would they follow this boy here?" She laughed merrily. "Forgive me, Ansa. You are a brave and handsome boy, but you are no Hael."

"Apology accepted," he croaked, taking a long drink of wine laced with a powerful painkiller. It kept the worst of the agony at bay without clouding his judgment too much.

"As for the Mezpans," Larissa continued, "—well,

that is just an interesting sort of warfare. Rather like fighting a machine, but what machine can prevail over splendid warriors led by an inspired king?"

" 'Interesting,' " Shazad repeated. "Is that really it? Do you people just love war?"

"We take pleasure in many things, as I explained to you back when you were my slave."

"Prisoner," Shazad corrected.

"It amounts to the same thing. There are two sorts of people: Islanders, who are warriors, and others, who are slaves. Anyway, we enjoy fighting, lordship, domination, all the really important things."

"Incredible. You really are as simple as you seem. But now, because I have you, it is time to negotiate."

"We negotiate well, too," Larissa assured her. "We do everything well."

"But always before, Gasam had you to guide him," Shazad pointed out. "It was always you I dealt with, never him."

Larissa laughed again. It did not seem to be forced. "Do you think Gasam needs me? I helped him with matters for which he had little taste, but he is the king and I am only his helpmate. We have been separated for months at a time while he was campaigning and I was reorganizing and consolidating our conquests. You really think having me gives you an advantage?"

"Yes," Shazad assured her.

"Do you not understand?" Larissa said with great earnestness. "All of you are our slaves! It is destiny that my lord and I shall rule over you all. Such as we choose to spare, anyway." She sat back, perfectly at ease.

"Larissa," Shazad said coolly, "it is good that you are so pleasant to look upon, because your fund of conversation is quickly expended."

* * *

That evening the queen, her counselors and commanders met in privy session. Ansa was there, propped up with fur-covered cushions and fighting to keep a clear head. As representative for his father's kingdom it was his duty, although he longed to be somewhere else, asleep. Being lionized as a hero was pleasant, but this was far more important.

"Gentlemen," Shazad said when all were seated, "let us not waste words or time. You all know of our new-won counter in the game, and you have had several hours to consider how to play it. Suggestions?"

They were somewhat startled at her abruptness, but they knew their queen was a woman of little patience at times of crisis and she did not stand upon ceremony during wartime. A grizzled army commander was first to speak.

"Kill her," he said.

"That would seem to reduce her value in negotiation, Lord Chutai," the queen said.

He snorted. "Your pardon, Majesty, but negotiating with the savages is foolishness. They will renounce every agreement without shame, as soon as it's to their advantage. But we know one thing about Gasam and Larissa: They're one animal. Kill her now and you mutilate him. I think the heart will go out of him, just as he'll lose a good deal more than half of his wisdom. With her dead, he'll be no match for us. Kill her now, is my advice."

"There is wisdom in such a course," she allowed. "But any such action is by nature irrevocable and if discovered to be mistaken it cannot be remedied. However, as long as we have her, this option is always open to us. Thank you, Lord Chutai."

"Your Majesty," Harakh said, "we must know

whether Gasam has halted his advance. If so, we know negotiation has a chance, because it means he is awaiting our next move. The initiative has passed to us. If not, it may mean that he refuses to be intimidated."

"What was the last report of our scouts?" she asked, looking to her commander of riders.

"We have had none since the woman was taken, but I shall forward such dispatches to Your Majesty the instant they arrive."

"Do so," she said.

"Majesty," said an elderly counselor, "you must get that woman away from here. As long as she is here, so near him, Gasam may be tempted to try a rescue. Send her back to the capital and clap her into your deepest dungeon and, on top of that, keep her location a secret."

"I agree," Harakh said. "Just having the slut around makes me nervous. The guards jump every time she speaks, because they think she's some sort of witch. If we're not going to kill her, let's at least get rid of her."

"But we could use her as bait," a general said. "Suck Gasam into another trap!"

"She's already bait," Harakh asserted. "He doesn't have to know she's been evacuated."

"This sounds like a good course to me," Shazad said. "Much as I value her company." The rest laughed politely, except for Ansa. Laughter made him hurt even worse. She looked at him. "Prince Ansa, I think you should go, too. We have no facilities for your care in this city. The physicians who survived the plague all fled at Gasam's approach. The doctors with the fleet are good field surgeons but the best of them are still in the capital."

"No!" he said. "We are still at war with Gasam and I must see it through to the end!"

"Ansa," she said tiredly, "we all appreciate your heroism but just now we have to carry you about like a sack of meal. How much advantage are you to the army in such a state?"

He fumed, but there was little he could say to that.

"Besides," she went on more gently, "Larissa's capture changes everything. There will almost certainly be long negotiations. I hate to do it, after raising this great armada so quickly and getting it into fighting trim, but we may sit here for months of protracted talks. The chances are good that you will be fully recovered and back with us long before any more fighting takes place."

"We know you want to represent your father in this," Harakh said, "but you've already done a splendid job of that."

"Aye, aye," said the others approvingly.

"So go back to the capital and let your wounds heal," the consort continued. "It's what I would do, bearing such wounds."

He had no strength to argue. "Very well. But send me back on the same ship with Larissa. I want to keep an eye on her."

"So you shall," Shazad assured him. He tried to follow the rest of the session, but he drifted off to sleep before the queen had finished another sentence.

"Esteemed King Gasam," Ilas read, holding the parchment scroll open before him, *"greetings and salutations from Her Majesty Queen Shazad of Neva."* He glanced at Gasam, who sat stone-faced on his folding chair, beneath a thatched canopy. Unlike his queen, Gasam had never mastered the art of read-

ing, considering it an accomplishment unworthy of a warrior.

"Go on," he rumbled, "read the rest. I'll tell you when I want you to stop."

Ilas cleared his throat. *"You know that our sister queen Larissa resides with us at present, as our honored guest. She is well, and sends you her loving regards. So much do I value her company that I shall part with her only upon certain unalterable concessions on your part."*

"Here it comes," Gasam said.

"Before we negotiate, I am bound to address a certain matter concerning the legitimate ruse of war by which the queen was captured and you so narrowly escaped the same fate. The ship employed by my loyal subjects and allies was one belonging to Queen Isel the Ninth of the land of Altiplan. I seized this vessel by force in order to employ it thus. Its appearance in the late military action is in no way to involve Queen Isel in our present conflict, nor is it to imply that Queen Isel is in any way in a state of alliance with Neva."

"What does that mean?" Pendu asked.

"Diplomat talk, I think," Gasam explained. "The foreigners don't want us to think they have taken sides against us." He chuckled. "As if it made any difference. They are our slaves like everyone else, did they but know it. Go on, Ilas."

"Our first condition: You are to cease all movement of your forces within the kingdom of Neva, save such movements as are necessary to effect evacuation of your forces by sea. Maneuvers undertaken for purposes of quitting our land shall not be molested.

"Our second condition: You are to cease all molestation of our subjects, release any you hold prisoner and return all property seized from them, and allow all

*our subjects within the land you have overrun to re-
turn to their homes in peace.*

*"Our third condition: You are to select an embassy
of representatives and submit to us, in writing, a list
of their names, together with description sufficient to
allow them to be recognized by our officers.*

*"Should you meet all these conditions to our satis-
faction, then you may send your embassy to us for negotiations of the terms whereby you may leave our
land and whereby your queen, our beloved sister
Larissa, may return to your side. Any attempt by you
to renew hostilities will be met with swift retribution.
Not only shall your queen not be returned to you, but
I shall not be answerable for her continued health and
safety. I pray you do not force me to this extremity.*

*"Send your messengers, and after them your em-
bassy, bearing white banners or white feathers upon
their staves. Their safe conduct is most solemnly guaranteed, upon the altars of the gods of Neva. I await
your answer."*

"And below is affixed her seal," Ilas concluded, ro-
tating the parchment to display the thick disc of wax
with the arms of Neva in low relief.

"This is degrading," Gasam said. "Must I really
deal with this woman, who was once my slave?"

"I fear so, master," Ilas said, greatly daring. He
was anxious that Gasam should begin to think of
him as a counselor. With Larissa absent, Gasam
might well look elsewhere for advice. Even the best
of his warriors were simple men, unaccustomed to
the ways and usages of courts. In such circumstances, who better to consult with than Ilas of Nar?

Gasam glared at him from beneath lowered
brows. "Say you so? That was more a comment than
a question. It did not demand an answer."

Ilas chose his words most carefully. "And yet, my

king, the matter should be addressed. There is enmity of long standing between yourself and the queen of Neva. There might be advantage to you in swallowing your pride to deal with her as an equal."

"Hold your tongue, pirate," said Pendu, who stood behind Gasam's chair, his great spear slanted across his arm. "Leave these matters to your betters."

"No," Gasam said, holding up a hand for silence. "I would hear what he has to say. Speak without fear, man."

Ilas's heart exulted at this opportunity. "Master, as you have said, Queen Shazad was once your slave. Years ago, you and your queen used her as your plaything, and rightfully so. Imagine, if you will, what a blow that was to a proud young princess."

"Of course," Gasam said. "That was the joy of it."

"Exactly. And for all the years since, she has brooded upon it. She has our queen now, and that must be a soothing balm to her wounded vanity. But, to her, your arrogance is unabated. Were you to humble yourself somewhat, I think that it could not fail but cause her own guard to lower."

"Humble himself?" Pendu said indignantly. "Unthinkable! Gasam, allow me to skewer this worm for you." He readied his spear, but once again Gasam held up a hand.

"Peace, Pendu. I told him to speak without fear. I will endure much to have my Larissa back. Revenge can always be exacted later, but its sweetness would sour on my tongue if I did not have her beside me to enjoy it." He leaned forward. "Just what do you mean, Ilas?"

Thus encouraged, the pirate went on. "My king, if having the queen in her hands is satisfying, think how pleased she will be if you . . . I will not say abase yourself before her, but at least approach her in a spirit of contrition? The exultation she will feel must surely cloud her judgment."

To his intense relief, Gasam was not angry but seemed to be pondering the suggestion deeply. "But," he said at last, "will this not increase even further the value of Larissa as a hostage?"

"It could hardly do so, because what more valuable prize could she have taken? She already knows that the value of Queen Larissa is all but infinite. No, for her the true prize is having you at a disadvantage, not in her character as head of state, but as a wounded woman."

"This bears thinking on," Gasam said, his eyes going narrow, sitting back and stroking his chin. "Always I have led as chief among warriors. Now I must act all but alone. Now I must think the way Larissa would."

"Exactly, my king!" Ilas concurred. This was working out better than he had hoped.

Pendu grunted. "You are both talking as if you can trust this Queen Shazad! Why should she not wring her concessions from you and then refuse to release our queen? Why should she not go ahead and kill her?"

Ilas fought down his impatience. He did not dare offend the most obscure Shasinn junior warrior, much less this powerful general. "Because she has made for herself the reputation of a just and merciful queen. Her father was a ruthless man who might well have done as you suggest, but not Shazad."

"He is right," Gasam said. "She knows she must deal with many rulers besides me. She would lose face with all of them if she broke her word to me. She would lose . . . what is the word?" He looked to Ilas.

"Credibility."

"Yes, she would lose credibility. She would lose her honor."

"Huh! She has no honor!" Pendu said scornfully. "Only warriors have honor. Only Shasinn warriors, at that."

"And yet, to their way of thinking, they are an honorable race," Gasam said. "In my years of dealing with foreigners, mostly through conquest, I have learned that, not only do they think differently than we, but the folly of their ways never occurs to them. And I have dealt with Shazad for a long, long time. Yes, I believe I can count upon her to behave with . . . what is the other word I need, Ilas?"

"Consistency, my king."

"Right, she will behave with consistency. She does not alter her policy to suit the circumstances, but rather she lets her 'honor' dictate to her, a foolish thing in anyone, much less a monarch. I can use her."

"It seems uncertain to me," Pendu said dubiously.

Gasam's expression became abstracted, almost dreamy. "It will be something new for me. I will have a role to play like the actors in the Nevan plays. I have been doing the same thing for too long. I think I shall enjoy this."

Ilas knew then that it was as he had suspected: Gasam was a child; a willful boy who had learned to manipulate others to conform to his desires. Such a man could be manipulated in turn, but until now only Larissa had done so.

"I have decided," Gasam said at last. "Ilas, get your writing materials. I shall send a letter to Queen Shazad."

"Gasam?" Shazad said, unable to believe it. "He intends to come and treat with me himself?"

"His letter says so, my queen," her secretary affirmed.

"Read it again," she commanded.

"To Queen Shazad of Neva, from King Gasam of the Islands, greeting:

"You have taken from me that which I value above all other things in the world, more indeed than the world itself. I am ready to treat with you, and upon receipt of your approval, the following embassy will call upon you, trusting to your royal honor and your safe-conduct:

"Chief of Embassy: King Gasam of the Islands." The secretary peered over the parchment at the queen, his eyes magnified by thick spectacles. "There follow the names of some five others. All the names sound Shasinn. And he wishes a blanket safe-conduct for his ship and its crew."

"A trick?" Harakh queried.

"How could it be?" she asked. "If he separates himself from his army and sails in here with no more than this negligible escort, he places himself completely at our mercy. We will know quickly if his army makes any move." She turned to her commander of scouts. "Are they still in place?"

"They have not advanced a mile since their queen was taken," he asserted.

"I do not know," Harakh said. "It is so unlike him, and we all know how bold he is. This could be part of some sort of . . ." He ran out of words. "I don't know what it could be. I do know I don't like it."

"Gasam is not subtle," she said. "Larissa is the schemer and I have her."

"Who cares what he plans?" said Lord Chutai. "Let him come in his ship. Then kill him when he steps ashore."

"No!" Shazad said, furious. "I'll not have my safe-conduct flouted. My name would be blackened before all the monarchs of the world."

"My queen," said an elderly advisor, "you must be reasonable. No true monarch regards this Gasam as a real king. He comes of no line, he is not part of a dynasty, he has no heir. His conquests have been ephemeral, and he owns nothing but a few wretched islands full of naked savages. He is a barbarian, an upstart and a pirate."

"My safe-conduct is sacred, whether granted to a king of Chiwa, to Gasam or to the lowliest rower on Gasam's ship! With Larissa it was different. She was captured in open combat and she is mine to do with as I will. Her death was an option open to us. His is not, if I extend my protection to him." She brooded for several minutes while they kept silence. Finally she spoke again.

"Very well. I have decided to allow his embassy to come here, with him at its head. They will be protected while here, and they shall leave at their own will without harm. I feel that we take no risk in this. Whatever he thinks in his overweening arrogance, he can do us no harm."

"I think," said the elderly counselor, "that Your Majesty underestimates that man's capacity to do harm."

Later, after they had gone, Shazad sipped at her wine and thought about her decision. She truly believed that she was perfectly safe with Gasam. He dared try nothing in the midst of his enemies, knowing that her guards and nobles were eager to kill him at the first sign of double-dealing from him.

But she knew that there was more to it. She was powerfully curious to see him at close range again. Being his prisoner, dreadful as it was, had been the most powerful experience of her life. The memory stirred her as well as shamed her. The prospect of having him come to her, voluntarily, when she wielded the whip hand was intoxicating.

For the tenth time she read over his letter. Over the years she had grown accustomed to threading her way through Larissa's amusing, duplicitous missives. The relatively few communications from Gasam had been blunt and aggressive. The most adroit of scribes had never been able to disguise the man's brutality. But this was different. This was Gasam speaking from the heart. This was Gasam wounded and vulnerable. Just reading his words was not enough. She had to see him.

"Your Majesty," said the guard outside the door, "Prince Ansa is here to see you." At her nod he signaled and four men carried in the prince's litter. She rose and went to his side.

"You should have sent word. I would have been happy to call on you."

"I get tired of the same four walls," he said. "Is the transport arranged?"

"Lord Sachu has agreed to take you and Larissa back to Kasin in his own flagship. At this time of year, his ships can sail south more readily than ours. They are not so dependant upon the prevailing winds. You will have a heavy escort of my own sailors and marines. Sachu is anxious to gather the riches I've promised and leave to report to his queen. Their own storm season will commence soon and he does not wish to be caught."

He glanced at the official-looking parchment on the table. "Have you received word from Gasam?" Making preparations for his departure, he had missed the hastily called meeting.

"Yes. He sent a list of his embassy's personnel. They will arrive in a few days, I think." She decided not to tell him that Gasam was coming personally. He would only try, like the others, to tell her she was being foolish.

"I am sorry I won't be here," he said.

"I am sure you will be missing nothing. Just go to the capital, rest and recover from your wounds. Rejoin us here when you are mended. Contact your father. Send him a report of all that has happened here. You may use my messenger service for this."

"I'll do that," he said, beginning to grow lightheaded once again from the medication he was still taking. He knew he would be asleep soon. He managed a brief farewell, and then was carried unconscious from the queen's chamber.

ELEVEN

T he wind blew a fine, salt spray over her as she paced the deck of the strange ship. She had always loved the sea wind. She had felt a special surge of elation when she and Gasam, still little more than children, had taken to the water to go and conquer the rest of the Storm Islands, having finished the conquest of Gale, their homeland. The vessel in those days had been a big war canoe, paddled by Shasinn warriors only then learning the skill. The sea was an alien environment to the Shasinn, who for generations had grazed their livestock on the plateau of the island's interior, only occasionally coming down to the shore to trade. They had not liked the idea of leaving dry land, and had been driven to it only by their king's remorseless will.

As in other things, Larissa had differed from the rest of her people in this. From the first she had loved the surge of the waves beneath the boat, the sense of movement and freedom it gave her. She had loved the wind streaming through her hair, and the salt spray. It felt strange to be feeling these things now, in this place, in chains. The surge of the wooden deck beneath her bare feet was slow and stately compared to that of a war canoe. Raised so high from the water, it seemed to be moving slowly as well, although she knew that in reality a canoe could go faster only in brief spurts. Only the wind and the spray were the same.

"Are you comfortable, Your Majesty?"

She turned to see Lord Sachu by her side. "As comfortable as I can be so decorated." She raised her hands and the chains draped all about her tinkled musically. "I had thought, after the hospitality I showed you on my island, that you would not have taken the part of my enemies."

He smiled tightly. "I have taken no part in this war between you and Queen Shazad. My ship was seized without my permission and neither I nor any of my command took part in that expedition."

"Yet you transport me."

"As cargo only. You are not my prisoner, but hers. It is lawful for me to supply transportation without involving my nation in hostility with yours."

"By your law, perhaps," she said, annoyed.

He shrugged. "What other law am I to follow? Now, be reasonable, Queen Larissa. Would you really be traveling on a Nevan warship or transport? They are less spacious and comfortable than mine, and they are full of folk implacably hostile to you. None of this escort dare molest you while I walk my own deck."

"Not to mention that you expect Shazad to win this war."

"You must admit your invasion came to a sorry end," he said.

Her face flushed. "A fluke. My capture might as well have been accidental."

"And I have learned that you have been pushed off the mainland before now."

"All rulers have temporary setbacks," she said, furious at having to defend herself to him, to appear weak before anyone.

"But I have never heard of a conqueror who, having lost lands once conquered, ever won them back again."

"Those may have been ordinary conquerors," she said, "but Gasam is not ordinary in any way."

"Then, should he regain all he has lost, and you be restored to him, it is with him that my queen shall deal. These are matters of statecraft and my activities here will not affect them."

"You can affect them very deeply," she said. "Deliver me back to my husband. You saw my treasure houses, some of them. Strike these chains off me and you'll have your pick. Take me back to Gasam, and your queen will be as my sister to the end of our days."

"Your offer is tempting, but such dealings greatly exceed the powers granted me in my queen's commission." He sounded more amused than tempted.

"What of that? Your queen will not care how you have exceeded your authority, as long as you bring her wealth and political favor."

"That may be so, but suppose I do things and your husband loses his war, anyway? I shall have made enemies of every other sovereign of this continent." He waved an arm eastward, taking in the great landmass in that direction. "For your husband, it seems, is the enemy of the whole world. What then? I'll tell you. My queen will hear my report, then she will listen to those of my subordinates, some of whom are not my bosom friends, and she will send me into the pit to entertain the royal bulls."

"The world could be yours!" she urged.

"Not all of us are like you, Queen Larissa. We do not need the whole world. Good day to you." With that he turned and walked away, leaning easily to the ever-changing tilt of the ship's deck.

She was not sure whether it was cowardliness, or lack of imagination, or rectitude behind his resistance, but she knew that he was not the only man aboard the ship.

Ansa lay in a bed built out of the wall of a tiny cabin. Every motion of the ship made him roll in the bunk and caused his wounds to ache anew. He was getting so accustomed to the pain that he barely noticed it now, save when an especially vicious twinge shot through him.

There came a rap on the door. "Prince Ansa?"

"Come in," he said, eager for any sort of company.

It was Sachu. "I trust you find your accommodations adequate?"

"More than adequate," Ansa assured him. "I was prepared to lie on an open deck."

"Oh, we can do better than that for a passenger of rank who has been injured in battle. I must say that this voyage has proven to be even stronger than I had anticipated. To trade, to establish commercial relations with new lands, this was all we expected. But to give passage to a wounded prince and a queen in chains, this is extraordinary, even on a voyage of exploration!"

"One sees some sights when one chooses a life of travel," Ansa told him.

Sachu laughed. "So one does. I was just speaking with Queen Larissa . . ."

"Be careful how you do that," Ansa cautioned. "That woman can charm a longneck out of its den and get it to eat out of her hand and then attack her enemies."

"She speaks persuasively," Sachu allowed, "but then she has more to tempt men with than most women."

"When I was a boy, I thought that my father exaggerated when he spoke of how evil Gasam and Larissa were, as he did often. When I met them, I knew that they were worse than I could have dreamed."

"Your father's kingdom," Sachu said, "what is it like?"

And so Ansa told him of his homeland, of its limitless, grassy plains and the heavily wooded hills of its northern belt, where his mother's people lived. He spoke of its great herds of game animals, the grazers and browsers and the predators that preyed on both.

Sachu listened intently. "An inland nation, you say? And it produces mainly livestock? Well, my queen will wish to establish relations, but I see little scope for trade. Our ships can carry only a few head for any distance. Gems?"

"None I ever heard of. We have furs in great abundance, and beautiful feathers, and some of the beasts are ivory-bearing." He was not used to talking this way, as a merchant.

"That is more promising. Metals?"

"We have steel."

"Steel!" Sachu straightened so fast that he rapped his pate on the overhead.

"Haven't people here told you of Hael the Steel King."

"I heard the honorific, but I assumed it referred to his character, as one might say 'Hael the Fierce' or 'Hael the Terrible.'"

"No, it means that he controls the only steel mine in the world."

"Steel mine! I never heard of such a thing. Steel is hoarded over the centuries and, once lost, cannot be replaced. Queen Larissa showed us her great arsenal of steel weapons, but I thought she must have robbed the world to get so much."

"She very nearly did. When I was a small boy, steel was the rarest of metals. Swords had blades of bronze with thin steel inserts in the edges. Then Father found the steel mine. Now steel is still valuable but a great deal more plentiful. I am surprised that Queen Shazad did not mention it."

"Between the plague—and I still do not believe we brought it—and her war, the queen has had very little time to speak with us. She prepared a formal letter to my queen and entrusted it to me and suggested that we return at a later date, strongly hinting that several years might be adequate."

"Justly or not, this plague has put you in bad odor with the Nevans."

"But your steel trade—has your father plenty to export."

"I don't know how the reserves stand, but he trades freely with all who want to buy. Well, not quite freely. I don't think he would trade with Mezpa."

"Is this yet another war?" He sighed with resignation. "It is difficult to establish relations when nations are in conflict."

"You should get used to it," Ansa cautioned. "We have been fighting each other all my life, and as far back as anyone remembers."

"But steel!" he mused. "For steel, I can put up with a great deal of negotiation."

The voyage was not swift, although the distance was not great. The winds blew from the south at that time of year, so there was a great deal of tacking and wearing to do, the ship making its way southward in a zigzag course.

It was slow, but the Nevans aboard marveled that it could be done at all. Their own ships had only the most rudimentary capacity for such maneuvers, and had to depend upon oars for complex movements where favorable winds were not blowing. Queen Shazad had put master mariners aboard each of the foreign ships to observe how they were handled. She intended to build an entirely new fleet incorporating these strange but useful designs, as soon as her war was over.

Larissa took only the faintest notice. She always enjoyed sailing, but the true utility of ships, in her estimation, was to ferry warriors from the islands to the mainland, where they could engage in the exciting and profitable activity of fighting and plundering. The hum of cordage and the creak of the masts were pleasant, but she never bothered to look overhead to trace the paths taken by the ropes in their spiderweb of rigging, to understand what they did.

Day after day she stood by the rail with the wind in her face and waited. The men aboard looked at her in awe. It was not often one was privileged to gaze upon a captive queen, beautiful in her chains. The Nevans were hostile, fearful and awestruck at the same time. The foreigners were unfailingly polite but kept their distance. This last she presumed to be at Sachu's orders.

One evening, as they neared Kasin, she lingered

long at the rail, after the sun had sunk in scarlet splendor in the sea to the west and the scarred face of the moon shone above the mainland to the east. In the darkness she admired the phosphorescent foam rolled up by the ship's bows. Huge, glowing eels swam about a few feet beneath the water, going about their business of feeding, mating and avoiding other denizens of the waters that wanted to eat them. A man walked up beside her and doffed his feathered hat. It was not Sachu.

"Good evening, mighty queen."

"Good evening, Lord Goss. I trust you do not address me thus in a spirit of sport?"

"By no means, Your Majesty!" he protested. "I knew you for a great queen when we met, and I think you one still."

"Even in my noisy adornments?" She jingled her chains.

"You are more beautiful in fetters than Queen Shazad in all her jewels and silk. Your current discomfiture is but a temporary setback. You and your husband, the great King Gasam, have, as I understand, suffered reverses in the past, yet have prevailed."

She warmed. "We have. And we shall again."

"A short time ago, Your Majesty spoke to Lord Sachu concerning these matters." His voice was low, insinuating. "I could not help but overhear. He was most obtuse."

"You have sensitive ears," she commented. "I did not see you anywhere on deck."

"You did not think to look below," he said. "You see that?" In the dimness she could make out his finger pointing to a grating set into the deck nearby, faint candlelight shining through its grillwork.

"That is a vent over the galley, to allow smoke

from the cookstove to escape. I just happened to find myself standing by the stove and looked up to see the sole of your comely foot."

"How convenient you just happened to be standing there. I'm sure your duties must call you often to the galley. And while inspecting the stove and my foot, did you hear all that passed between myself and Lord Sachu?"

"Every word. I hope you do not think me disloyal if I observe that Lord Sachu is lacking in both spirit and enterprise."

"Of course I cannot agree with you. He is my host."

"I, on the other hand, am a man of vision. My admiration goes out to dynamic leaders, to persons of vivid personality. Persons such as yourself, and your husband. It would be an honor for me to be the man who helps you to regain your rightful place."

She turned and smiled at him, her perfect teeth gleaming in the moonlight. "So it would."

King Gasam stood in the prow of *Seasnake*, leaning on his spear and surveying the spectacle ashore. The waterfront was lined with people, although the crowding was not so dense as would have been had so much of the population not fled. Soldiers lined the rails of the warships and transports in the harbor, all curious to see the spectacle of their queen welcoming the ogre king who had been their enemy for as long as many of them could remember.

A small but glittering reception party waited by the dock that had been set aside for his arrival: courtiers stiff in the formal gowns they took with them even on a military campaign, officers glittering in their dress armor, servants in colorful livery. They stood silently as the little warship was rowed smartly to the wharf. Ilas had been busy training replacement oarsmen and they made an acceptable show.

At the coxswain's command the oars were pulled in, then raised vertically as the ship quickly lost way, then nudged itself gently against the wet, fabric padding of the stone wharf. As it did, a stout courtier wearing a massive chain of office stepped to the edge of the wharf.

"Welcome, King Gasam and the embassy of the islands," the man intoned.

Gasam nodded to a junior warrior and the youth walked up the gangplank and onto the wharf. His spear was tipped with a great spray of gorgeous white feathers.

"By this token," Gasam said, his deep voice rumbling across the esplanade, "I proclaim myself to be under the protection of Queen Shazad of Neva, bearing her safe-conduct."

"Approach in safety, King Gasam," said the courtier in hieratic tones. "Queen Shazad extends her shield above you, and the gods of Neva protect you on all sides."

"Now," Pendu muttered beside him, "we'll see if the slut has any control over her subordinates. They are looking at us as if they want to drink our blood."

"If not," Gasam said imperturbably, "we shall have little time to worry or suffer. Let's go ashore." He stepped forth like a man without a care, walking up the gangplank until he stood before the courtier, who in turn had to look up at him. He ignored the man and gazed around to all sides.

"Why is Queen Shazad not here to greet me?" he demanded.

"King Gasam," the courtier said, "this is not a royal visit but an embassy. You have chosen to head your embassy personally, but a sovereign is not required to greet an embassy upon arrival. Rather, the embassy is conducted to the sovereign."

Gasam smiled at him. It was a chilling sight. "How good of you to remind me of a sovereign's duty. By all means, let us go meet with the queen of Neva."

"Just a moment," said a man in a general's cloak. "King Gasam, some of your men are armed. This is not proper procedure in an embassy."

"These are Shasinn warriors," Gasam said, "and they surrender their arms only in death. But you need have no worry. In this place, they will endanger no one unless you plan treachery. If you do, you are in such overwhelming force that our resistance must be futile. You should lose no more than ten men for each of mine."

"Twenty for me," said Pendu. "I have slain as many Nevans in an afternoon's fighting before, and fifty for my king. He is no common warrior."

The officer's face flamed between the cheek plates of his helmet. "My orders do not allow conducting armed enemies into my queen's presence!"

"Gentlemen, gentlemen," the courtier said, "this is not seemly. I am sure that our sovereign wishes us to honor the customs of our esteemed quests. Please, let us continue." The soldier glowered, fist on sword hilt, but he made no further objection.

The procession began from the waterfront and made its way along a broad avenue that led up a steep slope toward a cluster of splendid buildings that crowned the top of a superb hill, dominating the town. The people who lined the way looked on in amazement. There was no cheering, nor were there any demonstrations of hostility. There was only a nearly silent expression of wonderment, as if they were seeing something from a dream.

From a window of the mansion she had commandeered as her campaign headquarters and royal residence, Shazad viewed the spectacle below. She had a clear view of the harbor, and she recognized *Seasnake* instantly. Idly she wondered whether Ilas of Nar was in command. She would have to hang him if so. Then she remembered the blanket safe-conduct for the vessel's personnel. Another time, then.

Her heart hastened as she watched the small procession making its way up the avenue. So difficult to believe that this handful of arrogant men had made such a ruin of the world. How could it have happened?

"Your Majesty," said the lady at her elbow, "they will be here in a few minutes. We must prepare you to receive the savage."

"No, he can wait," she said. "I am the one with the power this time. I don't like this gown. Bring the black one."

While she was fitted into the elaborate gown, one of two score she took with her even on campaign, she tried to calm her anxiety. She was eager to see Gasam again, but there was something pleasurable in putting off the moment.

The mansion belonged to a family of wealthy merchants, the foremost family of this port city for many centuries. The men of the family were hereditary magistrates, and most of one floor was a great salon for holding court, used as a ballroom on festive occasions. It was not much smaller than her lesser throne room in her own palace, and served well in that capacity for this occasion. She sat in her portable throne atop the dais and inspected her courtiers and guards. Satisfied with their appearance, she nodded toward her steward and he thumped his bronze-shod staff on the polished stone floor. Two guards ceremoniously opened the double doors.

"Enter, honored Embassy of the Isles!" the herald chanted.

She held her breath as the Islanders swaggered in, their spears carried casually across arm or shoulder, looking about them with mild curiosity. Except for Gasam. He was somber and looked only at Shazad as he trod the narrow carpet to the dais.

She resumed breathing and forced herself to study him dispassionately. In his simple breechclout of scarlet cloth he was immensely more impressive than her officials in all their silks and cloth of gold. She saw the terrible scar on his chest, newly healed. That must be the mark of Hael's spear, she thought. The man was about of an age with her, but he looked at least ten years younger, possibly more. The deep reddish gold of his hair was only slightly faded from the days of his youth. The great scar down his face was far more noticeable than the few, small wrinkles. That was done by Ansa, she thought. It seemed that only one family was able to damage this man. For one who had devoted his life to war, he showed surprisingly few other scars. His people customarily painted their scars to show them off.

He halted at the foot of the dais and she stood. "Welcome, honored embassy of the Islands. Welcome, King Gasam." Because of the nature of his mission, she addressed the embassy first.

"Greeting, magnificent Queen Shazad," Gasam said, inclining his head a fraction of an inch. "I present my party."

She descended the steps and walked beside Gasam

as, one by one, he presented the men he had brought with him. Most were senior warriors. It galled her that she knew some of them from her days as his prisoner, when he had held war councils while she was chained by her neck to a wall, unable to rise from her seat on the floor. She came to the last man, much smaller, and not Shasinn.

"My shipmaster, Ilas of Nar."

Not by the slightest flicker did she betray that she knew him. "I see you have acquired another Nevan for your service."

"I wanted his ship, he wanted a master. We came to an accommodation. He is under my protection now."

"More to the point, he is under my safe-conduct." She turned away from the traitor with a swish of skirts. "It is nothing. Come, King Gasam, we must talk. There will be a formal banquet later. Please make allowances for our simplicity, we are under wartime conditions here."

"We value simplicity," Gasam said, falling in beside her. The courtiers kept their distance as the two warring monarchs conversed. "The years have been kind to you, Shazad. You are as beautiful as ever."

She smiled at him. "Don't try to charm me, you bloody savage. We are here to negotiate, not to flatter one another." She knew what to say, but she had little control over her feelings. She remembered the first time she had seen this man, just before the battle in which the barbarians had all but annihilated her father's army. During the pre-battle parley she had sat her cabo and he had looked her over as if she were a head of prize livestock. The raw, animal power of him was overwhelming. He was as handsome as Hael without the dreamy spirituality that made Hael something other than a man. To her horror, she found herself reacting just as she had then: with an erotic thrill that was little short of passion.

"Do not scorn my compliments," he chided. "I bestow them upon very few. And I find strength and character as attractive as the beauty of the flesh. You have both in abundance."

"From another man it would be flattery, indeed. But you have the most beautiful woman in the world for your queen."

"No, I do not. You have her." For a moment the pain showed behind his eyes. "I must have her back, Shazad."

"That is why you have come here. Leave. Go back to your islands and never cross the water again. I will send her back to you, and willingly."

He chuckled. "Then you are asking Larissa and me both to commit suicide. I was driven off the mainland once, and that was bad, but my people did not lose faith in me, because I was badly wounded, and it was Hael who did it to me, and my queen did the same to Hael. To my tribesmen, it was almost a matter of ritual, as when warriors challenged one another to the thorn circle in the old days. It was more like gods fighting, as I am told gods sometimes do."

He swung his head around, smiling as if they were speaking polite nothings. "But if I were to leave without a fight, waiting upon your pleasure to restore my Larissa to me, I will be nothing but a man, and a beaten man at that. Larissa would rather die as your prisoner than suffer that." Again the pain was in his eyes, and his voice as well.

"Then I fear we shall have very little to negotiate, for those are my conditions." She walked out onto a broad terrace, where tables of delicacies and goblets of wine had been laid out, with servants standing by.

The whole crowd followed them from the throne room, silent and staying just beyond hearing range. Only Gasam's warriors spoke among themselves, their voices low. They did not moderate their tones. The Shasinn were a village people who seldom raised their voices except in oration or battle-chant.

"Oh, come, now, Shazad," he chided. "You know as well as I that we shall make offer and counteroffer until we come to an agreement. If there were no room for negotiation, we would be engaged in battle right now."

She turned to face him squarely and the courtiers froze, tense. "How can I accept less than your instant evacuation, Gasam? You and your barbarians invaded my country!"

He smiled indulgently. "And your response was very swift. Incredibly quick, when I think of it. There you were, all unsuspecting, prostrate from a terrible plague, and you hear that I have arrived. Then, within a very few days, you are coming north with your whole fleet and your armies mobilized and gathered together."

His smile spread into a full grin. "Shazad, if I were a suspicious man, I might almost think that *you* have been planning to invade *my* homeland! That would make my little action—what is it your ancient military writers termed it? A 'preemptive raid'?"

"You have learned well from Larissa," she said, conceding the point. She turned away and a servant brought them wine in frosted goblets. The lavish mansion had an ice cellar.

"Who better to learn from?" he said, taking a cup. He held it lightly, flexing his long fingers against the cool surface. He took the smallest of sips. "Where is she?"

Shazad took a much larger swallow of her own. The Shasinn, she thought, were so good at controlling ordinary appetites while she was ruled by her own. "In a safe place, and quite comfortable. I am kinder to prisoners of distinction than you."

"Your memory is long, Shazad. We were all younger then. I was a wild warrior chief from the isles and to me the people here were just members of another tribe. I have learned a great deal in all these years."

She could not keep the astonishment from her face. Was Gasam venturing an *apology?* Even one as qualified as this?

"Your queen seemed as arrogant as ever when I spoke with her."

"You, too, were arrogant when all you had was your pride and your chains. Under those circumstances, what does a superior person have left but arrogance? Besides"—he chuckled, almost with a note of self-deprecation—"I enjoy being a king, but Larissa likes being a goddess. She comes as close as any human being can, but unlike her I cannot deceive myself that I am something other than mortal. The gray has appeared in my hair, I am not as strong as I was twenty years ago." He swept a long, elegant hand down his magnificent form from breast to knees. "My body takes a long time to recover from wounds now. No, I am mortal and I shall grow old and die. I no longer think like the young warrior king, Shazad, any more than you think like the heedless young princess you were."

"I wish I could believe you, Gasam," she said. "But you are the one thing in my life that seems never to change." She clapped her hands, the signal that preliminary talks were over, and the crowd began to mix indiscriminately. For a period all discussion would be casual. The procedure was somewhat irregular, but she needed some time to sort out her feelings and impressions. The presence of the man made this difficult. For many years she had taken great pride in comporting herself always as a sovereign with only the good of her realm at heart. It had rendered her uncommonly clear-sighted and firm of will.

Now she was letting her emotions overrule her. She was reverting to the sensual, impressionable young woman she had been. Harakh had been an adequate if dull consort. Comparing him to Gasam was like comparing a candle to a volcano. And why should she be making such comparisons at all? She did not bring Gasam here to seduce him. She had not invited him—he had chosen to come here on his own, entrusting himself to her honor.

After an hour of very uncomfortable socializing, the steward made the discreet signal informing Shazad that the banquet was in readiness.

"It looks as if we are ready to dine, Gasam," she said. "I fear we do not have any kagga milk and blood."

"I lost the taste for it years ago," he assured her.

They passed into the great banqueting room and soon were gorging. The dislocations of the times forbade anything exotic, but the fare, though simpler than usual, was abundant and the wine cellars of the mansion were lavish. The company marveled at the abstemious way the Shasinn ate, taking only tiny mouthfuls of meat or fruit, diluting their wine with water.

"My people think yours fear poison," Shazad said.

"They are always like that," Gasam said, eating in the same fashion. "As for the wine, I warned them to be easy with it. They prefer our native *ghul*, anyway."

"You didn't bring any of your warrior women," she noted. "I have never seen them."

"I acquired them since we last got together. No, I am afraid they are not right for an embassy. The sight of them would put your people off their food. They are wild and almost beautiful in their own fashion, but they lack the native dignity of my tribesmen."

"If you will not go," she said, plunging back in, "and I will not surrender Larissa, where does that leave us?"

"There are other avenues. We are sovereigns, we have armies, the world is large. There are things we can do besides tear one another to pieces. Have you considered an alliance?"

"Against Hael, you mean?"

He shook his head. "Hael is another part of my youth of which I am wearied. This great so-called enmity of ours is far more on his side than on mine. I do not covet his dusty plains or his wandering tribes. I would not have fought him last time, but he fell upon me without warning."

"You covet his steel mine," she pointed out.

He shrugged. "As who would not? I would try to take it from him, or from Mezpa, or from you, or from the king of Chiwa, if there were still such a king. It is the greatest treasure in the world and the envy of all."

"Then what would be the point of such an alliance? Would we fight Mezpa?"

"In time, perhaps. We might well contain their ambitions. But I had another foe in mind. Your shipyards are the greatest on the mainland. Can your shipwrights build ships to match those of the new foreigners?"

"They can," she said, seeing where this was leading. "Are you proposing an alliance against Queen Isel?"

"Does it not make sense? Why fight over the scraps of the old world when there is a new one?"

"Why should I wish to invade them? Queen Isel has done nothing to me."

"Has she not ravaged your country with the greatest plague anybody ever heard of?"

"Even if it is true, I can hardly hold her to account for it. These are not things people do to one another by design. It was a tragic accident."

"Maybe. But we need not even plan offensive operations at this time. How do you know that this man Sachu was only looking for new trading territories? He had a most warlike look to my eye, which is to be trusted in these matters. I think he was spying for Queen Isel, spying out land for conquest. When he goes back, he has a number of very interesting things to report: This mainland is very rich, for one. For another, it is split up among a number of squabbling kingdoms. For a third, it has just been devastated and vastly weakened by plague. And its ships are not as good as theirs. That sort of report could be tempting to someone in search of greater wealth and power."

What he said made sense, she could not deny it. "I cannot make assumptions about her merely on your suggestion."

"Do you do your nation any favor by neglecting to take precautions? You know better than anyone what happens when an enemy appears on your borders unannounced. With those ships, they could seize every one of your ports before you have time to summon your army."

"Are you suggesting that Neva and the islands ally against the foreigners?"

He leaned forward and said earnestly: "I am suggesting that these foreigners have provided us with a way out of this impasse. My people will not tolerate my immediate withdrawal from the mainland. Your people will not tolerate your allowing me to stay or advance. But if your people fear invasion by the foreigners, might they not find it a comfort to have the greatest warriors in the world close at hand, to aid them in battle with these plague-bearers?"

She had long known Gasam to be arrogant, imperious, masterful. She had never expected him to be subtle and persuasive. "I think you underestimate the fear and hatred in which you are held here in Neva," she objected.

"These things are always modified by changing circumstances. Did your people not rejoice when Hael came thundering in with his army of riders? Are they not even wilder-looking than my Islanders? They are certainly far uglier! Yet your people greeted them as saviors because they were so terrified of me. Let them fear the foreigners, who have killed many more of them than I have, intentionally or not, and they will welcome me with open arms. They will forget our past and remember only that we are the greatest fighters in the world. There is nothing like fear of an unknown foe to throw old enemies into each other's arms."

"You have never been so conciliatory before," she said, caught at a loss for one of the few times in her life.

"I have never lost my queen before," he said.

TWELVE

Something woke him. Ansa began to sit up in his bed, wincing at the way the motion pulled at his wounds, straining the stitches. Even so, he knew that he was healing quickly. If the man had no other good qualities, he thought, at least Gasam kept his spear scrupulously clean. There had been no infection. Besides that good luck, both his parents came from extraordinarily rugged tribes. Still, it seemed to him that a warrior spent an inordinate amount of time recovering from wounds. This was something they never mentioned to the eager boys, impatient to become warriors. It seemed to him that, since becoming a warrior, he had spent at least half his days in this condition.

But what had awakened him? It had been something about the motion of the ship. He was not greatly knowledgeable about ships, but he had grown accustomed to this one. Why had its pitch and roll altered? They were supposed to make the port of Kasin sometime the next day, but it was still dark. Outside his door, he heard stealthy footsteps and muttered words. Someone said something that sounded like "swimming bird" in Southern. He remembered that that was the name of one of the foreign ships. Something warned him not to call out.

He waited for a few more minutes, listening hard. There were scuffles and thumps, barely audible over the constant creaking as the ship's timbers worked. Very slowly he sat up and swung his legs out and down until his feet touched the deck. It was painful, but he knew that the real pain was to come. He took his sheathed sword from beneath the bed and put its tip against the deck. He placed his palm atop its hilt and slowly, agonizingly, pushed himself to an almost upright position. The overhead was too low to allow him to straighten fully, and at that moment he doubted that he could do so, anyway.

The pain washed over him but he forced it down. He knew that something was wrong. He had to find out what. After hobbling to the door of the tiny cabin, he opened it as slowly as he could. It creaked inevitably, but the vessel was so full of creaks that he felt one more would not be noticed. The interior of the cabin was so utterly black that the wash of moonlight through the door was dazzling. Except for the eerie lack of color, he could see almost as well as by daylight.

Directly before him was the ship's wheel. He saw that it was turning back and forth freely. Nobody stood by it, but there was a shapeless mass at its base. Using his sword as a crutch, Ansa inched toward the shape and saw, with little surprise, that it was the steersman. He lay on his back with mouth agape, sightless eyes rolled upward so that only the whites gleamed in the moonlight. His head lay in a black puddle that grew even as Ansa watched. His throat had been slashed in a wide crescent from which the blood welled steadily.

Ansa told himself to do nothing hastily. There was still the situation to assess. Whatever the ship's distress, it did not seem to be in immediate danger of sinking or capsizing. The night was fair, the sky cloudless. The faintest breeze tautened the sails. In the distance he could see the bow and stern lanterns of the other two ships.

Where was the watch on deck? Then he saw them: a half dozen bodies sprawled in the convulsive postures of violent death. There should have been a good seven or eight more of them, he thought. Perhaps they had been cast overboard. Craning his head upward, he could not see any lookout atop the mainmast.

A faint glimmer on the deck caught his eye. He shuffled over to the gleam and nudged it with his toe. On the polished boards of the deck lay a heap of thin chains. The moonlight was not strong enough to give them color, but he knew that when the sun rose, it would reveal them to be gold. He gazed out over the water and could just make out a small boat pulling up to one of the other ships. The larger vessel had taken in its sails and was falling steadily astern of the flagship.

Moving as quickly now as he could, Ansa hobbled to the wheel. Beside it was a bronze bell that rang out the hours and summoned the watch to turn out. He gripped the clapper's dangling cord and swung it back and forth violently. The pounding of feet began immediately. Sailors were never slow to meet an emergency. In seconds the deck was crowded with foreign seamen. After them came the Nevan escort, rubbing their eyes, still half-asleep. Two men sprang to the wheel and others swarmed up the ratlines. They babbled in Southern too fast for him to understand.

"What? Who sounded the . . ." Lord Sachu was on deck, the wood resounding beneath his heavy boots. Except for them, he wore only a long shirt. A sword was bare in one hand, a dagger in the other. He took in the situation with a swift scan of the deck and began to bark orders. The men at the wheel yelled something at him and he shouted back. To Ansa's surprise, they abandoned the wheel even as the men aloft took in all the sails except for the one that slanted from the mizzen mast to the main mast. Slowly the ship began to swing about to face into the wind.

"I sounded the alarm," Ansa said.

Sachu thumped over to him. "Tell me."

In a few words Ansa described what had happened. With each word, Sachu's expression grew more dismayed. His faced paled beneath its windburn, the change visible even in the uncertain light. When he stooped and picked up the chains, his mortification seemed complete.

"Goss!" The word was a curse. "He has done this! The traitor! This whole, long voyage he has defied me, subverted my authority . . ." He burst into a string of curses that meant nothing to Ansa.

"How?" Ansa asked.

The mariner forced himself to be calm. "He's been subverting and corrupting my men. Half those on watch tonight must have been his."

"Why has he done this?"

"He is jealous. He thinks his birth superior to mine. He thought he should be given command of the expedition, not I. His family have been rivals of mine for generations."

"But what does he hope to gain by this?" Ansa prodded.

"I think I can follow his devious thinking. Back in the islands, he sought to converse privily with that woman, but I prevented it. She and her king are unbelievably wealthy and their warriors make them powerful, savages as they are. The Nevans hold us responsible for the plague, while the Islanders are untouched by it. He sees great advantage to himself in forming an alliance with them. He thinks it is he who will reap the glory of this expedition in the eyes of our queen and our people."

Sachu pointed to the ship now far astern. "See? She has come about and sets sail for the north. *Swimming Bird* is his ship, captained by his own brother and crewed by his retainers. I tried to prevent this, but he has great influence at court. He planned this night's work well."

"Will you pursue him?"

Sachu shook his head slowly. "It would be futile. He took the precaution of cutting our steering cable. It was the quietest way of disabling the ship and we'll need hours to repair it. I've taken in all save the spanker to bring our bows into the wind." He sighed sorrowfully. "Her Majesty will be very displeased. I will denounce him in court as a traitor and call for his execution, but I may be the one who is clapped in prison."

"You could transfer to your remaining ship and chase him in that," Ansa said.

"*Swimming Bird* is the swiftest of our ships. Even if we could catch him, by then it would be too late to return home before the stormy season. We must go on."

"Can he believe that your queen would rather deal with those savages than the queen of Neva?"

Sachu gave him a long, sober look. "If things fall out as I think he plans, by the time he returns home, his ship laden with treasure, Larissa will *be* the queen of Neva."

By the rising of the sun the ship was under control again and *Swimming Bird* was out of sight to the north. All Ansa's pleading would not persuade Sachu to part with their sole remaining pinnace to run north and warn Shazad of the disaster.

"Your best course is to go to her naval yard and requisition a fast cutter."

"But they may all be with the rest of the fleet!" Ansa objected.

"Then find the swiftest merchant vessel you can," Sachu said obdurately.

Ansa spent the following hours in an agony of anxiety. That was not the only distress he suffered, for he spent much of the time pacing the deck, swinging his arms about, trying to work the stiffness of healing from his limbs and body. It looked as if he was not going to be able to convalesce in comfort, after all.

They came into harbor in late afternoon, the usually bright city gloomy beneath lowering gray clouds. The only joyous welcome came from the southern mariners who had given up Sachu's ships for lost. While the leader presented his documents from Queen Shazad to the port authorities, Ansa slipped ashore and made his way to the palace.

At the stables he requisitioned a string of cabos and some traveling supplies. He had had enough of ships. He was traveling north the way a plainsman should. The guards at the north gate gaped at the strange foreigner but they did not seek to hinder him when they saw his royal pass.

Bestriding a splendid mount, leading three others and in terrible pain, Ansa rode north along the high road through a warm summer rain.

Shazad's ladies prepared her for bed, a leisurely process that began with a long soak in scented, oiled water as hot as her flesh would tolerate. They blotted her with thick, soft towels and for the next hour she lay naked on a cushioned table while her masseuses kneaded the tension from her body. Last of all they draped a filmy, all but transparent gown around her and bowed their way out of the bedroom.

The covers were turned down and she was tired, the bed was tempting, but she was not quite ready for sleep. She treasured these hours snatched from her grueling schedule, when she did not have to bear the weight of her heavy gowns and massive jewelry, when she did not have the responsibilities of state pressing upon her life a crushing weight.

Idly she walked to the full-length mirror that stood before one of the frescoed walls. A gentle breeze that blew through the open balcony doors stirred the hem of her gown. She studied herself in the mirror for a long time. She had removed all her cosmetics, but the light of the single candle was flattering, and it did not reveal the gray in the hair that lay like a rich black foam upon her shoulders.

She tugged at the ribbon that fastened the gown at the base of her throat and it came free. The gown fell open gently and she spread it wide. She was pleased with what she saw. A lifetime of riding had kept her body taut, and the relative privations of campaigning with all its activities had caused her to lose some of her surplus flesh.

Her skin was still a flawless white, and it had no unhealthy sag. She had never borne children, and her gently mounded belly was unmarked. Her large breasts had lost some of their former proud jut, but they were full and soft, their broad brown nipples each as prominent as the boss of a warrior's shield. Her waist was small, her hips broad and between them lay a dense, perfectly proportioned black triangle. Her legs were not long, but they were shapely and terminated in slender ankles and tiny feet.

"Very lovely."

She gasped and whirled, closing the gown around her body as if it were defensive armor. Gasam was seated on the balcony rail, his long, powerful legs stretched before him, his hands widespread on the rail to either side, an insolent smile on his handsome, scarred face.

"You . . . you dare!" she gasped out when she found her voice. "How did you get here?" It sounded foolish to her even as she said it.

"I climbed up from my own balcony," he said reasonably. "I have always loved climbing, even as a boy. The vines on this wall made it easy. I assumed it was what you wanted me to do. That was why you gave me those chambers, and didn't post any guards on this side."

"That is absurd!" But she wondered whether he might not be right. Had she really intended this, without knowing it? "The lack of guards is quickly rectified. I shall summon them now."

His smile did not waver. "And what will that do to this historic conference of ours? Surely you will not imperil them because I embarrassed you?"

"Leave at once!" Her voice trembled and this

shamed her. She forgot that she was the one who held the power, that this was her palace, surrounded by her army, that she held a prisoner who was everything to this savage. She could only feel his overwhelming presence. Slowly, lazily, he rose from the balcony rail and came into her chamber. The candlelight flickered over his superb body, throwing the great, rolling muscles into high relief. His bronze-colored skin was so glossy it shone like the fresh-curried hide of one of her prize cabos.

"You do not really want me to go, do you, Shazad?" He stood before her, so close that she felt the warmth from his body. Lush though her body was, Shazad was a small woman and her eyes were on a level with the tiny nipples that sat low in the corners of the massive muscles of his chest. Beneath the sweet scent of the fistnut oil with which the Islanders loved to rub their bodies, she could smell his animal musk. Her knees trembled at his intense maleness. Suddenly the filmy gown felt unbearably heavy on her own nipples, swollen and aching.

"No," she said, not knowing herself what she meant by it.

His hands went beneath her arms and she was lifted, her substantial flesh magically transformed to something as light as thistledown. His mouth came down on hers and she was not sure whether his tongue was in her mouth or her own in his, so entwined were the two. Her arms went around his powerful neck, as thick-corded as a cabo's and she could not press her body against his hard enough.

He lifted her higher and, impossibly, held her there with one hand while with the other he tore the gown from her body, the fabric as insubstantial in his hand as the wings of a tiny insect. It ribboned away from her body and she felt wonderfully free, as if chains had been struck from her limbs. She forced her eyes open to see the top of his golden head, then her own head jerked back and her mouth fell open, gasping, as he sucked one of her throbbing nipples into his own mouth. His tongue laved it, tormenting her mercilessly.

She moaned as the torturous pleasure seemed to go on forever. She did not know when its focus shifted but her other breast was in his mouth, then the air was suddenly cool on her damp nipples as she was lifted higher and his lips trailed down along the gentle swell of her belly. Lazily his tongue swirled in her navel, sending rippling shudders through her. Still higher he raised her, straightening his arms with effortless strength.

Her hands rested on his rocklike shoulders, her fingers caressing, then digging in as she felt his mouth between her thighs, his tongue drawing pleasure from her the way a musician draws music from his instrument. Tears of pleasure welled from her eyes as she teetered on the brink of helpless ecstasy, but he knew exactly when to draw back.

As he lowered Shazad, her limbs seemed robbed of strength, her mind all but paralyzed, unable to think, only to feel. She licked the side of his face, her tongue tracing the long scar, going across his lips and teeth. She licked his neck and chest and his hard, ridged belly, tasting oil and sweat and maleness. Her legs would not support her and she fell bonelessly to her knees, her strengthless hands grappling frantically with his belt, almost weeping with frustration when it resisted her.

Then his hand went to his hip, and the belt and the cloth it supported fell away and she felt his hard power against her face, brushing her lips, too great for her mouth to encompass. Her hands went to the small of his back, slid down his buttocks to the backs of his thighs as she tried to give him the same pleasure he had given her.

Gasam stooped and his hands cupped the soft roundness of her buttocks, lifting her, spreading her. Her thighs opened and she fell back, unable to hold herself erect without his support. Vaguely she knew that the bed was beneath her back. Gasam stood, holding her hips as her legs encircled him, his great body looming over hers. She stretched her arms but could not reach him. Her hands fell back weakly, grasping her breasts, kneading them, twisting her painfully hard nipples. She felt taut with a tension that, if it did not crest soon, would surely drive her mad.

With a liquid flexion of his hips, he drove into her. She cried out as she was invaded, spread, filled. His body leaned over hers and he took her head between his hands. Her arms encircled him, her legs and his rigid maleness holding her lower body clear of the bed. His mouth opened on hers and she breathed into it while her interior loosened, relaxed, accommodated to his size and shape.

He pushed himself up and loomed above her on outstretched arms as he began to surge into her, withdrawing almost completely only to thrust himself back again, each rhythmic lunge arching her back, making her breasts roll back almost to her chin, so that once again she had to hold them. She was a helpless creature, unable to do anything except writhe, moan and feel the shock waves radiate through her from scalp to toes.

His relentless attack drove her farther back onto

the bed, until she felt the soles of her feet against the coverlet. Gasping for breath, she felt her strength come back and she began to thrust her hips up to meet his. They were both covered with sweat and their bellies slapped together, the sound somehow adding to her excitement. She was alive in a way she had not felt in years, the ending of every nerve tingling, every square inch of her flesh vital and awash with sensation.

With a groan her head went back against a pillow, her neck arching almost painfully as the pleasure pooled like red-hot liquid metal in her lower belly, then burst to every extremity. She wailed with joy at this ecstasy, and with sorrow that it was almost at an end.

For a few seconds she blacked out, unable to bear such utter intensity. When she came back to herself, the waves still coursed through her, more gently now, and Gasam was still above her, smiling and still moving within her in long, slow strokes. Dismayed and delighted, she felt the wonderful waves of pleasure building up again. Her hips churned frantically against him. This time, as she crested, she felt him go rigid in her arms. He drove impossibly deep and held there, pulsing, as she heard his deep, animal groan in her ear.

For many minutes she shuddered and trembled beneath him while her heart thudded, breathing so hard she thought she would never drag enough air into her body. She was a thing of pure sensation. Every inch of her felt bruised. Even her lips felt swollen. Slowly Gasam pushed back from her and she cried out, not wanting him to withdraw from her just yet.

She could scarcely believe the sensations of her

own body, that now seemed like somebody else's, so rich was its fulfillment, when he resumed the earthy, vital dance of life. She embraced him and gave herself joyously, purged of fear and sorrow, knowing that this man had made her his slave once again. And knowing that she loved it.

THIRTEEN

Ansa wondered whether this terrible ride made any sense. Could he reach Shazad before Goss delivered Larissa to Gasam? Even that would not be enough. He had to find Queen Shazad and get her to send out her fleet in time to recapture the woman. Could even the swiftest cabos get him up the coast faster than a ship could sail in the season when the winds drove powerfully north? And it was said that these foreign vessels had finer sailing qualities than the Nevan ships.

His only hope lay in knowing that sailing is a chancy thing even for the finest ships. Winds could fail or turn contrary even in the season when they were considered the most reliable. A tempest could force them to take in all sail, could blow them off course.

In contrast, his borrowed mounts were among the best cabos in the world, bred from royal stock for countless generations. They had never endured the periodic privations that made the plains breed smaller and tougher. Plains cabos were more enduring of hard conditions, but they could never match these magnificent beasts for sustained, long-distance running. As each cabo began to tire he switched mounts, swapping saddles on the run as he had been trained to since boyhood. If any creatures in the world could get him to Shazad in time, these could.

About their rider, he was not so sure. His wounds were seeping blood, but he had expected worse. He had to remind himself that it was only pain, that his wounds, large as they were, were only superficial. No organs had been pierced. The terrible, sharp edge of Gasam's spear had not slashed through the wall of muscle sheathing his belly. No nerves had been severed. When he got home he would be able to show off the longest single scar in the plains nation, and several smaller ones, but he would not die. He kept telling himself that.

Day blended into night as he rode, and the sun rose again, almost without his notice. He was aware of little save the road before him, the motion of the saddle and the beast beneath him. When he did not know whether it rained or the sun shone, he knew with the finest precision how his cabo was breathing, how its stride felt, whether it was beginning to falter. A plainsman born and bred, he felt that he drew strength from the powerful beasts. He had been half-dead on the ship, almost unable to move. Now he was making the ride of his life, although not in the shape he might have desired.

He was not sure how many days he had been riding when he saw the walls of the port city before him. It was not a large city, but extensive enough to have at least three gates. He rode up to the southern one and drew up, coming to a full halt for the first time since leaving the capital.

The guards atop the gate were surprised to see him, and an officer came out through a postern to examine his royal pass.

"How are things in the city?" Ansa demanded.

"All quiet," the man said, studying his pass. "No resumption of hostilities. The embassy is still at the palace."

That, at least, sounded promising. Surely Gasam would have resumed the attack if Larissa were already in his camp. The gates swung open and he rode through, leading his string of remounts. He remembered that the commandeered palace was atop the town's highest hill, but he soon wished he had thought to ask directions. The inland slope of the hill, unlike the seaward side, was a warren of houses, temples and multistoried tenements lining narrow, irregular streets. The soldiers he found in the streets knew the town little better than he, and the locals he encountered spoke a dialect he had a hard time in following.

At last he found himself riding into the marble-paved plaza before the great house. Its central fountain played as gaily as if the times were normal, but a company of royal guards were encamped around it, and their cabos watered in its basin. A solder took the reins of Ansa's mount and another took charge of his remounts. Waving his pass, he dismounted stiffly, amazed that he could move at all. For a moment he stood on half-numbed feet, the pavement feeling strange beneath the soft soles of his knee-high boots, long accustomed to the feel of stirrups.

"Do you need help, sir?" asked a trooper. He was an ordinary cabo rider, but like all members of the guard he was a scion of a prominent family, his accents and manners impeccable.

"Just help me get my weapons off the saddle," Ansa said. "I can walk." With his sword and dagger slung about his body he walked toward the palace door, leaning only slightly on his lance. The officer of the guard eyed him dubiously as he made his way up the steps. He took the pass from Ansa's hand and studied it.

"Let me in," Ansa demanded. "I have urgent information for the queen."

"I shall summon Lord Junis. He is the campaign steward," the officer said, unperturbed.

"I know who Lord Junis is! I am Prince Ansa! I have Her Majesty's pass!"

"Very true, but you are not a member of the royal messenger corps. Please wait here while I summon Lord Junis." The man whirled smartly, making his scarlet cape flare around his calves. He paced away and left Ansa fuming.

"Shall I call a surgeon for you, sir?" asked a young guard, pointing at the front of Ansa's tunic. He looked down to see that it was crusted with blood. Fresher blood soaked through the dust that covered him.

"It's nothing," he said, reminding himself he had to live up to his people's reputation for stoicism.

A few minutes later a gray man in long, rich robes arrived, his hands outstretched. "Prince Ansa!" he said, grasping Ansa's hands while a guard took charge of the lance. "You are the last person we expected here. Surely you were supposed to recover . . . Highness, you are sorely injured!"

"It's nothing," he repeated. "I must see the queen at once. I have information of the most urgent sort to communicate."

"Of course, of course. Come with me. No. Wait, I must summon a litter for you. You should not walk."

"I'll walk," Ansa insisted. "Just lead the way."

"Then be so good as to come with me." They walked through a great anteroom and Ansa bristled at the sight of several Shasinn warriors, lounging in the spectacularly arrogant fashion of which only the Shasinn were capable. Then he remembered that there were negotiations going on. Of course, he thought, there would be an island embassy here."

"How goes the parley?" he asked.

"Ah . . . it is most unusual, as you will find, my young prince. The queen . . . she is not quite herself, as you shall see."

"What?" He began to have a terrible feeling. "Is the plague returned? Has she fallen ill?"

"No, it is not an illness, as such, it is . . . well, you shall see."

The terrible feeling deepened as they wended their way through the labyrinthine mansion. Soldiers were everywhere. Courtiers stood in knots. Everyone conversed in low voices with an unmistakable furtiveness. There was an unease that had nothing to do with the uncertainties of war. He had seen Nevan courtiers unshaken in their adherence to decorum in the midst of catastrophe. War was a regular occurrence. These people were faced with something outside their experience and knew not how to react. The soldiers were grim. They had not lost a battle, they had not even been fighting. But they clearly felt something was wrong, as if they were somehow in disgrace.

In the throne room the crowd parted before them, Nevans and a few Shasinn mixed together. Then the front of the room was open and he saw Shazad standing at the foot of the throne dais, speaking with a big Shasinn. She turned to see who approached, her gown rustling slightly in the sudden, total silence that fell over the room. Her face registered a shock of recognition, but that was as nothing compared to the shock that went through Ansa when he saw the man to whom she had been talking.

"Gasam!" he cried, the name jerked involuntarily from his throat. His hand went as reflexively to his hilt, and the long sword began to hiss from its sheath. Instantly a pair of Shasinn spears crossed before his throat, forming a vee. A third clicked across them behind his neck, placing him in a deadly triangle of razor-edged steel. A single jerk on the weapons would behead him.

Shazad laid a hand on Gasam's forearm. "Do not harm him," she said quietly. "He did not expect to see you here, under my protection."

Gasam smiled gently and said something in the island dialect. The spears withdrew from Ansa's neck. Then, to Shazad: "Of course, my queen. He looks rather tired, and he is not in his right mind."

Slowly Ansa pushed his sword back into its sheath and his hand fell away from its hilt. There was a very slight easing of tension in the throne room. He studied Shazad, the way her hand still rested on Gasam's arm, the subtle attitudes of face and body that went back and forth between her and the island king. Ansa knew.

"Prince Ansa, what brings you here so unexpectedly?" Shazad asked. "You are still unwell."

"I have an urgent message for Your Majesty," he said, fighting to keep his voice under control. "It is for your ears alone."

She looked at Gasam.

"Of course, if you must, my queen. Please retire to hear his report. And you may wish to summon surgeons. My young friend may not be among us long otherwise."

She acted as if she needed his permission, he thought. The queen turned and left the throne room and he followed. Just past the great salon was a suite of lavishly furnished rooms he took to be her private chambers. She turned and faced him.

"Is it your father?" she asked. "Is King Hael dead?"

"Nothing like that. What has happened? Why is Gasam here?"

"King Gasam chose to head his own embassy, as was his right. He and his retinue are under my protection. You are to remember that."

"I mean what has happened between you and him?" he demanded angrily.

Her face and voice turned cold. "That is no concern of yours. I am here to receive your report, not to render mine. Now tell me what you have to say or be gone from my presence."

"What I just saw makes this easier for me to say, Shazad: You have lost Larissa! She is on her way to rejoin her husband!"

Shazad turned deathly pale. For a moment she looked even shakier than he felt. "How?" she said, almost sobbing the word. Quickly he told her of all that had transpired. As she spoke, she regained her composure. At the end of it she touched his arm gently.

"Injured as you are, you *rode* all this way to tell me. I shall dispatch our swiftest ships at once to intercept them."

"Of course," Ansa said, almost smiling, "they will be avoiding this place, looking for the island army. And now you have Gasam."

She stared sadly at him. "But Gasam is under my

safe-conduct, and I must let him depart when he wishes, or lose my honor. Now I must go to issue orders. My servants will take you to my baths and my surgeons shall attend you. I do not know how you have survived. Like Gasam's, the blood of Hael must be something more than human." She turned and walked to the door, then paused and looked back at him, her face infinitely sorrowful. "Ansa, I no longer know where my heart lies." Then she was gone.

Servants helped him to a large, beautifully ornamented bath, where steam rose from pools of varying heat. They stripped the filthy clothes from him and he descended the steps into the hottest pool. He laid his weapon belt on the mosaic floor next to the marble basin and lay back while expert attendants gently scrubbed the caked blood from his body with soft sponges.

While his hair was carefully washed, a team of surgeons examined his wounds and expressed amazement at how advanced was his healing. They pronounced his constitution to be as rugged as a longneck's. A barber shaved the skimpy growth of whiskers from his face, an easy task because his father came of a beardless race. In time he dismissed them all and lay soaking in the hot water, continuously freshened to keep it clean. At last he had absolutely nothing to do. He could not affect matters one way or another. It was a good feeling, but he wondered if it was the same feeling a warrior had lying on the field of battle, all his fighting over, as the last of his blood drained from his body.

He began to drift off to sleep, the events of the last months flickering through his head, as if the rigors of time had been lifted and all was in chaos, each event happening independently, with no connection to the others. He saw Gasam's spear slash toward him, and the Mezpan forces popping away with their ludicrous but deadly fire tubes. He saw the pirates cut the throats of the merchant sailors, and himself riding peacefully through Shazad's parks in Kasin. He was riding desperately through a rainy night, and picking up a tangle of golden chains from a deck. Then he was in a hot bath and someone was leaning in the doorway. Ansa's hand went to the hilt to his long sword.

"You make free of the queen's accommodations, Gasam. I'll wager that's not all you make free of."

"The ways of kings and queens are not for you to judge, child. We are not as other people." He leaned against the doorpost, thick arms crossed over his powerful chest, his head lowered a little to clear the lintel, his feet crossed at the ankles. He uncoiled from the pose like a huge serpent and walked into the room, unarmed but unconcerned about the weapon under Ansa's hand. He grinned down at the long scar that crossed Ansa's torso like a sash. "We have given each other the marks of honor." His hand traced his own scars. "It is only fitting, since your father and I are brothers."

"Foster brothers as children," Ansa corrected, "brothers in a warrior fraternity, perhaps. But not real brothers."

Gasam squatted by the basin, all his actions effortless, as if flaunting his strength before Ansa's infirmity. "But Hael and I share in ways deeper than the ties of mere blood kinship. Our taste in women, for one thing."

Ansa let it pass. "As kinships go, that is thin."

"Our mastery of men, for another. I cast him from the islands before he knew his power. He was just a boy then, far younger than you are now."

"I've heard the story," Ansa said. "You tricked him

into killing a taboo animal, used his own courage and skill against him."

Gasam smiled, nodding. "That is correct."

"He earned his disgrace in saving your woman's life. To save Larissa he killed the giant longneck, a thing never accomplished by any Shasinn, single-handed. And you used this to rid yourself of him. Are you completely devoid of shame or honor, you and Larissa?"

"Utterly," Gasam assured him. "Those are the concepts of fools and inferior people. They are for people who need others, who must have the good opinion of peers to feel safe." He looked up, stared at a mosaicked wall as if into a great distance either of time or of space.

"We were children together: Hael, Larissa and I. She was the headman's daughter. I was the son of an ordinary warrior. Hael was nothing, an orphan. Parentless children were despised in our tribe. My family fostered him because custom demanded it. He did not even want to be a warrior, but a spirit-speaker. But an orphan could not apprentice to a shaman, and so he went into the warrior fraternity when he was old enough.

"Larissa had to choose between two brothers, and she chose the greater. She chose me. She knew our destinies were intertwined. She knew that I was the man destined to rule the world, that Hael is nothing compared to me. Now Shazad knows it, too."

Ansa was relaxed, wondering that he felt no fear. "Where is Harakh?"

"With the fleet, as is his duty." He smiled again and chuckled. "Oh, he cannot challenge me to the thorn circle, or whatever the Nevan custom is. He is only a consort, and that is something much less than a king or even a prince. A reigning queen can discard them and take a new one as casually as changing mounts if they fail to breed children on her, and the two of them have produced no brats to sit upon the Nevan throne.

"You know, that has been a difficult problem for her here. Her nobles know she cannot live forever, and she has no heir. In a kingdom like this, that means the great families sharpen their knives for each other and for her. When she dies, they will fight for the throne. Some may take the opportunity of getting rid of her first. To a queen in that position, a great warrior king at her side is a comforting prospect."

"She has my father, who has always been her true friend," Ansa said.

"Ah, but Hael lies dying. I recovered, but he seems to hover between life and death. He may die at any time, if he has not already. And she must be realistic about these things. For a queen, a dead ally is no ally at all. Hael lies somewhere in the Canyon. I stand right here. Hael's warriors are scattered all over the plains and may no longer own him their king. My warriors are in her kingdom, and their loyalty to me is fanatical."

He looked down at Ansa, his eyes hooded and the smile on his lips colder than sword steel. "Tell me, boy: For a queen whose throne is very insecure beneath her shapely bottom, which of us is the obvious choice?"

"What is Larissa going to think of this arrangement?" Ansa said, hoping to sink a barb in the glossy impervious hide above him.

"I told you: The ways of kings and queens are not those of ordinary people. I will have my Larissa back, she will find this a fine way to reestablish our hold on the mainland." He rose, standing upright in a single motion. Ansa noted idly that his knees did not pop. Gasam walked to the door but he turned at Ansa's voice.

"Gasam, you and Larissa: Are you human beings at all?"

Gasam smiled broadly and shook his head. "Oh, no. We are something much better than that." Then he was gone.

"Galley to starboard!" the lookout shouted. Larissa walked to the rail and looked to see a low, lean shape in the distance. Its polished oars rose and fell, flashing with a steady rhythm, looking, she thought, rather like the wings of a beautiful insect. Lord Goss came to stand beside her.

"Can it catch us, do you think?" she asked.

"No, we have the wind. They can never row hard enough to maintain the speed they would need. And even if they could reach us, they could not capture us."

She liked his assurance, even if she despised the man himself. "But that is a warship and this is not."

He smiled his thin, superior smile. "These Nevans with their oared galleys and their crude masts and sails! We know secrets of ship handling they never dreamed of. We are more than a match for anything that floats in the waters of this continent."

Wait until you encounter the Mezpans, she thought. She watched the enemy ship straining to reach them, imagining the heart-pounding toil of the rowers as they hauled on their oars, the naked, sweat-streaming backs of them, writhing, flexing as they fought water with wood. It was a stirring image. She had always enjoyed lounging on the oar deck as such men rowed for her. Of course, her rowers had been slaves, unlike Shazad's.

Larissa wore a filmy bit of cloth that fluttered in the sea wind. The soft links of her chains had been cut away, but the rings at neck, wrist and ankle remained. Goss had offered to have them cut off as well, but she rather liked them. Being a chained prisoner had been a new and interesting experience. She had been a little disappointed in Shazad's icy decorum, the way the Nevan queen had insisted that she be treated by her captors with royal honors. She would not have minded a little mistreatment. She was sure that the boy would have liked to do worse, but he was too cut up to do much of anything. *Should have killed him before we left the ship,* she thought, regretting the missed opportunity.

"You are perfectly safe here," Goss assured her. "I shall deliver you to your king intact." His smile was insinuating, almost lewd. His attitude, his constant closeness and supposedly accidental touching, all repelled her. But she was used to the infatuation of men for her, and she knew well how to use it to control and manipulate them.

"Another galley, straight ahead!" shouted the lookout, pointing over their bowsprit. Larissa looked in that direction. A rocky cape jutted into the sea to their north. Even as the southern ship swung to port to avoid it, the prow of a light Nevan galley appeared around its point. As it spotted their ship, its oars began to churn in a burst of speed.

"This one will catch us, I think," she said to Goss.

"So its master thinks," he sneered. "Now you will see what I meant about the superiority of our ships. Perhaps Your Majesty had best go below. They may use arrows as they approach."

She shook her head. "They seem to have gotten word of my escape. If so, they can't risk killing me.

They have orders to recapture me. No, I think they will ram and board."

"As you will. Watch, then. This should prove amusing." He went to stand beside the helmsman. The three-masted ship sailed on, taking no evasive action, as if Goss intended to be rammed.

The galley sped toward them, details of it becoming clearer with each beat of its oars. The water foamed over a ram shaped like a cabo's head, its bronze turned green and crusted with barnacles. The paint of its sides shone bright and the marines on the deck glittered in their armor and weapons. In the bow the captain stood, pointing with a lance, giving directions to the helmsman while a man stood beside him with a speaking-trumpet, relaying his orders to the rowing master.

She braced herself, knowing that the impact was only seconds away. Goss said something to the helmsman and the ship's bow began to swing to starboard. The captain of the galley shouted something and the oars changed rhythm.

"You see how swiftly this ship answers the helm, compared to theirs?" Goss said. His eyes glowed with a fierce light and for the first time she understood how cruel this man could be. He barked something else and the bow began to swing back to port. The galley captain, thinking he was going to miss his first pass, had the vessel backing water and was caught slowing down and almost broadside. Larissa thought her ship would slip around the galley's stern and speed away with the wind. She admired the maneuver, but she was wrong.

The larger ship continued its starboard turn until its bowsprit loomed over the center of the galley. Men aboard the lower vessel screamed and some threw spears, as if this could somehow ward off the other ship. Larissa gripped the rail until her knuckles whitened, expecting an impact like that of striking a submerged rock. Instead, she heard a deafening rending of wood, a huge churning of water. The three-masted ship shuddered but it scarcely slowed at all. Bits of wood and snapped oars flew over the bows as the ship trod the galley underfoot.

Larissa looked down in amazement as half the galley slid past her, sheared cleanly from the other half. In its hollow interior she saw screaming men, many of them mutilated, thrashing and trying to extricate themselves from the wreckage. Then they were past and the halved galley was astern. Even as she watched, the two halves filled and sank. Only a few heads showed among the litter of shattered wood.

"A pretty maneuver, eh?" said Goss, beside her once more. His sailors were in the rigging, cheering and making gestures toward the drowned ship astern.

"But your ship has no ram!" she said, flabbergasted for one of the few times in her life.

"She needs none. We abandoned that sort of fighting many years ago. A ship that is rowed must be very lightly built or it is immovable. It runs for harbor in foul weather and sticks to coastal waters. A three-masted ship like *Swimming Bird*"—he slapped the rail with proprietorial pride—"is much more strongly built, to stand the strain of all her sails, and the deep waters of the high seas. Her timbers are thick, her keel is deep. A three-master must be higher, wider, deeper than a cockleshell galley. This ship is more than twice as large as that galley, but she is many, many times as massive. We must speak of geometry sometime. It was like a great stone striking a basket."

She nodded, acknowledging the power of the demonstration. "I impressed you with the sight of my treasury and arsenal. Now you have impressed me."

He grinned and nodded, doffing his beplumed hat in a sardonic salute. "It is so good that we understand one another."

They came to the little cove where she had been captured. To her great joy, Larissa saw that a heavy force of Islanders was encamped on the beach. They piled into their canoes when they saw the ship and paddled furiously. *Swimming Bird* lowered sail, drifted to a near halt and dropped anchor. The fierce warriors stood threateningly in their canoes, chanting and waving their spears. Then there was sudden silence when they saw the slight, fair figure standing at the rail. She beamed and waved her arms overhead and the men erupted into raving joy. A large canoe full of her personal guard rowed next to the ship and stretched their arms out toward her.

"Your Majesty," Goss said, "if you will tell your warriors to restrain themselves, I shall lower a boat to take you ashore."

"No need," she said. Larissa sprang lightly to the rail and balanced there, then she crouched, her arms stretched behind her.

"Don't!" Goss cried in terror.

Larissa ignored him. With a graceful spring, the queen of the islands dived straight out, her arms spread as if she were trying to fly, and she dropped straight toward the forest of spears that stood in the boat below. At the last possible instant the terrible, flesh-shearing points swept aside and she was caught by thirty or forty upraised hands.

Laughing, she was set upright and she embraced the young men like so many lovers. They touched her as if unable to believe she was there, unable to get enough of her presence. Then their hands were beneath her again and they raised her high overhead as the other canoes swarmed around them. Chanting ecstatically, the warriors paddled for the shore and she waved to Lord Goss. He waved back with a hand clad in scented gray leather, his sardonic smile back in place.

She stepped ashore and needed several minutes to get the frantically chanting and cheering men to quiet down. "Where is the king?" she finally shouted. Even as she spoke, a group of officers came into camp. She did not see Gasam among them but at their head was a familiar figure.

"What is all this noise about?" the tall warrior demanded. Then he caught sight of her. "My queen!" With a joyous whoop, he ran to her and took her hands.

"Pendu, where is my husband? I haven't been able to get these fools calm enough to tell me."

"But how did you get away? Oh, tell me about it later. I have much to tell you. This changes everything."

"Changes what?" she said, laughing, her eyes dancing. "Come, let's go find some quiet where we can talk."

They left the happy crowd and walked into the dim quiet of the forest that grew almost to the sea's edge. Overhead, only birds and small, furred animals made soft sounds in the evening coolness.

"The king is in the city where the queen of Neva has anchored her fleet. You must have sailed right past him."

She stopped in midstep, stunned. "What is he doing there?"

"He took an embassy to treat with Shazad, to secure your release."

"Of course there would have to be negotiations, but why did he go himself? Even Gasam is not so foolhardy!"

"I fear that he is, my queen. That pirate fellow, Ilas of Nar: he put an idea in Gasam's head. As always, the king turned it into a minor campaign."

It was always someone else's idea, she thought. But she would have expected Gasam to know better than to listen to someone like Ilas. She sighed. "Tell me about it."

"I was with the first group. We went in boldly, trusting to that woman's safe-conduct. I would never have trusted her, but the king insisted that her honor was reliable. When I reminded him that her jealous nobles might not be so delicate, he just acted as if that made it all more enjoyable."

"In some ways, Gasam will never grow up. Go on."

So he told her about the banquets, and how the queen had thawed toward Gasam, and how now the officers were free to come and go between the city and the Shasinn camps.

"So now Shazad hangs upon his arm and bestows her smiles upon him?" She dug her toes into the rich loam. It felt good after all the long days on ship.

Pendu looked distinctly uncomfortable. "Yes, my queen. I am sorry."

"Sorry for what? My husband did what he had to in order to get me back. He can bed fifty queens for all I care, if it is in pursuit of his destiny. He is not an ordinary man. Do you think anything he does with an ordinary woman alters what is between Gasam and me?"

"Of course not, my queen!" Pendu said hastily.

"Leave me for a while."

"As my queen commands." He bowed and strode away. She knew that her guards would be filtering through the forest, out of her sight but ready to deal with any threat.

She could understand how it had happened. She thought of Shazad, remembered the exquisitely beautiful young princess who had been such a joy to keep as her slave. Even then she had been a passionate, willful creature, spirited enough to rescue her own father from certain capture and kill his traitorous officers, directing a rearguard action to cover the old king's escape and being taken prisoner in the process. That was how she had come into Larissa's hands.

She would be a middle-aged woman now. The years and their responsibilities would have aged her, but not terribly so. The duties of office and the perilous times she had endured must have strengthened her, but they would have forced her to bank her formerly great appetites. Larissa knew better than anyone that those basic, animal appetites never went away. She had always indulged her own. In Shazad they would be like hot, glowing coals under a coat of ashes.

Gasam had known what the woman was the first time he had gazed upon her. What she still was. He had walked right into her court, and he had blown away the ashes. *She has been waiting for this all her life*, Larissa thought. *To feel Gasam upon her body has always been her secret dream. He was the faceless creature that came to her in the nights, so that she awoke with an ache in her loins.* Gasam, Shazad, Larissa, Hael: Their destinies and their bodies entwined over the years, changing the world each time.

She had not been entirely candid with Pendu.

Other women, certainly, but Shazad was not an ordinary woman. She was not as beautiful as herself, but Shazad would be passionate beyond the common run. And she was a queen in her own right. Shazad could actually picture herself seated at Gasam's side, sharing his throne. She was wrong about that.

But Larissa could not doubt Gasam's love for her. He was destined to set the world beneath his feet, and hers was to stand beside him in this. Let Shazad of Neva enjoy her dalliance with Gasam a while longer. She and Larissa had been deadly friends for many years, and the woman deserved to experience this rapture once in her life. Just as Larissa would enjoy killing her.

She shook the thoughts from her mind. Things, as Pendu had said, were radically changed. What would happen when Shazad found out that Larissa was escaped, alive and back with her Shasinn? Would she take Gasam prisoner in turn? She could not share his trust in her queenly honor. How to get word to him? She must get him out of that city, as quickly as possible. She thought hard, and she remembered Hael.

Ansa felt almost back to normal. Since returning to Shazad's headquarters, his healing had progressed with amazing rapidity. A royal physician opined that his headlong ride from the capital had stimulated the natural healing properties known to be located in the liver. Ansa was of the belief that there was nothing like straddling a splendid cabo to give a man strength; that plainsman and cabo were by nature a single creature, each receiving power and determination from the other. Whatever the reason, the pain of his wounds began to subside and they bled no longer. The long scar that slanted down his body was an angry pink, and the smaller cuts were already starting to fade.

He exercised, working the knots from his muscles. Each day, he drilled with sword, knife and bow, riding his cabos, picking off targets with his lance, wielded from the saddle. He wanted to be ready for battle when it came.

And he knew it must come soon. While Shazad dallied with Gasam, the situation was deteriorating. The soldiers chafed at the inaction, losing their fine combat edge. The court was all but demoralized by the presence of the Shasinn among them and at their queen's unwonted lethargy.

Worst of all, the fugitive ships from the southern fleet had been sighted heading north. There was a report that it had actually sunk a small Nevan pursuit galley. This last scarcely seemed credible, but it was known that the foreigners possessed secrets of seamanship that the Nevans could only guess at. Larissa had to be back with her Islanders.

Ansa's only hope was that the traitor, Goss, was holding her for ransom, extorting from the Shasinn some of the huge treasure they were rumored to have piled up in their islands. It would suit the man's character, as Ansa had heard it described. He felt it to be a forlorn hope. A queen of Neva with all her resources was one thing. He could not believe that a man like Goss with but a single ship and crew could keep Larissa from her warriors when they wanted her back. Ten thousand of them would happily throw away their lives for her.

On an afternoon when he was riding outside the city walls, hunting wild curlhorn, he was accosted on the road back to the east gate. Four mounted men blocked his path. He knew two of them: a high court official and a general of land troops. Of the others, one was in a naval uniform and the fourth in rich civilian clothes. He drew to a halt and kept his bow ready-strung by his knee.

"Good day, gentlemen," he said. "I see no hunting arms among you. Are you out for exercise?"

"We greet you, Prince Ansa of the Plains," said the courtier. "We and others of like mind wish to confer with you on most urgent business, touching the security of our nation and yours. Will you do us the honor of accompanying us to our meeting place?"

He knew that he might have expected something like this to happen. "Are you meeting in secret?"

"I fear it must be so," the courtier answered. "If you choose not to come with us, please say so and no more will be said. We ask only that you do not mention this to the queen."

"I speak very little with the queen these days," Ansa said. "Yes, I will come with you."

They took a narrow path that wound into the hills and as they did he wondered what would have happened had he refused. The men were squarely across his path and there might have been archers concealed in the brush that lay thick on all sides. Prince Ansa might have simply disappeared during an outing, perhaps picked off by an overeager island war party, or the victim of one of the roving packs of bandits that proliferated in the war-ravaged countryside.

They came to a clearing where a score of cabos were picketed. The same number of men stood or sat, some of them in folding camp chairs. All were important men, as was evidenced by the richness of their clothing and armor. At their arrival a grizzled veteran stood and greeted them.

"Good of you to come, Prince Ansa," the general said.

"I was expecting a summons of this sort, General Chutai," he answered.

"Good. Then you know what this is all about. Please dismount and join us." Ansa did so and Chutai made introductions. He had already met more than half of the men, most of them at royal councils. The others were high in the army and navy.

"We cannot be away from our posts too long," Chutai began, "so let's keep this brief. Our queen has been behaving strangely of late."

"I would use a stronger word," said the courtier.

"Whatever words we use, it is dangerous," Chutai went on. "Gasam, our deadly enemy of more than twenty years has the run of the campaign palace."

"He has the run of the queen!" said a fleet commodore. Others growled scandalized agreement.

"Let us say," said the courtier, "that the activities in the palace far exceed those proper for an embassy. There have been no negotiations over the release of our prisoner for some time, although the two sovereigns have spent no little time together."

"A moment," Ansa interrupted. "I do not see Lord Harakh here. Surely the admiral and prince consort should be here."

There was an uncomfortable silence. The courtier broke it. "Lord Harakh is the bravest and most loyal of warriors, respected by all, but in this most delicate matter we have determined that his involvement would not be justified."

A polite way of saying that a cuckolded consort was not to be relied upon, Ansa thought.

"Enough of that," Chutai said. "What are we to do? I'll countenance no treason against our queen, but at this time I do not believe her to be in her right mind. I think we are justified in taking some action to bring her to her senses."

"I must say that we should not balk at extreme measures," the courtier put in. "Deposing a monarch is a terrible action to take, but allowing the Islanders to overrun our land is a worse prospect."

Ansa wondered what the man's family connections were. Surely he would not have suggested a coup unless he expected to reach some advantage from it.

Chutai snorted through his broken nose. "That could mean civil war. Is there one pretender with a strong enough claim to the throne to take it without war? And does anyone think the Islanders will fail to take advantage of civil strife here in Neva?"

"No, there are no strong claimants," said a general. "Queen Shazad did away with all of them years ago."

"And good riddance to the lot of them!" Chutai said forcefully. "Come, my friends: We all want to do something, but we don't love one another enough to elevate one of our number to the throne! Let's speak in practical terms."

"I think Lord Chutai is right," Ansa said. "I am a foreigner among you, but my father and Gasam have been enemies almost since birth. I think Lord Chutai was correct in the first council after I captured Larissa." He thought it politic to remind them who had taken the woman. "He said she should be killed, and she should have been. She got loose and some traitor may have informed Gasam by now. Gasam should have been taken prisoner or killed as soon as he showed his face. I respect the queen's sense of honor, but it is misapplied where those two are concerned."

"Aye! Aye!" chorused many of those present.

"Prince Ansa," the courtier said, "while our respect for you is unbounded, and we of course value your counsel, you are, as you have said yourself, a foreigner. What is of great importance to us is your standing as a prince of the plains people. Your father, King Hael, and our queen are friends and allies of long standing. They have fought two great wars in alliance."

"What we want to know," Chutai interrupted, "is how your father is likely to react if we must take action against our queen. We don't want to trade an invasion of island savages for a storm of cabo-back archers from the plains. Granted, the state of King Hael's health is in question, but just a few months ago we had Gasam written off as dead, and look what happened."

"All must hinge," Ansa said, choosing his words carefully, "upon the nature of your actions. If Queen Shazad is restrained, placed under arrest until the matter of the Islanders is sorted out, then my father may be mollified. But if she is deposed, killed or in any way harmed, expect the worst." Actually he was not at all certain of this. Great as was the friendship between Hael and Shazad, his father might well consider the Mezpans too great a threat for him to spare much attention for Shazad. But Ansa felt that his words might help to moderate the actions of the most hotheaded and ambitious here.

"I, personally, will not allow our queen to be harmed," Chutai protested. Several others assented vigorously. But some looked doubtful.

"My friends," Ansa said, "we speak too much of Queen Shazad and her inexplicable actions. The evil here is Gasam. This is a man who seems able to corrupt anything and anyone. The Shasinn were a simple and noble race of herdsmen-warriors before he made himself their king. He has used the world as his plaything and has been checked only by his ancient foe King Hael." He saw the others bristle and added: "And, of course, the noble army and navy of Neva. The fact remains: get rid of Gasam and the queen will come to her senses."

"I'm for it," Chutai said.

"If her safe-conduct is violated," the courtier said, "heads will fall."

"Then this," Ansa put in, "will prove a test of just how much you are willing to sacrifice for your country." He looked around and detected little eagerness on that score.

"More than that," said Chutai, "that island longneck is not so easy to kill, and he is among his Shasinn. He is no god surrounded by demons, but I do not think it impossible that he could fight his way clear if the whole royal guard set upon him."

"Gentlemen, there may be an answer to this," said the courtier.

"Tell us, I'll be grateful," Chutai said.

"Well," the man began blandly, "while the queen would not hesitate to behead any of us for violating her safe-conduct, our young friend, prince of the plains, is a different matter. He is not her subject; he is the son of her old friend King Hael; his services in the wars with Gasam have been great. Twice he has engaged Gasam in personal combat. He personally took Queen Larissa captive." The man spread his palms in an appeal to reason. "Surely our queen would do no more than banish him from her court for a few years should he slay King Gasam."

Everyone looked at Ansa and he felt extremely exposed.

"Aye, he fought Gasam twice," Chutai said. "And that's more than any living man save his father can claim. But I point out that on neither of those occasions did he kill the man and on their last encounter the result was very nearly the opposite."

The courtier made a dismissive gesture. "I was not proposing anything so foolish as a duel. Single combat is a chancy thing. No, it strikes me that the plains warriors are famous throughout the world for their archery. Behold Prince Ansa's great bow, which hangs upon his saddle. So free is Gasam with the palace and its grounds that, surely, he must present a clear target before much longer."

"That's a coward's way!" protested someone.

"Don't speak foolishly!" Chutai barked. "Killing Islanders is exterminating vermin! If Prince Ansa can put an arrow or two through that beast, I'll put him in for every honor the Nevan military has to bestow. No one could ever question his bravery."

"Are we agreed, then?" the courtier said, much too hastily and smoothly for Ansa's taste. Even so, he was anxious for a chance to kill Gasam and rid the world of this evil once and for all. He was ready to forgo the honor of killing him in single combat. Like the others, he had doubts that the feat could be accomplished at all. As for Larissa, he thought it doubtful that she could hold the island armies together without a king.

"When?" Chutai said. "That island slut may be getting ready for an attack on the city and the fleet this minute. Gasam may learn at any moment that she's at large and make a run for it."

"The prince must kill him at the first opportunity," said the courtier. "We will do the rest."

"What 'rest'?" Ansa demanded.

"Why, we will ensure that you come to no harm because of this. We will deal with his Shasinn guards."

"That would be a good idea," Ansa said. "Even if I'm not seen, the fact their king has been skewered with arrows will let them know whom to look for."

His tone was dry but his words were deadly serious. He was amazingly recovered, but he was not deceiving himself that he was back in full fighting trim. A half score of enraged Shasinn would dispatch him handily.

"We shall see to all," the courtier assured him. Ansa was unsure of the others, but he was not about to trust this man.

He rode back to the city, taking a wide circle through the hills. All the conspirators were taking different routes to rejoin their ships or units or to return to the city. Ansa found the road leading to the north gate and began to trot along it, pleasantly tired, a plump curlhorn across his saddle.

A few miles from the city a Shasinn junior warrior passed him. Covering his shoulders was the brief cape of grass-cat pelt worn by Shasinn messengers, and to his slender, bronze spear was affixed the fan of feathers that proclaimed his immune status. He ran past the mounted man without sparing him a glance, his bronze hair worked into hundreds of tiny plaits and the plaits bouncing rhythmically upon his shoulders in time to his easy, loping stride.

Ansa greatly feared the message the boy might be carrying to Gasam. He took his great bow from his saddle and affixed an arrow to its string. Slowly he pulled it back to full draw, feeling his newly healed wounds throb in protest. The road was straight and it was a clear shot. In the light of the lowering sun the boy's glossy skin shone golden. He was slight, no more than fourteen or fifteen, by Ansa's estimation. The fluid grace of his movements as he crossed the green landscape made him a sight of heartbreaking beauty.

Gradually, an inch at a time, Ansa released the tension on his bowstring. Chutai had spoken truly

when he said that killing Shasinn was like killing
vermin. They were ravening beasts, the enemy of all
mankind. But there was something in their beauty
that made even this necessary act tragic. The heat of
battle was one thing, but Ansa could not commit
such a murder. He let the boy live.

Surely, he thought, he would have no such qualms
concerning Gasam. Gasam was different.

FOURTEEN

Shazad feared that she was losing her mind. The will, the strength in which she had taken such pride had melted away like wax before a searing flame. During the days, some of her old power would return to her. She would remind herself that she was a queen at war, that her enemy was within her gates, that she had lost the pawn that gave her bargaining power, that she must do something decisive, and do it quickly.

Then, in the night, he would come to her again and all her husbanded determination was drowned in the unbelievable sensual gratification that came from him as water from a fountain. With him she was weak, a quivering, mindless animal eager only for the next touch, the next sensation. It was insane. Only an idiotic young girl could allow herself to be so used, to forget kin and people for the sake of her own pleasures.

But, she thought, did she not owe herself something for the years she had sacrificed to the good of her nation? Had she not spent long years toiling over state papers and conducting state ceremonies, threading her way through the intrigues of her neighbors and of her own nobles so that Neva would be safe and prosperous? How could they deny her this pleasure so late in her life, when all the joys of youth had fled from her.

Sternly she reined in that self-indulgent path of thought. There were more practical, more sinister things to consider. Not only had she neglected the threat from the Islanders, but she had been indiscreet with her own court. When she was with Gasam in public, she could not conceal the signs of her infatuation. She was unable to hold herself rigidly aloof, expressionless.

It was all the ammunition her rebellious nobles needed. They saw that their queen was disloyal, that she had given herself to their enemy. They could overthrow her now, they could deliver her to the sword of the public headsman. And they would be right. She faced something more serious than scandal and scurrilous talk. She faced defeat in war. She faced death. It was time for an end to this.

She sat in her chamber as her ladies finished dressing her hair and she wondered how she could bring herself to do it. Would her knees go weak again when she confronted him? Would he smile down at her and make her insides go molten?

She dismissed the women. Alone, she rose and left her chambers. The sight that greeted her in the throne room made her stop, apprehension clutching at her. At one end of the room her courtiers and guards were clustered beneath the musicians' balcony, whence drifted gentle music of harp and flute.

At the other stood Gasam, arrogant as ever, one foot propped on her throne and surrounded by his Shasinn, all but one of them his elite master warriors. The exception was a junior warrior in the cape of a messenger. Fear clutched her bowels. What message did the boy bring from the Shasinn camp? Distantly she heard some sort of clamor in the city, but she had no attention to spare for it.

"King Gasam," she said as she approached. "Is all well with your people?"

He turned, looked down and smiled at her, but this time it caused her belly to quiver not with passion but with fear.

"All is well, indeed, Queen Shazad."

He knew. It was over, she thought. What had she done?

"Come, join us, Shazad," Gasam said. "We have much to talk about."

Slowly, but without overt reluctance, she climbed the dais. Her courtiers began to drift toward the throne end of the room. One step at a time she approached him, feeling the menace that radiated from him and from the other Shasinn. Their easy, diplomatic demeanor was gone now, replaced by the barbaric deadliness of the Islanders. They were hostile, and they were hugely outnumbered, in the midst of their mortal enemies. Why were they confident?

She ascended the last step and stood before Gasam. Whatever she had brought upon herself, she would meet it face-on. If this was to be her death, she would die like a queen.

"I see matters no longer lie smoothly between us, King Gasam," she said. "What has changed?"

"Everything," he said. His smile was now truly terrible. Whether he had truly loved her, whether it had been a mere pose, masterfully done, he had reverted now. He was the savage king in truth. His hand came up as if to brush her cheek, but the long fingers closed on her neck. The playing of the musicians halted abruptly and there was a rattle of action from the guards. "You see ..." Gasam began, but the junior warrior in the fur cloak cried out in a shrill voice, pointing to the musicians' balcony. There stood Prince Ansa, his bow at full draw.

The clamor from the city was very loud now but its pitch seemed to deepen as everything Shazad saw began to happen very slowly, as if everyone were moving through deep water. Gasam's face registered surprise and his fingers loosened from her neck as he turned to face the balcony. The arrow was already in flight. The range was not great: less than a hundred feet. Nothing could save him.

The junior warrior who stood by Gasam's side leaned forward, a frown of concentration compressing the level black brows. *Strange brows for a Shasinn*, Shazad thought irrelevantly. The boy's move was incredibly precise as he brought the long, swordlike blade of his steel-edged bronze spear across the king's body. It caught the arrow on the shaft, just behind the head. Shazad saw a curling sliver of wood shaved from the shaft as it changed course and she was overcome with admiration even when she realized what was going to happen. *These Shasinn*, she thought, *are simply not mere human beings*.

The arrow struck Shazad in the left side, at the bottom of her rib cage. She felt as if a piece of ice had been slipped beneath her bodice, and a numbness spread from the spot. She looked down and saw that no more than two inches of shaft and the feathers protruded from her body. The sight did not distress her greatly. She would probably take some time to die from this wound and she had things to do.

Gasam stared at her with shock as his warriors closed in front of him, ready to stop any more arrows. Shazad felt as if she were floating. She fell backward and knew that there was an arm behind her back, supporting her. She looked from Gasam to see that it was the junior warrior. Holding the queen with one arm, the spear outstretched in the other, the fur cap swung open and she saw the firm, shapely breasts. Then she knew why the black brows had struck her as strange.

"I am sorry, Shazad," Larissa said. "I did not intend for you to be hurt." Her skin and hair had been darkened masterfully. She moved like a warrior so well that the illusion was all but complete. The island queen leaned forward and kissed her on the lips, then drew back. "I love you, Shazad. I hope you live. No one should kill you but me. I don't want to share this with a son of Hael. I am going to go kill him now. I will avenge you." Then Gasam was lifting her, holding her easily in one arm as pandemonium reigned in the throne room.

Someone burst in from outside. "The barbarians are inside the city! They've taken the north gate!"

Ansa stood, stunned, almost paralyzed. How could it have happened? It had been one of the easiest shots of his life. But instead of his enemy, he had killed his friend. Overcome with dread and guilt, he hardly heard the commotion below. Some people were pointing at him, but most had other matters to concern them. There was a great clamor and people shouting something about barbarians in the city.

His numb brain tried to sort out what was happening below. The knot of Shasinn warriors had closed around Gasam and were carving a path for him toward the door. Their great spears flashed like the blades of some incomprehensible mowing machine and the guards fell back before them. Even in his stuporous state it seemed to Ansa that the guards were not fighting very hard.

Then he saw Shazad. Gasam cradled her in the crook of one arm, where she was curled like a child. Her hands were clasped to her side and the fletching of his arrow rose from them as if she were holding a flower. His stomach sickened when he saw the rest of the arrow thrusting from her back, more than a foot of it slicked with her blood. The barbed tip dripped red onto the floor.

The spear almost got him as he stared with sick horror at his handiwork. The faint noise and the flash came as if from a great distance, but the years of warrior training did not require the working of his conscious mind. He twisted and blocked with the only object at hand: his bow. Steel-edged bronze bit deep into wood and horn. At the other end of the spear, amid the litter of instruments the musicians had dropped in their flight, stood the Shasinn junior warrior he had spared that afternoon. The fur cape was gone and he saw the warrior's face three feet away and he knew.

"Larissa!" Holding the spear wedged in the split wood of his bow, he dragged at his long sword. She was not a large woman, but she had both hands on her spear while he held the bow with only his left hand. With a twist of her whole body she wrenched the bow from his hand just as his long blade cleared the sheath. She knocked the bow against the balcony rail, freeing her blade, then swung the butt spike against the side of his head.

Ansa reeled back, blood soaking his hair, frantically blocking with his sword as the blade slashed across again. The metal rang and through the vibrating steel of his blade he felt her grip loosen on the spear shaft. Weakened as he was, he was still far stronger than she. Once again she threw her whole body into her weapon, lunging toward him and binding his blade.

"I spared you today!" he gasped. "I had my bow drawn at you and let you live!"

"I could have put my spear through your back as I ran past, but I had more important duties. We both have regrets. You shamed me and you've killed Shazad!" she snarled, sounding more animal than human. Her knee came up viciously into his groin, making the world spin with sickening agony as light flashed behind his eyes. By main strength he pushed against her, his greater body weight forcing her back against the balcony rail. Their weapons pinned flat between them, he wedged her buttocks and pelvis against the rail with his thigh while he pushed her backward, bending her over. If he could not cut her down, he would break her back.

Her head twisted back, Larissa began to scream: a high, piercing sound of pain and rage. Past her up-turned chin, Ansa saw the Shasinn below him. They had fought the length of the room, leaving a litter of bodies, male and female, behind them. Gasam looked up and saw them. He called out something and a Shasinn whirled, aiming a spear, but Ansa straightened and jerked Larissa in front of him. Gasam yelled another command and the warrior lowered his spear.

Maddened by his fury, Ansa jerked Larissa around and pinned her wrists behind her with one hand. He heaved her up, clearing the balcony rail, and lowered her on the other side, so she hung dangling above the Shasinn party. As he lowered her his broad blade went beneath her chin, biting into the tender flesh. A thin curtain of blood began to run down her neck. He needed but to drop her and her head would be sheared away. The tableau held for long seconds as no one dared make a move. Chaos roared outside, but in the throne room all was stillness.

"Trade, Gasam?" Ansa called out. Larissa quivered and twitched in his grip, which was weakening.

"Trade!" Gasam said, his face, for once, registering only concern.

"You first. Quick now, my arm is weakening and that woman you hold may be dead."

Gasam stepped a few paces from his men and laid Shazad gently on a bloodied carpet, carefully, so that the protruding arrow did not touch the floor. He stroked her hair gently, then went to stand beneath the balcony, his arms upraised.

Ansa swept the blade away from Larissa's neck and released her. Gasam caught his queen easily and set her on her feet. He threw Ansa an insolent salute and the island contingent erupted into violence once more. Prudently Ansa stepped back from the rail, lest a Shasinn spear reach him.

Slowly, achingly, he went to the stair and descended into the throne room. There was an arras running along one wall so that the musicians could enter the room and go to the balcony without being seen. He realized that this was how Larissa had made her way from the dais to him, bypassing the swarming guards. He could not fault her eye for terrain.

He pushed his way through the knot surrounding the fallen queen. The court wailed amid the carnage but he had eyes only for Shazad. Dropping his sword, he fell to his knees beside her.

"Forgive me, Shazad!" He tried to say more but could not.

Her eyes opened slightly. "Everyone wants me to forgive them today, even the savage queen, but nobody is doing anything about this shaft in my side."

"Surgeons have been summoned, Majesty," said a weeping court woman.

"They'll be busy men this day." She looked at Ansa, barely able to turn her head. "You violated my safe-conduct."

"Gasam was attacking you, Your Majesty!" someone said. "The prince only sought to protect you. It was an accident!"

"There are no accidents in this matter. The gods are involved." She smiled weakly at Ansa. "You, your father, Gasam, now I. Have any royal people since the days of legend done such harm to one another?"

An armored man bulled his way through the crowd and glared at Ansa. "Fool!" he said.

"Hold your tongue, Chutai," Shazad said. "I sense your doing in all this and there will be a reckoning, but later. What has happened?"

"They took the north gate, Your Majesty," Chutai said, shamefaced. "As men came to join Gasam here, not as many left. Someone was not counting. They hid here in the city and tonight they overpowered the watch. The woods were full of them and they stormed into the city before we could stop them."

"We shall all pay," she said tiredly. "I for being a fool, you for failing in your vigilance, Ansa because he tried to commit murder. We shall all pay."

A team of surgeons arrived and set swiftly about removing the arrow. One clipped its point off and

Shazad's personal physician drew steadily on the shaft until it came free. Shazad groaned and blood blossomed from the wound.

"I am cold," she said. Then, to Ansa: "It was Hael. He was her inspiration."

"What do you mean?" he asked, thinking she had left her senses.

"When they had me captive in Floria, he came into the city alone to bring me out. She did the same to fetch Gasam. They have such a fine grasp of the splendid gesture." Her eyes closed and she said no more.

Slowly Ansa rose as the queen was borne off by servants and physicians. The sounds of mayhem had faded from the palace. He was wearier than he had ever felt and, for once, he had no urge to run toward the sounds of battle.

Gasam and Larissa were truly happy. All around them was swirling chaos as men screamed and cut and stabbed. The chanting Shasinn raised a terrible music, all but drowning the shouts of Nevan officers trying to bring their men to bear against the Islanders. The center around which all this wildness swirled was the royal couple, and they were in a state of exultation.

Surrounded by their master warriors, they stood shoulder-to-shoulder, plying their spears wherever an especially stout Nevan managed to get through the whirling blades of the masters. A few doughty heroes managed this feat, to die on the great steel spear of Gasam's or Larissa's smaller bronze weapon.

Larissa felt that, should she die at this moment, she would be content. Always, she had wanted to stand by her husband's side as a warrior in mortal combat, but he had forbidden it. She had had to watch the battles from afar, touring the battlefields after the danger was past and the blood that stained her feet was already drying. Now she was experiencing her dream, and combat was never more mortal than this. She could see by the smile on Gasam's face how pleased he was with this battle, which they might still lose.

The Nevans were crowding in from all sides, packing the streets, their shields making a wall before them. The Shasinn fugitives carved their way northward, where they could hear the invading force just a street or two away. Nevan reinforcements were pouring in through the east and south gates. The narrowness of the streets made it impossible for the Nevans to use their greater numbers to crush the Shasinn in spite of all their warrior skill and valor.

One by one the master warriors fell, each buying his sovereigns a few more strides northward and depriving Neva of a number of soldiers. They fought their way to a small square where four small streets met and there the last of the master warriors died. Gasam and Larissa, too busy to exchange words, stood in the middle of the square, back-to-back, hewing to right and left.

She knew then that they would die here and it did not sadden her. They were killing enemies, together and at the height of power and beauty, living fully, as they had always lived. A Nevan officer in a bronze casque snarled before her and she leaned aside from the thrust of his short sword. Using both ends of her spear in the Shasinn fashion, she knocked his shield a few inches to one side and turned the move instantly to a downward slash through the gap she had created, parting his throat, sending him to the pavement in a gush of blood. A shape hulked to her left and she slashed blindly. Her blade clanged against a long spear held rock-steady and she was staring into a grinning, familiar face.

"Have I committed treason that my queen wishes to slay me?"

"Pendu!" she shouted, throwing her arms around the man as he almost casually speared a Nevan who sought to run her through from behind. Then a storm of howling warriors surged past them and they were safe.

Gasam grinned and embraced her. "It is good, little queen! Life is right once more."

"We've come through it again," she said, smiling with adoration into his eyes.

"More than that," he said, his bloodied arm across her shoulders as they walked toward the north gate. "Our warriors have seen us fighting alone, side by side, against our enemies. They know I am as powerful as ever and the gods, if there are any gods, smile upon me." He turned to Pendu. "Have we enough men to take the city?"

"No, just enough to hold this part of it for a while. That was as many as we could get through the forest unseen."

"Then hold them for a little while longer and we will fall back to rejoin the main army." Over the low hills he saw a glow coming from the direction of the harbor. "What is that?"

"I sent a small force in canoes," Larissa told him. "They were to fire some ships and cause as much confusion over there as they could. I didn't want marine reinforcements coming to the palace. They could get there faster than the soldiers from the camps outside the walls."

"You think of everything, little queen! Come, let's go find our warriors. Life is good and we will con-

quer the world!" Happily, the two left the city
through the north gate and walked through the
night toward their destiny.

His bow was gone and Ansa vowed never to travel
again without a spare. Lance and sword would have
to suffice. At least he had a good cabo, the best of
the string that had carried him so magnificently
from the capital. His few belongings were packed in
his saddlebags. He was ready to ride. Assuming, he
thought, that he would be allowed to leave. As he
swung into the saddle a group of tired, smoke-
stained men strode toward him across the small esplanade that fronted the mansion that had made
such an ill-starred campaign palace. In their forefront was Harakh. By him was Lord Chutai and
among the others were some of the conspirators he
had met with only the day before. It seemed far
longer, but Ansa knew that, in times like these,
things could happen in an impossibly short time.
They stopped before him and upon none of their
faces did he detect a smile of welcome. Harakh was
first to speak.

"The physicians say she will live. Myself, I doubt
it. If you were not Hael's son, I would have you
killed right now. But she lives yet, and you performed fine service until last night, and you were
not alone in this." Ansa wondered how long he
would last. A cuckolded consort would command little respect, for all his years of loyalty.

"To the end of my days the memory of my deed
will shame me, though it was not by intent."

"Because of that," Chutai said, "we allow you to
ride from this place. That, and because some of us
feel equal to you in guilt. We put you up to this deed
because we were too cowardly to do our own dirty

work. There is plenty of blame in this matter. Go. The people do not yet know what happened last night and you will be unmolested. Once they learn, you are safe nowhere within the borders of Neva. Shazad is a much-beloved queen."

"What will you do now?" Ansa asked.

"Fight," Harakh said. "We prepared for an invasion of the islands. We might just carry on. Perhaps they'll go back to protect their homeland. And you?"

"To the Canyon. I must find out whether my father lives. Perhaps Gasam and Larissa are unkillable. Perhaps others are forever destined to suffer for their deeds and die in their place. We are just mortal human beings. In all the world only King Hael is a match for them."

Chutai stepped close. "Go, Prince Ansa," he said, not unkindly. "Find your father, do what you can. We have a war to fight and you have no place in it now. It is as the queen said: The gods are in this. Perhaps we'll meet again in better times."

Ansa saluted the stony-eyed men and wheeled his cabo. He rode through the confused city, where bands of soldiers stood watch on every corner, and out through the south gate. He longed to return to his home in the plains, but his road was now to the Canyon, and his father who might be dead, and Lady Fyana, who had the gift of life in her hands. Behind him was bitter, indecisive war. Until the wounded king was whole again and could set things to rights, he knew, the world would be plunged into madness. The evil gods were at large once more.

FANTASY BESTSELLERS
FROM TOR

☐ 52261-3 BORDERLANDS $4.99
               edited by Terri Windling & Lark Alan Arnold   Canada $5.99

☐ 50943-9 THE DRAGON KNIGHT $5.99
               Gordon R. Dickson   Canada $6.99

☐ 51371-1 THE DRAGON REBORN $5.99
               Robert Jordan   Canada $6.99

☐ 52003-3 ELSEWHERE $3.99
               Will Shetterly   Canada $4.99

☐ 55409-4 THE GRAIL OF HEARTS $4.99
               Susan Schwartz   Canada $5.99

☐ 52114-5 JINX HIGH $4.99
               Mercedes Lackey   Canada $5.99

☐ 50896-3 MAIRELON THE MAGICIAN $3.99
               Patricia C. Wrede   Canada $4.99

☐ 50689-8 THE PHOENIX GUARDS $4.99
               Steven Brust   Canada $5.99

☐ 51373-8 THE SHADOW RISING $5.99
               Robert Jordan (Coming in October '93)   Canada $6.99

Buy them at your local bookstore or use this handy coupon:
Clip and mail this page with your order.

Publishers Book and Audio Mailing Service
P.O. Box 120159, Staten Island, NY 10312-0004

Please send me the book(s) I have checked above. I am enclosing $ _____
(Please add $1.25 for the first book, and $.25 for each additional book to cover postage and handling.
Send check or money order only—no CODs.)

Name _____

Address _____

City _____ State/Zip _____

Please allow six weeks for delivery. Prices subject to change without notice.